Dog Meat

By the same author

Dog Meat

Robert T. Price

ROBERT HALE · LONDON

© Robert T. Price 2005
First published in Great Britain 2005

ISBN 0 7090 7846 3

Robert Hale Limited
Clerkenwell House
Clerkenwell Green
London EC1R 0HT

2 4 6 8 10 9 7 5 3 1

Typeset in 10/12½pt Stempel Garamond
Printed in Great Britain by St Edmundsbury Press
Bury St Edmunds, Suffolk.
Bound by Woolnough Bookbinding Ltd

─PROLOGUE

The road was little more than a car-wide track through the woods. A large black car rolled slowly along it, silent but for the occasional crack of a fallen twig. Inside, the five occupants of the car were even more silent; too tense to speak. The driver leaned forward anxiously, nose almost touching the windscreen as he concentrated on guiding the vehicle through the dark tree-framed tunnel with only the low-level glow from the sidelights to guide him.

When the car emerged from the wood, there was a collective release of pent-up breath, but no lessening of the tension. A degree of visibility was restored, courtesy of a partial moon riding high in a clear starry sky. They were in an open area of rough grass and scrub. Off to the right, the edge of the wood was a black diagonal slash; to the left, the scrubby grass angled upwards to become the slope of a hill. They could just make out the contour of a footpath which seemed to offer a zigzag route towards the top of the hill.

No sign of human habitation was visible in any direction; no distant lights; not even that glow in the sky that points the position of a town – any such tell-tale must have lain in a direction obscured by the trees.

As the vehicle drew level with the lower end of the hill footpath, the man in the front passenger seat tapped the driver lightly on the shoulder. The car stopped. The man who tapped the driver's shoulder got out. Before closing the door, he turned and leaned back into the car. 'Wait,' he said quietly – the first word spoken since they entered the vehicle. It had the tone more of a request than an order. Nobody answered. The driver stopped the engine and switched off the lights.

The man from the front passenger seat turned up the collar of his jacket, although the night was warm. He walked up the hill, following the line of the footpath. A recent spell of dry weather had made the ground hard, removing any possibility of footprints. He did not look back during the few minutes it took to reach the summit, at which point his erstwhile companions might just have been able to make out a small vague silhouette against the sky. If they had still been trying to follow his progress.

The man turned to face back towards the car, which he could no longer distinguish against its stygian surround. For a few heartbeats he stood motionless. Then his left hand slipped into the inside pocket of his jacket. It emerged holding an object about the size and shape of a mobile telephone. The man slid aside a section of the casing of the object to uncover a recessed push-button. He stabbed the button with his right index finger.

A fireball blossomed – silent at first. The ear-shattering sound followed a long quarter-second later.

The man on the hill did not bother to watch while the remains of the car and its contents were reduced to a blackened amorphous mass. The petrol in the tank fuelled further explosions to add to the raging conflagration. He continued down the other side of the hill to where his new transport is waiting.

He would have been surprised – not to mention disturbed – had he been aware that he was not the only live human witness to the recent violent event.

—CHAPTER ONE——

'Kenny, there's a mysterious-looking bloke oot there. He's asking for you.'

Senga's curly red head followed her Glasgow accent round the half-open door of my office. I looked up from the newspaper I was reading while ostensibly checking last week's job sheets.

'What does he want? And what do you mean by "mysterious-looking", anyway?'

Senga was the foreman (foreperson?) in the Lone Harp Auto Repair garage, of which I am the proprietor; not that being the boss gets me any respect from her. She brought the rest of her five-foot-one frame round my side of the door.

'Well, he's dead weird. He looks kind of … as if he's knitted his own hair an' whiskers, and made a right bad job of it. A twenty-four carat nutter, if you ask me.'

'So why didn't you just send him on his way?' I said, 'Or get Bill to go out and have a discouraging word with him? That usually works.'

'The thing is, Kenny,' she said, 'this weirdo says he's a friend of yours – and we've got used to seeing all sorts of shady characters coming in here to pass the time of day with you.'

She started to turn away.

'Right, then, if you don't know a tattie-bogle look-alike with a serious hairiness problem, I'll go and get rid of him.'

I sighed and gave in to my curiosity. I never seem to learn anything from my previous mistakes.

'Hang on a minute, Senga. Better bring him in, though I haven't a clue who the hell he could be.' I tossed the newspaper on to the filing cabinet behind me, and prepared to meet my visitor.

What I had realized was how unusual Senga's attitude was. I mean, normally when somebody comes to the garage asking for me, she doesn't say a word – just gives a vague wave towards my office door with a mole wrench or whatever other tool happens to be in her hand at the time. So this visitor must have plumbed some pretty advanced boundary of weirdness. This was something I couldn't miss.

When he arrived at my office, I waited a silent moment to give myself the full benefit. A bit shorter than me at around five-seven or eight, you could tell he was probably quite thin, or at least wiry inside the layers of wrapping. His hands were thrust deep into the pockets of a thick black overcoat which looked as if it could stand up by itself. Below coat level, I could see an inch or two of faded jeans, followed by a pair of muddy trainers.

But the crowning glory was the area north of the coat. There were three separate hairy sections. The beard was long, black, and improbable. It didn't match the sad grey moustache – nor the reddish strands of hair that poked out under the brim of his straw hat. I couldn't tell anything from his eyes because they were crouching behind dark sunglasses.

Not really a weirdo then – more like a loony.

Speechless as a result of trying to keep a straight expression on my face, I waved him towards my visitor chair. Once he'd got himself settled down, he opened his mouth for the first time, and spoke in a gruff voice.

'I need your help.'

I was still gazing at him in disbelief. It was a moment or two before I could compose myself sufficiently to get my voice into gear. Finally, I made it.

'Bloody hell, Nick,' I said, 'considering the way you look, you're miles beyond help.'

That got to my visitor. He slumped in the chair, as far as his overcoat would allow, and added a crestfallen air to the mixture of signals he was bristling with.

'What ... how did ... did you know it was me?'

Now that I was past the first flush of mirth, I could talk without too much risk of bursting into laughter.

'Why don't you just peel off a few layers, and let me into the secret. What are you so shit-scared about?'

Nick Pearson was somebody who had been a fairly familiar figure in town for goodness knows how many years – the town in question being Stratford-upon-Avon, where we both live and work – part of my criminal past, I suppose; a reminder of the days when I used to nick cars for a living. Nick Pearson was a reasonably competent breaker and enterer by trade. However, it was his readiness to do pretty well anything short of violence for a few quid, so long as no actual work was involved, that made him useful to the Midlands criminal fraternity. He could occasionally be useful as an errand boy and general low grade utility villain.

'I'll keep this clobber on if you don't mind,' he said firmly, 'the bastards might have followed me here.'

I felt like pointing out that if the bastards (whoever they might be) were following him, they must already have seen through his disguise. On second thoughts, I kept my mouth shut, realizing that something must have scared Nick Pearson so much that his normally low intellectual capacity had deserted him altogether. Instead, I waited patiently for him to tell me what he thought I could do for him. Which he duly did.

'I need someplace to lie low … what with all we've been through in our time, you an' me … I thought you might be able to … you know … help out an old mate when he's in trouble.'

Now, I want it known that Nick Pearson and I have never been close, nor noticeably friendly, nor even drinking buddies, as such.

I said, 'Look, Nick, you and I have never even been drinking buddies, as such. Any time our paths have crossed in the past, it's been through some shady business. Well I'm a legitimate businessman now, and I'm not having the likes of you dragging me into a life of dishonesty.'

Kendall Madigan, the well known sanctimonious git – that's me.

'No, no,' he protested, 'nothing like that, mate. All I need is someplace to keep my head down, like … just till it all blows over.'

He whipped off the sunshades, to reveal his beady black eyes pleading at me from deep within the facial jungle. In spite of myself I was starting to feel some curiosity about what was going on.

'Tell me all about it,' I stupidly said, and remembered to add, 'But no promises, mind.'

Nick Pearson is not noted for getting straight down to the point. In fact, a mate of mine once said that if Nick Pearson can't find a bush to beat about, he'll plant one and wait for it to grow. So it took another fifteen minutes of dragging him back from side excursions, before I had a reasonable idea about what had turned him into a high-profile fugitive.

It seemed that late the previous night, Nick Pearson had been minding his own business – the burgling business, that is – in the grounds of a large private house in one of the many villages in the nearby countryside. This was maybe seven or eight miles outside of town. A so-called mate had tipped him off about this house the occupants of which were so lax in the security department that they would often leave ground-floor windows open at night and some-times didn't even bother to lock the back door.

Well, Nick Pearson may be a bit mentally sub-average; no doubt about that; but he is not quite stupid enough to take that kind of information at face value. So he naturally checked it out for himself by casing the joint on a couple of dark nights without attempting to go inside. It was all true. However, being Nick Pearson, he did not do a complete research job. For instance, it never occurred to him to find out who lived in that house – or for that matter why his 'mate' was so anxious to hand out seemingly valuable knowledge for free.

So there he was, approaching what he hoped would be the scene of the crime.

... Nick Pearson was being ultra careful. He parked his battered old Vauxhall behind two other cars where the road widens in front of Lower Pebbington's village hall. He then walked along the unlit sleeping Friday Street to the single track private road leading to his target, which was the last habitation at the edge of the village. This tarmac driveway led nowhere except to the house. Off the public highway, the night turned even blacker under the canopy of foliage held aloft by the trees lining both sides. Sounds of the night-time countryside could be heard from all directions, but luckily Nick Pearson lacked the kind of mental equipment that would have had many a more imaginative criminal turning tail and heading for home.

At one point in his planning, he had considered bringing a wheelbarrow to transport potential loot the half-mile from the house to his car. However, even Nick Pearson was well aware that this was not the kind of residence where the most valuable items are the TV and video recorder waiting to be nicked by some opportunist villain who will end up flogging them for peanuts in the pub. With any luck, this place would be harbouring jewellery and valuable antiques. Nothing too heavy; so all he had in his pocket was two large black plastic bin-bags.

He kept as far as possible to the right side of the tarmac drive in order to maintain a comforting contact with the top bar of the wooden boundary fence, even at points where the road widened to provide a passing place for vehicles. At first it was all just the same as on his reconnaissance visits. But in the blink of an eye, everything changed.

Nick Pearson was not yet halfway to the house, when he heard footsteps and voices from behind – catching up on him. He might have climbed over or through the fence into the unknown countryside, but that would cause unpredictable noise. He could have stepped up his pace to increase the gap, but that way he would feel he was being herded towards danger, or at least discovery. Which is why he simply remained motionless where he was – huddled against the fence.

Shadowy black shapes against the slightly lighter black of the night. Two men, guided by a downward pinpoint of flashlight dancing on the tarmac. They drew level with Nick Pearson, still talking.

'... in and out in ten minutes. Dirk must have cut the land line by now, but somebody could still use a mobile phone.'

Inaudible reply.

'Right, element of surprise. They won't get time to think about it. You keep the daughter covered. I shall pluck him from the bosom of his family. With any luck, he won't have to waste time getting dressed ... what the fuck was that?'

'That' was an involuntary cough emanating from Nick Pearson, who was suddenly dazzled by a bright light sweeping across his face. A harsh voice behind the light said, 'Don't move.'

The instruction was not necessary – Nick Pearson could not have twitched a muscle if his trousers had been on fire.

The other voice, the first one again, joined in, using the same quiet conversational tone, but with the unmistakable stamp of authority. He spoke to his companion.

'This must be the fellow whose car we noted back there – the only one with its engine still warm. He must have been creeping around listening to our conversation. We can't take any chances; he's probably one of Simmons's goons. They must know more about our plans than we thought.'

The rougher voice said, 'Could he just be a Poacher, do you think, boss ... or maybe some other mystery player we don't know about what wants to join in our game?'

The boss voice replied, 'No way. It's too much of a coincidence to be anything else but the opposition ... Christ knows how they found out. Just do the necessary and let's get on'.

The rough voice addressed Nick Pearson again.

'Right, you ... nothing personal ... blame your bosses for thinking you could get away with it. Sorry mate, but you're dog meat.'

The flashlight beam wavered as its holder switched it over to his left hand. That waver afforded Nick Pearson a glimpse of a gun emerging from a pocket. The fright of that sight following on the heels of the dog-meat threat, made our hero flinch backwards. Unfortunately there was nowhere for him to flinch to, since his back was already firmly up against the fence.

There was a loud crack as the woodworm-riddled top rail of the fence gave way. Nick Pearson had no control over what happened next. He flipped backwards over the lower rail. In the instant he did so, there was an even louder second crack – a gunshot this time. He landed on the ground on the other side, at the top of a steep slope. Down which he rolled, gaining momentum as he went, wondering how badly he had been wounded. By the time his progress halted, he was in the middle of a clump of bushes a good distance downhill from his starting point.

He waited, paralysed, incapable of any activity beyond breathing, which he tried to do as quietly as possible. His pursuers were reluctant to give up the chase, so he was able to hear them blundering around for what must have been ten minutes. By the end of that time, two things had become obvious to Nick Pearson: he was uninjured; and the two hard men were not going to find him easily. He heard the boss call the thug by name. They regrouped not far from Nick Pearson's personal bushes, and he was pleased to hear the boss say, 'Come on, we can't spare the time for side issues. You've got a note of his car number ... no great harm done if it takes us a couple of days to find and deal with him. Right now we'd better get back to the main business – Dirk will be wondering what's happened to us.'

Nick Pearson went on cowering in the bushes, waiting to give the pair time to be far enough away. Then he crawled out, struggled back up the hill, where he clung to the fence so that he could follow it back out to the road, but stayed on the field side of it rather than the more dangerous driveway side. This he accomplished, with only one hitch. That was when he had to duck behind a tree to avoid being caught in the headlights of a large car which roared down the drive, presumably from the house. On attaining the comparative safety of the public road, he abandoned his car, and walked all the way back to Stratford.

'Wow,' I commented when I'd extracted all the facts, 'you don't do things by halves, do you?'

A miserable shrug was the best Nick Pearson could manage. I thought for a couple of minutes. Could he really have been shot at? Why not? It must have been well away from both the house and the village. Besides, a gunshot at night in the country is not likely to attract much attention. Farmers are probably out there at all hours taking pot shots at foxes for all I know … and poachers are far from extinct in this neck of the woods. I asked for more detail in order to check the story for consistency.

'Sounds like you got their names though, didn't you say the dog meat man was called Dick … and what was the boss's name?'

'No, that was Dirk. He was the one supposed to be waiting at the house – and the boss was just called Boss. The one that tried to shoot me, the dog-meat bloke – his name was Blossom.'

'Blossom?'

'Yeah, I thought it was a bit funny, not that I was laughing, mind. But the boss wasn't far from my bushes when he shouted for Blossom to come back.'

I was convinced. Nick Pearson hasn't got the brain cell capacity to make up stuff as unlikely as that. We sat there looking at each other for a minute or so.

'Look,' I said eventually, 'have you stopped for a minute to think – just think about this … about what happened to you last night?'

He didn't say anything in reply, which led me to guess there must be a confused expression going on under his foliage. So I went on, 'I mean, from what you've told me, it sounds as if you parked your car near some others in the village … well away from the driveway. Right?'

A response this time; a nod and some words.

'Yeah, but it wasn't that far away – and my car would be the only one there with the bonnet still warm.'

'All right, but think about it. I don't think there could have been anything to link your beat-up old banger with the way into a posh estate. Did you see any other car nearer than yours, and close enough for anyone to associate it with that private drive? If there was, that means they must have been talking about some car other than yours, and it also means that when they trace the owner, it won't be you – it'll be some other poor bugger. Get it?'

That got a bigger nod.

'I … I think so,' he said, not sounding too convinced.

'So, were there any other cars parked anywhere near the entrance to that private road when you arrived? Come on, you must have noticed – you were on your way to break into the place, for Christ's sake; you were bound to check out the surrounding area.'

'Yeah, well, there was only one, a black BMW, quite small, not one of the great big ones. It was on the grass verge near the private road … but the same car was there, in the same place the other nights when I went to have a shufty. So it was … like … a normal part of the furniture.'

'Well, there you are then,' I said, 'That'll be the one those guys picked up on. They'll be off after some other poor sod, just as soon as they find out who owns that Beamer. Congratulations; looks like you're in the clear.'

'It's still bloody horrible gettin' shot at,' grumbled Nick Pearson, though I could detect the relief leaking back into his demeanour.

Anyway, that was the end of it – or so I thought at the time. I got Nick Pearson to dump his idiot disguise, and supplied him with a mug of coffee to steady his nerves. As I watched him trudge out through the garage, I felt a good solid glow of satisfaction at having brought sunshine back into the life of a fellow human being – even though the alleged human being in question was a particularly undeserving specimen.

I went back into my office and picked up my newspaper from the top of the filing cabinet which the former owner of the garage used to refer to as a credenza. Might as well read it again, I thought. There could have been some information there that I'd failed to pick up the first time. But no; the newspaper was as short on facts as everybody else. They just fluffed it out by going on at great length about the country house and how many bedrooms and bathrooms it had. The actual story contained about three pieces of real or imagined information and a small amount of speculation.

One: person or persons unknown had broken into the house of a prominent Midlands businessman in the dead of night.

Two: the intruders had scared the living daylights out of the businessman's wife and daughter by pointing guns at them.

Three: the businessman, a Mr Gerald Plank, had been forced at gunpoint, to get dressed and leave with the aforementioned intruders.

Those were the so-called facts. The speculation had to do with Mr Plank's alleged recent activities in assisting the police by pointing the finger at some of the country's most notorious criminals. Actually, it was only the fear of libel actions that prevented the newspaper from saying outright that Mr Gerald Plank is not your ordinary businessman, but is known to be the biggest criminal gang leader between Oxford in the south, and Sheffield in the north. In the shady world of criminal society, his lack of stature caused him to be generally known as Short Plank, though nobody who valued the continued benefit of their teeth would dare to use that name in his hearing, nor within earshot of any of his numerous tall associates.

He didn't need to bother about security at his house; no sensible villain would dare to try burgling it. As for assisting the police – well that was in the same ballpark as Goldilocks and the Three Little Piggies. I reckoned Nick Pearson had a lucky escape.

Oh, well! None of it had anything to do with me, thank God. There was a period in the past when I was up to my ears in villainous activities – when I used to make a living by stealing cars to order, for instance – not to mention getting inadvertently mixed up in several more serious situations. But that was all behind me by this time, and I had plenty of my own concerns to look after.

This particular day was a case in point, because I was a man short at the garage. Petesy Curtain, the young bloke who runs the second-hand car side of the business (Madigan Motors, named after me), had failed to turn up for work. I decided he must be pretty sick for that to happen, since Petesy was as keen as a mustard poultice, and even got quite miffed at me when I wouldn't allow him to open for car sales on Sundays. Not that I'm religious, as such, you understand – it's just that I think it's not good for people to work all the time without having at least one day off every week.

──CHAPTER TWO──────────────────

B arry Thomas is feeling pretty pleased with the way his life is moving along. Now that the central control of the organization he works for is breaking down, there could well be some chance of the advancement he yearns for. Barry's ambitions soar beyond the capabilities of a – reliable, but pedestrian – protection enforcer. He can see himself as boss of the protection business, a vision not shared by any of those locked in the current struggle for control of the shards of Mr Plank's empire.

Although ostensibly in the employ of Eastshire Eagle, a respectable debt collection agency (if such a thing is possible), Barry is one of several muscle-men whose efforts in the Leicester area are really for the benefit of the East Midlands half of Mr Plank's organization, under the iron-fisted control of Rod Simmons, Mr Plank's East Midlands representative. Eastshire Eagle is one of Plank's relatively straight businesses. For several years it has operated successfully, not only as a viable business in its own right, but also as a vehicle dedicated to transmuting the proceeds of the protection racket into legitimate profits. Now that Mr Plank is believed to be moving out – or rather onwards and upwards – the possibilities are wide open. If Simmons can manage to move himself into the space vacated by Mr Plank, then maybe Barry's current boss, the sadistic Andy Kelp, could be the one to get promotion into Simmons' job – and that would in turn create the vacancy which Barry Thomas would happily give his few remaining teeth to step into.

These are the thoughts occupying Barry's brain as he emerges from the Taj Mahal restaurant, which has just added its contribution to the growing wad of currency in his back pocket. He would probably have failed to notice the van even if he had not been preoccupied by career planning. All it is, is a van bearing the logo of a ubiquitous express delivery service.

The three men grab Barry from behind, and boost him through the van's rear loading door before he knows what is happening. The vehicle is already moving away while its back door is still closing. No one in the vicinity notices anything unusual. Inside the van, Barry is swiftly coshed into unconsciousness, so he does not hear the satisfied grunt of 'Gotcha! Now you're dog meat, mate.'

It is bad luck, pure and simple. The killers are not particularly bothered which of the eastern faction's wide selection of thugs gets the chop. However, about six months previously, during a combined hijacking operation, Barry happened to be the one who was insensitive enough to get up the nose of a prominent member of Mr Plank's western organization.

Barry is discovered by a farmer early the next day in a ditch at the edge of a field of oil-seed rape. He is still well-dressed in his dark blue suit and silk tie. He has lost the money from his hip pocket, and gained two neat bullet holes in the back of his head.

'That wasn't fair ... you surely should at least have let Nick Pearson know who he was trying to burgle,' said Aileen.

We were having a microwaved Marks & Spencer dinner for two in our brand new town-house in Stratford. Since we had both been out at work all day, there wasn't much time left for cooking in the evening. Over dinner is when we tell each other about anything interesting or funny that happened at work. Well, it's mostly Aileen who has things to tell, since she's the one who meets the public all day. She works at Jonathan Philips, that posh shoe shop in Sheep Street, so she can't avoid having to deal with all kinds of stupid idiots. She says the customers who think they are better than everyone else are the ones who make the biggest fools of themselves.

But for once, I was equipped with what I thought was the really funny story of Nick Pearson's disastrous robbery attempt – but Aileen surprised me by taking it very seriously. (As usual, she was siding with the underdog, though as far as I'm concerned, Nick Pearson is more of an underweasel.)

She went on, 'Besides, if what he told you is all true, he could easily have been killed and that's no laughing matter. So you should think of others and show a bit more sensitivity, Kendall Madigan.'

Faced with one of Aileen's sobering thoughts, I realized it was time for me to shut up. Even so, I felt it necessary to point out that

I actually *had* helped Nick Pearson in his hour of need; and that he left the Lone Harp garage a much happier incompetent burglar than when he arrived.

Having delivered what my Auntie Ursula would have called my plea of mitigation, I changed the subject, and told Aileen about Petesy not turning up for work. As it happens, Aileen is rather fond of Petesy – in a kind of big-sisterly way, I think. They are both around twenty-five, about seven years younger than me. Anyway, she was immediately all concerned over Petesy, to the extent of insisting on trying to call him at home in his flat to see if he was all right. No reply, of course, just as on the several attempts I had made in the course of the day.

'You see, love,' I pointed out, 'he'll be shacked up with some girl, probably at her place. They'll have been hard at it all day. You'll see ... he'll turn up at the garage tomorrow morning, too shagged out to do a stroke of work.'

Petesy really was quite a lad for the girls (though he tended to refer to them as 'chicks' or 'babes'). He reckoned he could pick up any woman he wanted; anytime he wanted to. So there was a pretty high likelihood that my guess was on target.

In case you were wondering, Aileen and I are not actually married, as such. We talked about getting hitched, around the time we moved in together. About two and a half years ago, that was. I was up for it, but Aileen said no why don't we wait and see if you grow up and I said what did she mean by that and she said never mind she was only joking. Which I thought was a bit strange because a sense of humour isn't really Aileen's strongest suit. Not like me.

Anyway, I had recently been thinking it might be time for us to take a second look at the marriage option. Life had changed for us in a lot of ways. Back then, I had just been made redundant at the lawn-mower factory, and was making a precarious living as a small-time criminal (not a great choice career-wise; the only positive aspect being its tax-free status). We were living in a rented maisonette in a pretty down-market part of town, when I was recruited by Quinn, the previous owner of the Lone Harp Auto Repair garage. He was an Irishman who had lived in Texas for some years. He gave me regular employment, ostensibly as a mechanic, but my real job was nicking cars to order.

As it happened, Quinn had his fingers in loads of criminal activities which were a lot more dicey than car theft. Not to mention him turning out to be dangerously unbalanced. In the course of some unpleasantness with another mob from London, various people got murdered, including Angus, who was the foreman at Lone Harp, and a friend of mine. In the end, I managed to close down Quinn's operations, recovering a load of stolen jewellery in the process. The insurance companies paid out a reward which came to Aileen and me. We used most of the reward to buy the Lone Harp garage from the receivers at a bargain price, and we gave a share of the money (and Angus's job) to Senga, his widow. The police claimed all the credit, of course, and leaned their size twelves on me for a while.

Now at last we had taken the next step and got ourselves on to the mortgage hamster-wheel, so if that's not a stable relationship, I don't know what is.

We had just got the dinner table cleared and the dishes dumped in the sink and were settling down in the living-room, on our new sofa, about to turn on the television, when the doorbell rang. I answered it, and was not terribly surprised to find Petesy on the doorstep. He came in, looking as if he had just run a marathon with the cares of the world firmly settled on his shoulders. Aileen took one look and went off to make coffee. Meanwhile Petesy sat down on the sofa, and I took a seat on a packing case opposite him, the sofa being the only living-room furniture we had so far, apart from the table holding the television, and a floor-standing lamp that Aileen insisted on calling an uplighter which consisted mostly of metal tubing.

Petesy and I sat looking at each other. He was content to sit there, all pale and limp like a droopy prawn, without saying a word, while I was quite willing to wait until he had his coffee and was ready to start offering explanations for his absence from work. As far as I was concerned, he should be anxious about how the boss (me) was going to receive his – no doubt feeble – excuses.

I should have known Aileen would put her personal oar in. She came straight in with three mugs of coffee, handed one to me, one to Petesy, and went all sympathetic over him.

'Woman trouble, Petesy? Well, never mind – there are plenty more. She obviously didn't deserve you.'

Petesy was too busy gulping coffee to answer right away, which allowed time for Aileen to fuss over him a bit more.

'I've got the very vitamins you need to get the roses back into your cheeks. I'll just put a week's supply in a freezer bag for you.'

Aileen is very hot on her vitamin tablets and mineral supplements and all that kind of health food stuff.

Petesy spoke for the first time since he arrived.

'Don't bother, Aileen,' he said, with what I thought was a particularly pathetic sigh. 'There aren't enough vitamins in the world to save me this time.'

I was opening my mouth to say something sarcastic, but I never got it out; luckily I suppose, since I can never seem to make sarcasm work. All of a sudden, Petesy was ready to talk.

'It's not woman trouble this time ... well, actually it is – I mean there is a woman involved ... this wonderful girl, Daphne. But she's not the problem; I mean, none of it is her fault. What it is, you see – somebody is ... they'll be trying to kill me as soon as they find out my name and address.'

I groaned aloud.

'Not another one. I'm surprised you're not wearing a false beard and wig.'

'Hold your tongue, Kenny,' said Aileen. 'Can't you see poor Petesy needs our support and sympathy – not your cynical gibes?'

Cynical gibes, for Christ's sake. Anyway, we persuaded Petesy to begin at the beginning. Of course, it did start with a woman; 'A real babe' apparently. Petesy had met this Daphne chick about a month earlier, and in the last week the affair had reached the torrid stage, with our lad being smuggled into Daphne's bedroom each night, and slipping out in the early morning. Daphne, being only nineteen, still lived with her parents.

'Don't tell me,' I said. 'Her father caught you, and came after you with a horse-whip.'

He shook his head.

'No, it was nothing like that. The trouble started when these villains broke into the house during the night, and kidnapped her dad.'

Bloody hell. I suddenly understood what he was going on about.

'Did you know who her dad was ... is?'

'Not then,' he said. 'I found out later on, but I can't blame Daphne for choosing the wrong father. She's still the only one for me, and—'

'Never mind the commercial,' I said, 'just tell us exactly what happened.'

'Well, I had gone to the loo – in the en suite attached to Daphne's bedroom. I had just switched off the bathroom light and was about to get back into bed, when there was this almighty crash and a lot of confused shouting from somewhere else in the house. I froze on the spot, just inside the bathroom … which turned out to be the right thing to do, because he never saw me.'

'Who never saw you?' That was Aileen.

'This enormous fat bloke in a mask who opened the bedroom door and switched the ceiling light on. He pointed a gun at Daphne – luckily she was under the covers with only her head showing – and he told her not to move if she didn't want to become … oh, pet food or something.'

'Dog meat,' I corrected him.

'Yeah, that's it! Dog meat,' agreed Petesy, giving me a funny look.

'Anyway, there was loads of noise … doors banging and such. This guy's mates were obviously checking all the rooms. Well, I was lucky, or so I thought, because it never occurred to him to look in the bathroom. The stupid git was too busy leering at poor Daphne trapped in her bed, and he made a nasty remark, something like: "That looks like a nice cosy empty space beside you, miss … if only I had a bit more time". Then he went on to say a load of nonsense which I didn't know what he was going on about and neither did Daphne, she told me later. But I remember his exact words.

'"I've just realized who the pillock was we met outside. It was your boyfriend on his way out thinking what a lucky lad he was. Well, don't worry … we're not going to torture you to find out who he is – we'll find that out soon enough."

'I suppose it was all just to confuse and scare Daphne. But then there was a shout from the landing, and the stupid idiot shut the door and left.'

'Why'd you reckon he's a stupid idiot?' I asked.

Aileen answered that. 'Because if he had been doing his job properly he would have checked the bathroom … thank God he didn't … and also because Daphne or Petesy could have used a mobile phone to call the police.'

She turned to Petesy. 'Did you?'

'No,' he replied, 'we were too scared ... and we didn't think of it until afterwards and I had left mine in my car – I mean, the last thing you want is for parents to hear an alien ring tone clanging out in their daughter's bedroom. Anyway, the break-in only lasted about ten minutes altogether, then we heard a car driving away from the house. We found out later it must have been Mr Plank's Mercedes and he had been kidnapped.'

Aileen was looking puzzled. She said, 'I can see how it was a terrible experience, and it's a shame for your girlfriend's family – but the intruders didn't even catch sight of you. How can they want to kill you, when they don't even know about you?'

I told her how:

'It was Petesy's black BMW that was parked near the entrance to the private driveway, wasn't it, Petesy? They noted the number and they'll use it to find out who the owner is. These professional villains usually have a tame contact in the police force, who will do all kinds of small favours for them.'

Petesy, gave a glum nod.

'Yeah, and just wait till they discover who I am. That will definitely have them believing I was not there just by accident.'

That was true. Petesy used to do a lot of dirty work for his late uncle, who was a notorious crooked businessman known as the Wheel – come to think about it, I suppose this Short Plank bloke must have arranged for himself to be drawn into the vacuum that was left when Petesy's uncle was killed. It was around that time that I gave the lad the chance to make an honest living – if you can call the second-hand motor trade an honest living. Anyway, the point is that there must be quite a few members of the Midlands villain community who still remember Petesy, or at least his name. A lot of them used to call him Peachy, which annoyed him no end.

And I hadn't told him yet that his situation was worse than he knew. Last night's intruders had taken a pot shot at Nick Pearson, but they must now believe (or would believe as soon as they traced the ownership of that car) that the person they tried to kill then was none other than our very own Petesy.

'All right,' I said, 'you can kip down in the back bedroom upstairs. There's no bed there yet, but we were going to have to buy one for it sooner or later ... might as well do it tomorrow. A blanket on the floor will have to do for tonight.'

'I'll get you a nice soft duvet,' Aileen told him.

'Thanks,' said Petesy, mainly looking at Aileen. He added, 'There's no way I could go back to my flat, the way I feel now.'

I was beginning to realize just how much danger the lad could be in – maybe. Anyway, there was no harm in taking simple precautions.

'Another thing,' I said, 'since they obviously know about your car, you'd better use one of our second-hand motors for a while. Drive your BMW to work in the morning and lock it in the unused service bay behind the garage.'

This one-car bay had a separate entrance behind the garage; it was where Quinn, the previous owner, used to process stolen cars to give them a new identity. I used to call it the moonlight bay, but nobody else saw the humour in that.

'Remember,' I told Petesy, 'it's just for a few days ... until the whole thing blows over, and we prove that nobody's interested in coming after you. I'm sure they were putting on a bit of menace just for effect.'

While saying that, I couldn't help imagining a large dark silhouette firing a gun at Nick Pearson, so it's quite possible that I didn't sound as reassuring as I wanted.

Later on, in bed, I had another thought. I mentioned it to Aileen. If the mystery men were on to Petesy, there was every chance they would turn up at his flat sooner or later. Perhaps they already had.

'It might not be safe for Petesy to go back to his flat,' I said, 'but there's nothing to stop me going there tomorrow. I can pack a case for him with changes of clothes and such.'

'What's the point of you going rather than Petesy?' she said. 'I mean, won't the nasties, if they're keeping an eye on the flat ... won't they just think you're Petesy if they see you going in there?'

'I don't think so,' I replied. 'Some of their own gang probably knew Petesy in the past. I bet they'll have a description of the lad by now. After all, if they've got his address ... and anyway, I can use one of my disguises.'

Silence. Aileen has about fifteen different kinds of silence in her larder. This was the kind she uses when she's waiting for me to finish stabbing myself in the foot. Sometimes I don't know when to back off and let nature take its course. I went on the defensive.

'Well, you can't deny it's fascinating. Wouldn't you like to know what's going on? I mean, there's no chance of you and me becoming sucked in this time, not as such. Not this time. We can just be the interested by-standers watching from the sidelines.'

A big sigh from Aileen, and I could sense her shaking her head in the dark before she finally gave me the benefit of what was on her mind.

'You don't see it, Kenny, do you? Think it through … put yourself in the place of the kidnappers. Let's say they find out who Petesy is … they must also know that he used to work for his uncle who was a big-time gangster. As far as they're concerned, it's going to look as if he's close to this Plank character … shagging his daughter for goodness sake. What do you think is the next question they'll think of?'

I've said it before and I'll say it again. My Aileen has a brain like a steel trap. She's got this way of turning a subject around and finding ways of looking at it that haven't occurred to anyone else. But I was catching up fast.

I said, 'You mean they'll start wondering who Petesy is working for now?'

'Exactly. It won't take them more than five minutes to find the answer to that one. And you'll be in the boiling water up to your neck. As usual. And before long they'll have your description as well as Petesy's.'

'Yeah,' I said, 'but they'll see that my garage is a legitimate business, and then they'll lose interest.'

I actually faltered a bit while saying that, because I was starting to remember uncomfortable bits of the past. So it wasn't absolutely necessary for Aileen to put the boot in, as such.

'Of course they will,' she said, in a voice loaded with sarcasm, 'and they'll obviously agree it could never be used as a front for nefarious villainies – again.'

Nefarious villainies, indeed. I muttered something about going to Petesy's flat tomorrow anyway, on account of Petesy having too much work to catch up on to spare the time.

Aileen turned round into her sleeping position, and about two minutes later began snoring gently – leaving me alone with my thoughts and some new nagging worries.

*

25

How ironic can you get? This is the inevitable uppermost thought in Stella Galloway's mind as she taps in the number Vince has provided. It is a welcome sign that she has been accepted into the fold, to become a trusted member of the gang. Here she is making a telephone call to one of the organization's tame crooked cops. His private mobile number. Vince wrote it down for her, along with the information that the unnamed policeman will be off duty at this time. It is answered after three rings.

'Yeah?' The masculine voice gives nothing away.

She speaks the password – also provided by Vince.

'Right,' the voice replies.

'Black BMW 320,' she says. She follows up with the registration.

'Call back. Two hours,' says the voice. The line goes dead.

Stella checks her watch. Six fifteen. Her assigned task is to track down the owner of a car that has been spotted near Mr Plank's house, and to find out as much as possible about the aforesaid owner. Vince has not bothered to inform her that he and his sidekick have come face-to-face with the owner of the car.

Nor did he mention that the man they confronted had cleverly evaded their clutches. His only comment was that the vehicle belongs to a close associate of Mr Plank, who might be involved in the abduction of the boss. No mention of the close associate's status as the boyfriend of Plank's daughter.

Having nothing else to do for the moment, Stella passes the time by lingering over a lasagne and a glass of red wine in the nearby Pasta Piazza. By 8 p.m. she is back in the office of Ecological Recycling Ltd, the Redditch-based company that has spent the last three years as one of the Plank organization's pseudo-legal fronts. It is the nerve-centre of the Western faction of the now disintegrating Plank empire.

At the crack of eight fifteen, Stella makes the call, gives the password, and writes down the information that comes back up the phone: Oliver Peterson Curtain, the address of a flat in Acock's Green.

And a bonus nugget:

'... no convictions, no arrests, but known to the police as a relative and former associate of Alphonse Turner, a prominent Midlands racketeer who was murdered in the course of an outbreak of gang warfare two years ago.'

Bingo, thinks Stella. This Oliver Curtain sounds like somebody who would likely be associated with Plank in a criminal role. She decides her next logical step would be to pay a call on his flat – preferably when its occupant is not in residence. With a bit of luck she will be able to present Vince with the detailed low-down on some of Mr Plank's secret connections. It seems unlikely to Stella that this Curtain character would be working on his own – tip of an iceberg, more likely.

Besides, she really needs to ingratiate herself with the movers and shakers of this set-up. How else to move up the tree and keep herself informed of every new development in what seems an increasingly confusing situation.

—CHAPTER THREE————————————

Petesy lives in a flat in Acock's Green, which is a southern outskirt of Birmingham, not far past Solihull from our direction. It was his compromise when he moved out of the flash apartment near Hagley Road in the middle of the city. He couldn't have kept that without the high income that comes from being fast-track trainee management in a criminal organization. At the time, I suggested he should move to the Stratford area, but he couldn't tear himself that far away from the Birmingham clubs which he regularly attended in order to pull the most desirable chicks.

Armed with Petesy's key and his instructions as to which items of his extensive designer wardrobe were most essential, I drove the twenty miles to Acock's Green and parked near the flat. I put my disguise in place before getting out of the car. Well, it wasn't really a disguise. Not as such – but it worked better than any false moustache and wig. What I did was, I clipped to my lapel a large white ID badge with the name of a gas company in large red lettering. It identified me as Arnold Belcher, mains inspector (don't ask me where I got it or any of my other assorted ID badges). That badge together with the clipboard which I tucked under my arm, made me virtually invisible. Nobody ever bothers to take a close look at officious-looking employees of utility companies. As my Aunt Ursula would have put it, all that glitters is probably just a rose by another name.

The whole building was pretty quiet, being occupied mostly by young and youngish singles and childless couples, most of whom would be out at work on a Wednesday morning. Petesy's door looked innocently closed but, as it happened, I didn't need the key – not to get inside the place, at least. The door swung open in response to my light push.

I was immediately on my guard. The opposition must have got

here sooner than I could reasonably have expected. Well, perhaps not so surprising – they'd had a whole day and a night to chase up Petesy's car registration. My inevitable next thought was that the intruder (or intruders) might still be here. In fact, just thinking about it, I realized how likely that was. A professional criminal in search of information would definitely leave the door locked when he departed.

I thought at first my most sensible course of action would be to go outside and watch the building from my car until the coast was in the clear. Then I would be able to follow Petesy's burglar when he came out. But that wouldn't work: how would I recognize him – he probably wouldn't be carrying a bag marked swag over his shoulder? In other words, there could be all sorts of people emerging and how would I know who was the right one to follow?

My brain cells flashed through that set of arguments in an instant, enabling me to plump wholeheartedly for the most stupid course of action available. I knew the layout of the place, having helped Petesy when he was moving in. It was pretty small, consisting of one bedroom, a living-room which also had a dining table, a bathroom and a tiny but well-equipped kitchen. I tiptoed inside and flattened myself against the wall beside the first door – the bedroom. Carefully peering in through the half-open door, I found it unoccupied. The bathroom and living-room both delivered a similar result. While checking the last of these, I heard a noise which could only have come from the kitchen, the door of which was slightly ajar.

Found him, I thought. I squinted through the narrow gap, and was just able to make out, against the bright daylight from the window, a burly figure bending over Petesy's waste bin. I've heard it said that the best way to get the complete low-down on a person is to examine their rubbish. Here was someone obviously acting on that principle.

I had the advantage of surprise on my side. What else could I have done?

Throwing the kitchen door wide, I leapt in and grappled the intruder from behind. My left forearm went round his neck, putting pressure on his throat to prevent any chance of a shout while my right hand was twisting his right arm behind his back.

My strength was obviously superior. There was very little resistance beyond some gurgling noises, which seemed to be an attempt at speech. I risked loosening my grip in the hope of hearing something interesting.

''Ere, what's going on? … Lemme go you bastard swine … Me purse is in me coat hanging in the hall … No, don't rape me …'

About this time it was beginning to dawn on me that the intruder I had captured was a plump middle-aged woman in an apron. I released my stranglehold on her and stepped backwards.

'Who the hell are you – and what are you doing here?' I asked, though by now I was forming a pretty good idea of the answer.

'I'm Marlene, the cleaning lady. I come in every Wednesday morning for three hours …'

'Oh, Christ, I'm sorry,' I said, feeling a bit shamefaced. 'I thought you were an intruder who'd broken into Petesy's flat.'

She was looking at me in what I can only describe as a suspicious manner, with quite a lot of nervousness thrown in. I retreated towards the living-room, and she followed at a safe distance. We stood awkwardly facing each other; me in the middle of the room, she just inside the door, poised for a quick dash to safety if necessary. I decided more explanation was needed.

'Look, Marlene,' I said, 'I'm Kenny … Petesy – Mr Curtain – is a friend of mine. He asked me to pick up some of his things … See? I've got a key.'

I held it up and she must have recognized it because I saw her relax a little. Suddenly I had the presence of mind to whip my Arnold Belcher badge off my lapel and slip it into my pocket.

'Maybe,' she conceded, fortunately still eyeing the key, 'but what was that you called him there … Peachy or something?'

'Petesy,' I told her, adding, 'you must know his name, surely?'

'I've only met Mr Curtain two or three times. He didn't tell me his first name … but his business partner called him Oliver and that sounds a lot different from Petesy.'

Marlene was renewing her suspicious glare.

Suddenly, a whole herd of alarm bells was going off in my head. On account of being his employer, I happen to know Petesy's full name, which is Oliver Petersen Curtain. I was also aware that nobody who knew Petesy ever called him Oliver. Not to mention the fact that the term business partner has no meaning when applied to Petesy.

I asked, 'Who is this business partner then? How do you know about him?'

Marlene corrected me.

'His business partner is a her, not a him ... a very nice Scottish lady actually ... you would know that if you really were Mr Curtain's friend. She was here already when I arrived this morning. She dropped in to collect some papers he asked her to pick up.'

That clinched it. I had to phone Petesy at the garage and persuade Marlene to talk to him. With great reluctance, she agreed to trust me, and fill me in on her encounter with Petesy's so-called business partner.

It seems that this woman – slim, thirtyish, pin-striped business suit with short skirt, brisk business-like manner – had already collected some of Mr Curtain's papers into her briefcase. Most of the stuff that 'Oliver' had asked her to bring ... it would be suffi-cient, she told Marlene. A few pleasantries were exchanged, and on the way out, the nice lady had picked up Oliver's telephone and address book from the table in the hallway, 'Just in case he might need this'.

Aileen was right. Any number of pointers they might find among Petesy's papers could lead the nasties in my direction. Given the kind of luck I was having, they would soon know all about my past criminal associations.

And Petesy's too, of course, if they didn't know about that already.

But no point in dwelling on what might happen. Driving back to Stratford with a case full of Petesy's best clobber, I reviewed things from a more level-headed perspective.

I decided I wouldn't spend too much time discussing the situation with Aileen. If her previous night's reaction was anything to go by, she would be inclined to the gloomy side, which is not really like her usual reaction. Anyway, I reminded myself, there was actually nothing to discuss. The whole thing would most likely fizzle out and dissolve into a storm in a tea-bag. No need for Aileen coming up with way-out ideas like going to the police, which was possible since her friend, Sally, married CID policeman Neil Cornfoot.

The last thing I needed was to have an over-educated copper poking his nose into my business – even though I had nothing to hide. Not any more.

Don't get me wrong, Neil is a perfectly nice bloke as such – when you meet him socially. Detective Inspector Neil Cornfoot. There was a time in the past – well, a few times – when he was an over-ambitious sergeant, and pressured me into solving cases for him, which culminated in me helping to clear up half the crime in the Midlands so that he could get his promotion. Well, I suppose it was better than being arrested for nicking cars, which was the kettle of fish that Neil has held over my head in the past. This time there was nothing to interest him – well, nothing that would do me any good.

So what I would do was, I would just carry on with my life as usual. We would buy that new bed tonight after Aileen finished work. Petesy could stay at our house for a week – maximum. Then, once it was clear that nothing else was going to happen, he could clear off back to his own flat in his own car. And everything would be back to normal.

Definitely no point involving the police, especially not Neil. So I made a mental note to remind Aileen to avoid any mention of this stuff to him or Sally.

—CHAPTER FOUR———————————

I was a little bit late finishing up at the garage that evening, what with having a tray full of accumulated paperwork to tidy up ready for Mrs Torrance who comes in twice a week to do the book-keeping. By the time I got home, Aileen and Petesy were already there discussing my morning's adventure at Petesy's flat, and who on earth that 'business partner' might have been. Not to mention why, and what it all had to do with the recent outbreak of bizarre events around Mr Short Plank.

It took a bit of effort on my part to change the subject, but I managed eventually to get the three of us out. First there was the boring part which consisted of choosing one out of about forty identical beds for delivery at some unspecified time in the future. Then we had a reasonably enjoyable meal in a pub restaurant. Altogether a pleasant, ordinary evening – though I think we were all aware of an unspoken shadow hanging in the background.

Back home, Aileen asked Petesy about the status of his current romance, now that fate had thrown a spanner into the ring. He just sighed and said, 'Daphne and I have been talking on the phone … several times today … she's quite upset of course. We've decided to give it a day or two and see what happens. But we agreed that for the moment we must stick together as much as possible, especially since Daphne has to go back to college in a few weeks.'

It might be better for everyone concerned if they didn't bother getting together again, I thought. Of course, I didn't dare say a word.

Once Petesy had retired to his sleeping bag, I confided to Aileen that I, in my own way, had come to the same conclusion as Petesy – that we should simply do nothing, and wait for the whole thing to fizzle out. To my surprise, she didn't agree.

'That's right,' she said, 'go ahead, you and Petesy – bury your heads in the beach, like a couple of stupid ostriches and then you'll be amazed when the tide comes in and drowns you. Honestly, you men are all as bad as each other.'

Before continuing, Aileen put on her determined expression and did that jerk of her head to the right to flick what she called her golden tresses away from her eyes.

'Well, thank goodness one of us has enough sense to know when to blow the whistle. I've arranged with Sally for us to go over to their place on Friday after work. We can tell Neil the whole story and get his advice. After all, he probably knows about this kidnapping from the police point of view, so maybe some of what you can tell him could be of use.'

'Aw, come on, Aileen ...' I started to protest, but when Aileen gets the bit between her legs there's no stopping her. She talked right through me.

'If these people, whoever they are, really mean to harm Petesy and you ... well, maybe Neil could use you as bait. You know, keep watch, and when the villains come after either or both of you, Neil and his men could nab them ...

'... or something,' she added with a flap of her hand, as she ran out of steam.

I was speechless for a while. Eventually, I said, 'What about Petesy? He might not agree with you throwing a copper into the works – and he might not fancy being bait. I sure as hell don't.'

'Oh, I don't think we need to tell Petesy, do you?' she said, quite shamelessly. 'I certainly don't want him along with us on Friday ... it's just the two of us going out to spend a pleasant evening with friends.'

She quickly switched to what she must have thought was a more positive side of the subject.

'Anyway, just think how much safer it will be for Petesy and you when you have the police on your side to protect you.'

I did what I think of as my hollow laugh. In my experience police protection is about as useful as tits on a nun. But Aileen had made the arrangement, so I would just have to go along for the ride. Anyway, I was well aware that coppers are not allowed to discuss current cases with all and sundry, which means that Neil would have to be non-committal and just nod wisely at anything Aileen might tell him.

Use Petesy and me as bait, indeed. Where does she get these ideas?

'I hear you may have some information for me ... about various members of our criminal fraternity. So what is it all about, Kenny?'

Neil handed me a bottle of Beck's as he asked the question.

'Thanks,' I said, taking a swig from the bottle to give myself a little thinking time. I had been hoping that any mention of Mr Plank and our little local difficulty would be laughed off with no more than a couple of sentences among the four of us. But it seemed that Aileen must have exaggerated the importance of the thing by dropping the word to Sally, who would in turn have set Neil up for a major consultation.

I should mention that at the point where Neil broached the subject, the girls had tactfully left us alone together while they went on a cruise through Sally's wardrobe. But they would have done that anyway, in spite of the fact that there was no question of clothes swaps on account of Sally being several inches taller than Aileen, and very skinny – sorry, I'm not allowed to say she's skinny, or even thin for that matter – what I really mean is slender. (And I have to admit that she looks very attractive, sexy even, although she's not my type at all.)

So what with one thing and another, and without really intending it, I ended up telling Neil what I knew about recent events at the Plank house, and the fallout that seemed to be heading towards Petesy and me through no fault of our own. I even mentioned Nick Pearson's nasty experience, while managing not to divulge his name. Not that our caring policeman gave a monkey's about anybody's suffering – nor any potential mayhem either.

He said, 'Well, it's great that you've already started to get a handle on the Plank situation, Kenny. That, together with the fact that they're already coming after both you and Petesy – well, it saves us having to point them in your direction. And it shows that they're afraid of you.'

I was a bit flabbergasted.

'Afraid of me!' I said, 'Not as bloody afraid as I am of them, mate. What happened to the police duty to protect the public – which includes me and my friends?'

'Oh, come on, Kenny,' he replied. 'We all know you're well able to look after yourself. Anyway, you wouldn't be able to fulfil your function for us if they could see that you're well protected?'

'Function?' I asked.

'For you?' I asked.

'We appreciate your offer, Kenny. My group down at the station have been working out how best to take advantage of it, ever since Aileen passed on the good news via Sally.'

Neil stopped for breath while I was still too stunned to get my mouth into gear. At this point, my Auntie Ursula would have been going on about his words not buttering many parsnips, or something. Anyway, he took my silence as the green light of assent, and got his mouth into its stride.

'So what I really need to do now is bring you up to speed with all the data we've amassed on the Plank case, as well as sketching in the background as far as possible on the current activities of the whole Plank organization.'

I was on my feet now.

'Bollocks to you and your sodding group down at the station. You can look somewhere else for your fucking stooges in future. I'm out of here.'

I up-ended my beer bottle over his trousers, and dropped the empty after it. Neil yelled in protest – something about the new sofa – but I didn't really catch it all because I was already through the door.

'I don't care what you say,' I told Aileen, 'if I listened to that bloody bureaucratic busy with his "bringing you up to speed as regards the ongoing Plank scenario", I would find myself getting sucked in to some god-awful dangerous … state of danger or something …'

This was when we were back home in bed later that night after I had walked back from Neil and Sally's house, leaving the car for Aileen. She used my momentary excess of indignation to take control of the conversation.

'Kendall Madigan …' she began, in her most serious tone of voice. When Aileen uses my full name like that, it's a warning for me to shut up and listen or suffer the consequences.

'Kendall Madigan, you're as stubborn as a mule in a china shop, you know that? You're just sticking your head under the duvet. Can't you see that you're already up to your ears in the ongoing

Plank scenario, and you could do a whole lot worse than listen to what Neil has to say – he's a professional law-enforcement officer. But will you listen? Oh no, not Mister Know-it-all Madigan ... and now you've burned your britches and you won't know what to say to these ... er, Plankers when they come after you and—'

Human flesh can only stand so much of this. I had to do something to stop the flow.

'Plankers!' I repeated incredulously. 'You definitely said Plankers. How in hell did you ever think up that one?'

That knocked Aileen off her stride. She floundered a bit before coming up with, 'Well ... I wanted to include Plank's gang and his kidnappers, either or both ... and I couldn't call them plonkers because that would make them sound harmless, and I didn't want to say wankers – you know what I think about gutter language – so it just came out as Plankers ...'

She tailed off as I laughed out loud.

'It's a great word,' I said, kissing her neck. 'From now on, they're all Plankers. Right?'

Aileen giggled and I felt her head nod in the dark. She said, 'I've got to admit it was funny, though. Sally and I came down the stairs to find out what the commotion was all about, and there was Neil red-faced, rubbing at the front of his trousers with a tissue and leaving white specks all over his flies. Once Sally was satisfied the sofa wasn't stained, she started laughing and told him it probably served him right for being pompous.'

It sounded as if Aileen was back on my side. I reached out to give her a hug, which led to one thing after another. Afterwards, as she turned round into her sleeping position, she had the last word, as usual.

'Don't forget what I said, though, Kenny. I think this could be a really dangerous business. I hate going through life having to worry about you ... I mean I know you'll always keep me safe but that's not enough any more.'

The next morning was Saturday. Aileen only gets about one Saturday in four off work, so she was out early, heading for the shoe shop. Petesy, in his keen as mustard way, was off to open up the used-car side of the business. I quite often go in to the garage on Saturday mornings, just to make sure everything is cleared up all ready for business on Monday. But today, I had something else to do. It's one thing to get a feeling of satisfaction by pouring beer over somebody in the heat of the moment, but you're liable to end up with no friends if you don't make some attempt to repair the breach.

I called Neil and arranged to meet him around lunchtime in that pub in Stratford Old Town that I can never remember the name of – the one that used to be grotty, but has recently been refurbished to attract the smart yuppie set. I thought Neil would feel at ease there.

So I bought him a pint of Old Crapper, or whatever the so-called guest ale of the week was called, and a lager for myself and we took them out the back to a table in the garden where we would be less likely to be overheard. Somehow I got the impression that Neil was still sulking, which caused me to try to cheer him up.

'Come on, Neil,' I said, 'you're a copper. You must be used to people wanting to do a lot worse than pouring beer on you.'

'I could have you inside, charged with common assault, you bastard,' he growled. But I just kept looking him in the eye, watching until his scowl changed to a reluctant grin. Then we both relaxed and took a swig of our drinks.

Neil wiped his mouth daintily with a paper napkin from a dispenser on the table and said, 'All right, Kenny ... I accept your apology.'

This was devious, considering that I had not actually apologized. It was really his way of apologizing to me without actually doing so, and that meant he really needed my assistance – or he thought he did, which amounts to almost the same thing.

'Right,' he said crisply, 'here's the low-down on Plank, as we see it. First of all, there is a strong aroma of dead mackerel surrounding the man's alleged kidnapping.'

That's what you get from coppers who have degrees – metaphors on wheels instead of straight dealing in facts.

'Are you trying to tell me it was a put-up job – the kidnapping?' I asked.

'Got it in one,' said Neil. 'My ... er, our interpretation is that Plank arranged to have himself "kidnapped" by members of a loyal faction within his own organization. It would be very convenient for him to disappear for a while, considering the shake-up that's going on currently in the criminal community.'

He finished this speech and put on the smug look of someone who has just come up with a complete explanation of the Leghorn Mystery, whatever that is. From where I was sitting, all he had done was to add some new items to the growing list of questions buzzing around in my brain.

'Don't you think it's more plausible that Plank was kidnapped by members of a disloyal group in what you call his organization or – even more likely – by some rival gang of thugs?' I asked.

Neil continued to look smug while he drank down what he probably thought was a well-deserved gulp of real-ale cat pee. Then he came back with, 'Well, I would suggest that both of your scenarios are a touch improbable in the light of the paradigm shift which is at present driving the restructuring of the crime industry in this country.'

I mentally scored myself a point when he actually said the word scenarios? And what about paradigm shift, for Christ's sake? I pretended to go along with whatever he was talking about.

'All right, Neil … so you've got some inside information. Why don't you fill me in on the background so that I can feel superior too. It might help if I knew what the fuck you're talking about.'

'That's what we're here for, Kenny,' he said cheerfully, obviously enjoying himself. 'If you'll just keep quiet long enough, maybe you'll learn something.'

Supercilious bastard. I glared at him as viciously as I could manage, but kept my mouth shut in the hope that he might actually get on with the business of saying something useful, interesting, or even understandable.

He began, 'See, it's like what the rest of British industry has already gone through – the move out of manufacturing and into services. Not that the crime industry ever produced anything useful … what it means for them is getting out of the tough and dirty end of their business. No more risky and labour-intensive robberies, extensive shop-lifting operations, truck hijacking, fencing stolen goods, drug smuggling, etcetera. Even when they are successful, these activities leave the perpetrators with most of the job still to do. Right?'

I nodded. 'You mean they don't get their hands on any actual money until they do the hard work of finding a market for the stuff they've nicked.'

'Exactly, and just think about the expense of moving it around. Warehousing and storage costs too ... and so many people to pay out of the profits. No wonder they get to thinking the game isn't worth the candle any more. That's why a clever crook like your friend Plank is shifting his commercial base – he's leaving traditional crime to the amateurs and small-time villains ... anybody who wants to fill the vacuum, including his own former employees. Especially them, in fact, because he's also pressing on with what the legitimate industries have taken to referring as downsizing – in other words, dumping large numbers of employees who lack the appropriate skills in an increasingly technological business environment.'

In spite of the high-flown jargon, it was making reasonable sense, except that I couldn't imagine the likes of Short Plank personally getting into anything as hi-tech as, say, computer fraud. I pointed this out to Neil.

'I can't imagine the likes of Short Plank getting into anything as hi-tech as computer fraud,' I said.

'No, of course not,' he almost sneered. 'He wouldn't understand how to hack into bank networks or anything else, and he didn't get where he is today by trusting anybody else to do his dirty work for him. Anyway, it depends what you mean by computer fraud – his start-up enterprises are certainly fraudulent, and they rely on computers for their day-to-day running, just like any communication-based business.'

It sounded to me as if Neil was about to start telling me all the details of how Plank was about to find new ways of separating money from its former owners, when I interrupted to point out that we were both in dire need of having our glasses refilled – and it was his shout.

When Neil came back with our drinks, I used the interruption to move the discussion back to more interesting ground.

'So, tell me more about the ructions caused by Plank's slimmed-down mob of desperate hoodlums,' I said.

'Well, the rank and file are about as disgruntled as any group of workers who know that most of them are on the brink of becoming redundant ... with the additional features that, first, this lot won't be in line for redundancy handouts; and, second, they are a murderous bunch who are not inclined to take things lying down.'

'Ah,' I said, 'so you think they've kidnapped the boss to make him change his mind?'

'Well, that's one possible starting point, but I don't think it's that simple. See, there are two separate groups – we believe that Mr Plank deliberately keeps them apart and even encourages the rivalry between them – so if he really has been kidnapped, it could be the work of either of the two factions. There's never been any love lost between these two bunches of Plank villains, but it has hotted up in the last month or so. They've been at each others' throats for weeks now, and the tit-for-tat body count is growing almost day by day. It's quite possible that either of the two groups could have staged a fake kidnapping to protect Plank from the others.

'Or – my choice, as I said before – maybe he arranged it himself.'

'That's all very well,' I said, 'but from where I'm standing, the only important question is how you propose to protect me from whatever bunch of murderous bastards is coming after me.'

'It must be the bunch responsible for the kidnapping – or disappearance, who would threaten you,' said Neil, in that smug way he has.

'Yeah, but it sounds as if it could be just about anybody.'

'Exactly,' he said, 'and that's why we would like you to cooperate – so we can find out what's really going on.'

I asked, 'You seem to know quite a lot of the low-down on this mob already. Why don't you get the rest of the information the same way?'

'I wish we could. All the background data we have came from our own copper we put in there to infiltrate Plank's mob – oh, a couple of months ago, before the kidnapping. It was already obvious that there was a flurry of increased activity in the criminal world, so we wanted to know more about it.'

'So why would you need me to help?'

Apparently it was a sore point. Neil looked a bit sheepish.

'Well, just at the moment, we don't actually know what's become of our undercover cop. I'm not supposed to tell you this, but we haven't heard a word for more than a week now … so that's something else you might be able to help us with—'

'You bloody stony-hearted bastard,' I broke in, 'Your poor sod of a cop might be lying dead in some ditch, and here you are trying to pressure another mug into replacing him.'

'Look, Kenny,' he said forcefully, 'I'm only trying to help you. Whether you like it or not, you're already in this up to your bollocks … and you've got a history that makes it possible for you to get on the right side of these villains. They must need your kind of talent for illegal chicanery.'

Neil can't resist putting on a bit of drama sometimes. He paused to pour the last of his pint down his throat, and banged his empty glass down on the table before delivering the final persuasion, which somehow failed to fill me with enthusiasm.

'Anyway, I'm pretty sure our undercover operative is still alive and active. We don't think she's become a victim of the recent flurry of gang warfare. At least she hasn't turned up among the latest crop of mob bodies – not the ones we've found anyway. Stella Galloway is capable of looking after herself; she's a very resourceful person. Quite like yourself in a way.'

That was just about it, then. I could only think of one more question.

'What exactly is this new business that Plank is setting up?'

Neil shrugged and tried not to look embarrassed.

'We don't actually know, except it's something that doesn't need large contingents of mentally challenged muscle,' he said. 'I suppose we'll find out all the details sooner or later.'

So we parted with Neil promising to keep in touch; he would get some specific instructions to me very soon, he said. He seemed to think I was now committed to his cause, but as far as I was concerned, I was still my own man.

Kenny Madigan, the stranger in a fool's Paradise.

─CHAPTER FIVE──────────────

Having completed her successful mission to Acock's Green, Stella bears her prizes back to the Ecological Recycling office in Redditch. She is pleased to find that Vince himself is not present, as she particularly wants to present him with a completed piece of work; every i dotted, every t crossed. It also means she can use Vince's office and desk, not having one of her own, and Dirk being in residence, fiddling with his electronic bits and pieces in the spare office.

Eagerly, Stella opens her briefcase, to shake out on to Vince's desk all the booty she has collected in Oliver Curtain's apartment. Besides the telephone and address book, there are a number of domestic bills – gas, electricity, credit cards, and so on – as well as an assortment of pieces of paper. Most of the stuff is useless, but that is to be expected.

A careful marshalling of the available paperwork, combined with the address book, enables Stella to put together a partial view of the suspect's life. (Annoyed, she corrects herself. Mustn't think of him as a suspect; it's a police habit.)

It seems that the er … this person is known to his friends as Petesy, not Oliver. Clearly a bit of a lad, at least in his own estimation, judging by the predominance of female names and numbers in the address book. Surprisingly, he works at an apparently legitimate job running a used-car operation. This is deduced from a draft newspaper advertise- ment which gives the address of the car dealer and concludes with the message: 'For the best deal on wheels, steer a route to Petesy Curtain at Madigan Motors'.

Not that the used car business is always straight by any means, thinks Stella.

Detective Constable Stella Galloway is rather enjoying this job despite her awareness of being in a potentially dangerous situation. She has been seconded from a Scottish force in response to Inspector Neil Cornfoot's request for a resourceful copper with zero risk of being recognized in the Midlands. Cornfoot does not actually expect a woman, but quickly persuades himself that she will be so much better than any man for the work he has in mind.

His arguments are: considering the current spate of bloodshed among the criminal fraternity, an undercover male might well be required to prove his mettle to the villains by taking part in murder – which is definitely not on for a policeman, no matter how deserving the victim; whereas a woman will most likely escape that requirement, given the politically incorrect attitudes of organized crime. Furthermore, Neil reasons illogically, an attractive young woman is less likely to be in physical danger from a bunch of big strong male thugs. Conveniently, he does not bother to consider what other dangers might lurk in the path of a female copper.

'See if you can make your Scottish accent just a tiny bit coarser; that'll give you a bit more credibility as a criminal,' Neil tells her, unaware how close he comes to physical danger at that moment. Luckily for him, he thinks better of another – even more sexist – remark he almost comes out with. But only as a joke, of course:

'If you find yourself in a tricky situation, you can probably defuse it by flashing your tits.'

In the event, Stella has infiltrated the Plank empire without too much difficulty, using the criminal background and references which have been set up for her. Now she has to admit to herself, she is really enjoying the job. At the same time, she finds it somewhat disconcerting to be working with such enthusiasm for the wrong side. Loyalty is a quality which plays a fundamental role in Stella's character, so she instinctively wants to do a good job for her current bosses. This is all very fine, and she gets a glow of satisfaction from the knowledge that she is a warrior in the fight against crime.

But it comes to her as something of a surprise, revelation even, to feel the same kind of loyalty towards Vince Moorhouse, boss of this western section of Plank's little empire. Admittedly, he is a lot more intelligent than the general run of thugs who work for him. Stella's lip curls at the thought of the personality-free zone known as Dirk; but even he is infinitely preferable to the leering, sneering presence of the one she cannot help thinking of as 'the ugly fat bastard', apparently Vince's right-hand man.

Vince's thin veneer of urbanity is not sufficient to conceal the ruthless drive which has taken advantage of a perceived loss of grip on the part of Mr Plank to pursue his own power struggle against the other half of his own (or at least Plank's) organization, the East Midlands mob led by the despised Rod Simmons.

Stella has been lucky enough to become the third member of Vince Moorhouse's personal staff, joining Dirk and the ugly fat bastard. What she is doing turns out to be quite absorbing, and is to her surprise more akin to real detective work than any of her former duties as a normal detective constable. She has now followed the trail leading from a sighting of a particular car, all the way, not just to the identity of the car's owner, but into his lifestyle, and beyond that to the owner's employer, a Mr Kendall Madigan of Stratford-on-Avon.

Stella has, of course, informed Inspector Neil Cornfoot of the general situation she finds herself in. Her first few reports on becoming established covered all that. However, she has not yet had the opportunity to meet Mr Plank in person. Her knowledge of his disappearance is limited to what she has been able to read in the newspapers; so either Vince knows nothing or he is not yet prepared to trust her with the really important information.

Since there is nothing she can add to the existing police knowledge, there is no point in taking unnecessary risks to submit null reports – until now, that is. Suddenly the inspiration springs full-blown into her mind – wouldn't it be a good idea for her to know more about this ominous pair, Petesy Curtain and his shadowy boss, Kendall Madigan.

This strikes Stella as a productive train of thought. She lets it roll on a bit further to see where it might end up (that Stella Galloway, they used to say back in Largs, has too much imagination to make a successful career in the police force). Her reasoning goes like this: since Vince himself seems to have no knowledge of these people (Curtain and Madigan), it may well be that they represent Plank's new business direction. They could be the reason why Plank is dumping his old organization ... both west and east parts of his old organization. Maybe Curtain and Madigan could provide a clue to the nature of Plank's future enterprise. Being a very astute criminal, Plank would choose his associates carefully. So these two, together with any comrades they might bring to the feast, must be very good at whatever they do.

Stella decides she needs access to all available police resources to get the low-down on Curtain and Madigan. She will have to pass on some of the resulting information to Vince – things she could have discovered for herself, or gathered from criminal connections – but the best bits will be kept for her own potential use. Knowledge is power.

Mindful of the likelihood of the offices at the Ecological Recycling

Company being infested with bugging devices, Stella goes outside for a smoke in the wind-blown carpark (but shrewdly does not get into her car, just in case). She uses her mobile to make the call to Detective Inspector Neil Cornfoot on his private mobile number, which she has memorized.

Aileen listened attentively to my account of Neil's garbled tale of cops and robbers. We were at home after work, mopping up the remains of our chilli con carne. Petesy had gone somewhere else straight from the garage, which Aileen thought he was doing so as not to be constantly what she called 'living in and out of our pockets' while he was staying at our house.

I finished my story with one of my best derisive snorts.

'So you can see how Neil is trying to use me for his own purposes, as usual. I would be crazy to get involved in all that stuff – wouldn't I? Don't you think?'

'Kenny,' she said in that kind of pitying tone that she puts on to annoy me, 'now you're being the protester who … er, protests too much.'

I had to admit she was probably right, though not out loud; just to myself. But she wasn't finished.

'Bring these plates and we'll get the washing-up done while we discuss this thing. So, what did he actually tell you? I mean, what real information did you get?'

Aileen supplied her own answer without waiting for any contribution from me. She counted them off on her fingers while I ran hot water into the sink.

'*One*: the criminal gangs change their organization and look for new kinds of crime. *Two*: some of the plankers get overheated about being left in the dust. *Three*: the police become so desperate to know what it's all about that they send some poor woman into the jaws of jeopardy. Wow!'

A bit bemused, I boggled at *jaws of jeopardy*. And then it came to me that Aileen was dead right, as usual. In a few words and about twenty seconds she had summed up all the information it took me a whole lunchtime to pry out of Neil. I nodded my head, thinking carefully before I would open my mouth. As it happened, I never got the chance to say a word, because Aileen wasn't finished yet. Her eyes narrowed as she squeezed yet more creative thinking out of her brain.

'Not much to go on, is it? What about all the stuff he didn't bother to tell you … like what exactly is so different, and so great, about the new crimes these villains have invented? I bet he knows quite a lot about that. I mean, I quite like Neil and he's a good husband to Sally and everything but …'

She left the *but* trailing, just switched to a different track, and ended with: 'Not to mention *why* he "forgot" to tell you any more. You just leave it to me, Kenny – I'll find out through Sally.'

We finished up drying the crockery and cutlery in silence, each, I suppose, preoccupied with our own thoughts.

Later on, we were on the sofa, half watching some rubbish gardening programme on television (Aileen's idea because our brand new house came complete with a back garden – well, it could be a back garden if we ever managed to remove the builders' rubble which was only hidden from view by a thin layer of topsoil), when the doorbell rang.

'That'll be Petesy being considerate,' Aileen said. 'He'll probably go straight up to his room without disturbing us.' Sure enough, a few seconds later, Petesy opened the front door with the key we had given him, and we heard – not just his footsteps coming inside, but also another set. By the time the tap came on the living-room door, Aileen was dashing around tidying up odds and ends in honour of the unknown visitor.

Petesy came in, ushering a girl – well, a young woman I suppose, though she looked about fifteen to my thirtyish-year-old eyes. This vision was introduced to us as Daphne, whom I immediately recalled as being the daughter of the missing gang boss. Daphne Plank then. I reminded myself that she was nineteen and had to admit she was worth a second, third, fourth, etcetera, look. Even though she could have been no more than five foot one, she was perfectly proportioned, and looked up at the world with big dark eyes below a tumbling torrent of jet-black hair.

'Little Daphne Plank, I presume,' I said stupidly, shaking hands with her. Exceptionally gorgeous women always leave me with all the wrong words, and this one was well up in that league – her figure made her what I think is called a Pocket Venus. Petesy really does have good taste in girlfriends, if in nothing else.

Aileen was her usual practical self, ushering our guests on to the sofa (where they perched, holding hands in a particularly nause-

47

ating way) and then bustling through the archway into the kitchen to set up coffee and biscuit production.

Once we were all sorted out and provisioned, Petesy could wait no longer. Through a shower of Hob Nob crumbs, he began.

'Daphne ...' He shot a moonstruck calf kind of glance sideways to his loved one, as if overcome by the sound of her name.

'Daphne and her mother are very upset about the disappearance of their ... er ... her dad ...'

'Yes, I can see how awful it must be for both of you,' said Aileen, switching her attention to Daphne. She's really good at sympathy, my Aileen.

'Right,' said Petesy, slightly frowning at the interruption while Daphne merely nodded. 'Well, I mentioned you, Kenny ... and how you've solved a few things for people in the past.'

He looked at me expectantly, as if it was my turn to pull a rabbit out of my coffee mug. I took a sip from it instead, while I tried to think up some devastating reply which would get me off the hook. I failed.

'Yes,' I admitted, 'but that was ... well, there was no other way out at the time and ...'

'That's what I mean – it's like that again,' Petesy said. 'You and me, Kenny, we've probably already fallen foul of the punks who kidnapped Daphne's dad, so it can't get any worse for us – right? Anyway, I've promised her mum – Mrs Plank – that you'll go over there and have a chat ... see what you can come up with.'

He gave me a sickly smile and added, 'I'll take you to see her tomorrow morning.'

I was left floundering and dumbstruck while Petesy transferred his attention to Aileen. She's such a sucker for his so-called charm. Yes, she supposed it would be all right for them to bring Daphne's stuff (including sleeping-bag) into Petesy's room; did Daphne's mum know where she was spending the night? Well, yes, mothers are usually well aware of the fact that their daughters are smuggling a boyfriend into their bedrooms, and no, they don't always tell the dads, do they?

I wasn't really paying attention to this conversation on account of I was still thinking about being hustled into going to 'have a chat' with the wife of the biggest big chief in the Midlands criminal fraternity. Other people were taking over the planning of my Sunday without regard to any preferences I might have.

*

Sunday started quietly enough, with the four of us having an early breakfast in the kitchen. Not too many words were spoken, which suited me very well, since morning is not my best time – unlike Aileen, as you know. It didn't seem to apply to our two guests either; they were both looking more lively than anybody has a right to look at that time. Especially as Petesy and Daphne must have enjoyed something of a torrid night judging from the cow-eyed expressions and adoring glances.

The lovebirds were already dressed up ready to face the day; Petesy resplendent in his designer casual gear and Daphne in an emerald-green crop top to reveal a lot of waistline skin and tight white shorts which emphasized her tan legs. As soon as I reasonably could, I slipped away, accepting the pair's offer to cope with the washing-up. Aileen followed me upstairs to 'have a quiet word'.

'Aren't they cute?' were the first of her quiet words. She was grinning fondly. 'Give them a few months and they'll be spending their Saturday afternoons in garden centres.'

I waited for Aileen to get on with whatever she really wanted to say, which was not long in coming.

'Take it easy with Daphne's mum,' she said. 'Remember she must be in a terrible state, what with not knowing what on earth has happened to her husband.'

Considering the circumstances, I thought I was very restrained. I paused in the middle of buttoning my new dark blue linen shirt from NEXT.

'Maybe you should come along and operate me ... I'll just move my mouth when you say the words.'

I was quite pleased with that remark, actually. Sarcasm doesn't usually work so well for me, as you know. Aileen came out with a straight answer, though.

'No thanks, I'm quite happy to stay here and get on with some urgent hoovering. It's just that you leave a lot to be desired in the tact department ... you're liable to stick your foot right in the treacle tin if I'm not there to stop you.'

I maintained my dignity by not saying another word.

─CHAPTER SIX─

Petesy drove us in the Madigan Motors Renault he was using temporarily instead of his own. When he turned on to the Warwick road, I protested.

'Hey, this isn't the way to Lower Pebbington,'

'Mum's staying with my Aunt Rachel in Leamington,' said Daphne from the back seat. 'She needs the company ... and besides, the police have been paying a lot of attention to our house lately – they're probably still watching it.'

'They would have followed your mother. They'll be watching your aunt's house now,' I pointed out.

'No,' she said, 'Aunt Rachel came over to visit, and Mum left with her, hiding under a blanket in the back of the car. They didn't follow.'

Christ, I thought, what chance have the coppers got against a family like this. Daphne must have guessed what I was thinking, because she said, 'It's not illegal to leave your own house ... anyway, it was Mum – well, both of us really – who reported the kidnapping to the police ... and no they haven't followed Petesy and me either.'

That last bit was in response to my turning round to look out of the back window. No doubt she was right; the cops don't have enough resources to keep tabs on everyone connected with a crime. They would definitely have followed Mrs Plank though, if they'd got the chance.

It was that thought that made me decide the kidnapping must be self-inflicted by Mr Gerald Plank; which in that case his wife's first priority would be to side-step the attentions of the police so that she would be free to contact him. And, surprise surprise, that's just what she had done. You can see why I jumped to the obvious conclusion long before we turned in at the driveway of a large detached stone house in a quiet road on the north side of Leamington.

The door was actually opened by Daphne's nondescript Aunt Rachel, but she was swiftly replaced by a younger woman who was identifiable as Mrs Plank by the fact that Daphne ran to hug her, asking, 'Are you feeling better? Is there any news about Dad?'

She shook her head in reply, and Petesy said, 'We've brought my friend, Kenny ...'

He started into an awkward introduction, but Daphne's mother took over.

'Pleased to meet you Kenny. I'm Debra Plank. Come on in.'

We were ushered into a large comfortable front room, not what you would call smart, but well supplied with cushiony sofas and armchairs.

Mrs Plank was not what I expected, though I have no idea what I would have expected her to be like if it had occurred to me to have any expectations at all. The first surprise was that she appeared to be about my age. Well, all right, a well-groomed forty-year-old woman can look like she's in her early thirties – especially if she has the same dark good looks as her daughter, and can afford to deck herself out in up-to-the-minute fashions.

Once we were all seated, I took a closer look at this woman's face. I fancied I could detect lines of stress around her mouth, and a certain puffiness under her eyes, which could be the residue of tear-filled sleepless nights. Or maybe she was an accomplished actress, I added mentally – but it was hard to think of a reason why she would put on such a performance for my benefit.

She got straight down to the matter at the front of all our thoughts.

'Kenny, I don't know why I'm getting you involved in this thing ... except that I'm so desperate, and Petesy tells me that you have some talents which might be of use. If you don't want to get involved, I'll quite understand. But I am so desperately worried about Gerry ...'

Pause. At the end of which, she added unnecessarily, ' ... my husband.' She stopped, shrugged her shoulders and put a pathetically helpless expression on her face. She got up and went over to an old-fashioned piano which stood against the wall opposite the windows. From its high top, she picked up one of several framed photographs. She handed it to me. I saw Daphne looking like a high-school girl, so it would be about two years old. Behind Daphne were the grinning proud parents holding hands. So this was Gerry; just a well-dressed businessman much like any other except that the dark-haired top of his head was on a level with his wife's nose. I realized with a start that I was studying his features, so I hastily handed the picture back to Mrs Short Plank.

'Look, Mrs Plank ...' I began.

'Debra, please,' she corrected me.

'All right. Debra, then. Surely you must know many people who would be better placed than me to provide help... for instance, what about your husband's, er, business associates?'

She was shaking her head.

'Yes, but no ... I believe some of these people may be part of the problem. I don't know who I can trust because the kidnappers themselves are probably people who either are or have been his so-called associates ... nobody seems to be taking this kidnapping seriously. Gerry's friends, his business associates, even the police – they all act as if they believe it's all been set up by Gerry himself. God knows what they think he could possibly gain by faking his own abduction. Anyway, he wouldn't want me to suffer like this, not knowing ... or his daughter either. He dotes on Daphne, you know.'

My opening mouth was closed by the opening door of the room, through which Aunt Rachel appeared bearing a tray of goodies. I watched in silence as the aunt poured tea into cups, invited milk and sugar options, and handed round a plate of biscuits. Rachel didn't look the least bit like her younger sister. She was blatantly middle-aged, with the beginnings of grey in her hair. Her flowery apron amounted to an emphatic anti-fashion statement. At the end of the chore, I expected her to take a seat and join the rest of us, but no, she retreated back to the inner regions of the house, closing the door carefully behind her. Doesn't want to get involved in what Aileen would call nefarious goings-on, I decided.

Silence while we bit into our ginger nuts. Well, really just Petesy and me I suppose. Eventually I was sufficiently crumb-free to carry on.

'Mrs ... ah, Debra, can you assure me that your husband's disappearance is a genuine kidnap, as far as you can tell?'

'Absolutely,' she said. 'I would definitely know if he intended to pull something like that.'

I was watching Debra closely, and she made no attempt at eye contact with me during that speech. Now, it's a known fact that when someone wants you to swallow a major porky, they look you straight in the eye with a sincerity-soaked expression on their face while they tell it. On the other hand, perhaps Debra Plank knew that too – or knew that I knew it, or ... OK so it probably means nothing at all.

'Convince me,' I insisted.

'Well, I'm sure you know very well from your own experience, Kenny – you being an entrepreneur yourself – that in business it is sometimes all too easy to sail a bit close to the wind ... even occasionally to inadvertently be dragged into something a bit, shall we say, a little bit illegal. Well, that is as far as it went with Gerry, in spite of what certain malicious rumours said about organized crime and gang bosses and all that nonsense. Though actually I must admit ...'

She stopped for breath, and filled in the silence with a nervous gesture that involved smoothing her hair back using both hands like five-toothed combs. Bloody hell, I thought, it sounds as if she really believes that Short Plank is just a successful businessman. Aloud, I encouraged her.

'Go on. You're doing fine.'

'What I mean is, some of the people who worked for Gerry turned out to be downright dishonest, and it caused all kinds of trouble. Well, the upshot was that Gerry decided he had finally had it up to here with the whole thing – all the hassle of having a large number of people working for him. That was why he started planning to move into the world of high-tech, where his employees would be just a few well-educated whiz-kids instead of all these low-life yobbos.'

I refrained from pointing out that low-life yobbos are one of the more useful options when your business includes hijacking trucks, faking designer clothes, large-scale wholesale of smuggled booze and cigarettes, shady night-clubs – not to mention running protection rackets and a fleet of call-girls. Instead, I helped Debra's story along, so I wouldn't have to listen to much more of her misguided views.

'So you think that the former members of er, Gerry's organization were so disgruntled about being fired, that they've kidnapped the boss in an attempt to make him change his mind. Is that right?'

'Well, I suppose that sums up what I think about it in a nutshell,' she said, 'though it's really a bit more complicated than that … for instance, there seem to be two groups of former staff who are at loggerheads with each other. I don't know which lot have got my Gerry, but it seems that both groups are mad at him, which is a bit thick after all he's done for them … but as Gerry says, you don't get any gratitude these days, so you might as well look after number one. Anyway, these two bunches of … er, employees are both potentially dangerous …'

Potentially dangerous, indeed. These murdering thugs are as vicious a bunch of villains as have ever been gathered together. I'm not too surprised they're 'at loggerheads', though I hadn't realized that loggerheads includes killing, maiming, shooting and stabbing. I was thinking how the best thing the police could do would be to leave them alone to get on with eliminating each other – any outsider in danger of getting caught up in that scene would be better off going down to his local butcher and asking permission to put his head in the mincer. I was wondering how soon I could get out of there without causing too much offence. I had tuned out Debra's voice, which was still droning on in the background – until something she said snagged my attention. I did a quick replay to catch up.

'… so I'll be forever in your debt, Kenny. If you're half as good as Petesy leads me to believe, you can get the whole thing sorted out, and save Gerry for me. I'll gladly pay twice your usual rates, and I'm quite sure Gerry himself will make sure you are well rewarded for your efforts.'

That's the kind of reward I don't need. What was I in danger of being dragged into? I certainly had no memory of agreeing to do anything for anybody – least of all Debra, the potential Widow Plank. I started wondering how much it costs to go and live in South America for three months. Would that be long enough?

'I don't see that there is any way I can help you, ah … Debra,' I said, feeling a bit pompous as I said it, not to mention wondering what on earth she meant by that stuff about my usual rates. Mrs Plank surprised me again.

'So what the fucking hell are you doing here then?' she burst out. She's taking refuge in anger, I thought. And waited.

She waited.

We both waited, looking at each other. Me in amazement; she, flushed with what looked like fury, hosing me down with hot glare.

Eventually, she gulped, 'Why don't you bugger off then? I'll get another private detective who can do what I need doing …'

Incredibly, I didn't take the sensible action of getting up and walking out of that house without another word. I glanced sideways at Petesy, who was looking decidedly uncomfortable. Not as uncomfortable as he was going to feel later on when I got him alone. I held up my hand towards Debra Plank in a stop-right-there gesture.

'OK, OK,' I said. 'You've convinced me you're serious … I'm really beginning to believe that you think your husband's kidnapping is genuine – I came here with the presumption that he had staged it for some devious purpose of his own.'

No, I don't know why I did and said such a stupid thing either.

Kenny Madigan, the shining knight on a tin horse.

Mrs Plank subsided, and looked expectant. Petesy reached into a pocket to produce a notebook and pencil.

'I'll take notes, boss,' he said. 'You'll be needing them to refer to later on.'

Being already a long way down the one-way street, I sighed and took the hint.

I told Mrs Plank, 'You'll have to give us' – I carefully included Petesy – 'something to go on, Debra. What are the names of your husband's associates, as far as you can remember? Where can we contact them? And anything else you can think of that might help – oh, and give us your best description of the kidnappers.'

I looked over at Petesy and put a serious tone in my voice when I told him, 'You and I will go over the whole thing very carefully when we get home, my lad.'

At the time I didn't really mean it, of course.

By the time Debra showed us out, Petesy had filled several pages of his notebook with what I was pretty sure was trivia, sprinkled with a few names and places which might or might not be relevant.

As the door was closing behind us, I turned back with a final question.

'Debra, what exactly is the nature of this new high-tech business that er … Gerry is moving into?'

She pulled the door wider and shrugged, sending tremors around her bust region – which was quite a lot more interesting than her reply.

'Sorry, Kenny, I haven't a clue. The only thing I can tell you for sure is that it's become necessary for him and his new partner to bring in somebody with lots of computer knowledge and experience.'

—CHAPTER SEVEN—————————————

Stella has never been in Evesham before. She simply follows Inspector Neil Cornfoot's very detailed instructions: leaves her eight-year-old Golf in the open-air car park accessed from a back street; selects the recommended pedestrian exit from a choice of about five; through a narrow alley about thirty feet long – a backward glance is enough to verify she is not being followed; then a left turn on the pavement of the main street when she emerges into it, and into the pub two doors along.

The King's Arms is an old pub which has managed to retain its old-fashioned gloomy discomfort, largely because of being too small for easy conversion to a viable economic unit in any of the chains of pleasant café-bars that now blanket the country. Stella buys a half-pint of her namesake lager from the sullen barman and takes it to a table from which she can watch the door. As it is Sunday pre-lunchtime, she has forsaken her business outfit in favour of a more casual jeans and sweat-shirt combination. She lights a cigarette and waits.

Neil arrives about five minutes later. He goes to the bar, carries his pint to Stella's table and sits down. He wrinkles his nose pointedly at the smoke wisping up from Stella's cigarette. He says, 'Sorry about all this cloak-and-dagger stuff. But it's for your own protection, after all. Your safety is most important to the force.'

Stella nods impatiently. She doesn't need a lecture. They spend a few minutes on her report of activities, which boils down to 'no real progress as yet on the Plank front, and very little new information to report'.

She glosses over her recent activities relating to following up the Petesy Curtain connection. She presents it as not directly connected with the Plank case – just something that will increase her standing with Vince, if she delivers the goods. Neil is, of course well aware that it has everything to do with Plank, but makes no attempt to correct her.

Report out of the way, Stella moves on to what really interests her.

'What have you got for me on this pair of tossers, Curtain and Madigan?' she asks curtly. Although in her head she knows it for the nonsense it is, somehow she cannot rid herself of the feeling that she is betraying Vince Moorhouse by talking to the opposition. Maybe it's because Vince is a damn sight more pleasant to her than this pillar of the law.

Into the continuing silence, she adds, 'Come on, Guv, get on with it. You promised you would get me a run-down on them by today.'

She stubs out the remains of her cigarette in the ashtray.

'Yeah, yeah, I'm just thinking it through. You know I can't let you have anything in writing. So make sure you keep your ears flapping.'

Neil looks up towards the brown smoke-stained ceiling for a few moments, getting on with marshalling his thoughts and deciding what and how much to tell, before bringing his gaze back to her face. He starts his briefing.

'Curtain first. Oliver Peterson Curtain, usually known as Petesy. He is the nephew of Alfred Turner, a businessman/criminal boss known as the Wheel. Now deceased, the Wheel was at the height of his powers a couple of years ago. Curtain worked for his uncle, and was hoping to step into his crooked pin-stripes. When we broke up Turner's organization the nephew somehow slipped through our fingers. He finished up working for Kenny, er … Kendall Madigan in his car business.'

Neil stops for breath and to gather his thoughts for the next bit. Stella, for some reason is still feeling uncharacteristically nervous – more nervous in the company of this supercilious copper than she is among Vince and his villains.

'Right,' she says. 'That seems to cover the Curtain guy … what can you tell me about this Madigan character?'

'Hmmm …' goes Neil, wondering how to begin. 'Well, for a start, everybody calls him Kenny and he's got this girlfriend, Aileen … oh, don't get me wrong – we've never managed to pin anything on him, and the girlfriend is straight as a die … but any time there's a big flurry of activity among the criminal fraternity in this neck of the woods, you can bet Kenny Madigan will turn up close to the action with unbelievably clean hands … he's practically bullet-proof.'

'You're not trying to tell me he's really quite a nice inoffensive wee man, are you … wouldn't hurt a fly, kind of thing?' Stella interrupts.

'Bloody hell, no,' Neil exclaimed, aghast. 'Quite the reverse. Kenny's definitely not inoffensive by any means. He's about as slippery a customer as you'll ever meet. Don't ever underestimate him … he's bright enough to run rings around most of the other villains.'

Neil takes a swig from his pint, thinking about the beer Kenny poured all over him. He adds, 'And half the police force as well – so if I've answered all your questions I'll be on my way now. Lots to do – villains to catch.'

He puts his beer mug down on the table, still a third full, and gets to his feet.

Stella says, 'Just a minute, Guv – one more question. Is Madigan's garage a genuine business right enough, or just a front for, er, criminal activities?'

'Oh, it's a real business – right enough,' Neil replies, mimicking her accent, not very successfully. 'It's where I get my wife's car serviced, ye ken … they do a good job. Keep in touch.'

And Detective Inspector Neil Cornfoot is off – away out the door before she can say another word.

Stella lights her third cigarette. At this rate her whole day's quota will be ash by mid-afternoon. She glares through a cloud of blue smoke at the still-closing door.

'Fucking tosser,' she mutters.

She sits on in the King's Arms for a while, although her glass is now empty. Absently, she blows a couple of smoke rings, while absorbing and digesting the information she has just received from Neil; plugging it into the framework of everything else she knows about the situation. It makes a pretty ramshackle structure, which, pending real information, will require some imaginative cement to lend stability.

Thinks: funny how these local cops can't put two and two together when the evidence is right in front of their eyes. It shouldn't need a newcomer like me to suss out that this Kenny Madigan bloke must be some kind of master criminal. If he's involved at all, he's surely at the centre of this whole kerfuffle … and we know that Petesy Curtain, his tame sidekick, was on the spot when Mr Plank was kidnapped. Add to that the fact that I have no reason to believe Vince knows anything about Mr Plank's present location. *Ergo* – it seems to me that Madigan is likely the man in charge.

Stella nods as if in the process of convincing herself by means of this train of logic. Which, of course she is.

Thinks: but wait a minute; suppose one or other of my bosses – Neil or Vince – or even both, are holding out on me. Maybe neglected to pass on to me everything they know. All right then – what about Neil? We're on the same side, so he would have no reason to hold back on any relevant information. No, if anyone is being economical with the truth, it would have to be Vince … after all, he is a known criminal. But if he knows more than he admits, why is he concealing it? After all, he is just as anxious as anybody else to rescue Mr Plank – or so he says.

I guess I've just got to go along with what I know. My priority must be to find out all I can about Kenny Madigan and Petesy Curtain. Then I'll be in a position to make my own judgement.

So the sooner I get to meet one or both of that pair, the better. Meanwhile, I'll have to report some of this information back to Vince; I've still got to keep in with him and get him trusting me enough to let me in on whatever it is that is taking up so much of his time.

Back home, we told Aileen all about our meeting with Daphne's mother. Petesy produced his notes, which Aileen immediately pounced on. She studied them with Petesy's help – his abbreviations were not easy to understand, and the writing was atrocious. Meanwhile Daphne and I busied ourselves making coffee. Don't ask me why; I felt as if I hadn't stopped drinking coffee all day. I suppose it was just for the comforting ritual.

'Hang on a minute … I'm just reorganizing Petesy's notes,' Aileen said, in reply to Daphne's 'What's up?' that accompanied her mug of coffee. And so she was. Aileen was making her own set of notes, as if Petesy's weren't good enough. And Petesy didn't seem to mind at all – in fact, he was gazing at Aileen in admiration as if he thought she could wring some extra facts out of his notes just by writing them down in a different order. The rest of us obediently kept our mouths shut and waited until the oracle was ready to speak.

'Right,' she said eventually. She leant back and took a sip of coffee to give her more time to scrape her thoughts together, before giving us the benefit of her thinking.

'Right, let's review what we know about *The Mystery of the Missing Mobster*.'

Like a bloody who-done-it, for Chris'sake. Nobody said a word; we were a captive audience.

'First thing that strikes me is the actual kidnapping. Why do you think they were wearing masks?'

She wasn't asking anybody in particular, but I couldn't resist answering.

'That's bloody obvious ... so they wouldn't be recognized, of course.'

Aileen turned to look at me.

'So you think Daphne or her mother would have recognized their faces without the masks.'

It wasn't actually a question as such, more like a conclusion, but I answered it anyway.

'No ... well, maybe ... I don't know. Perhaps it was only Plank who might know them. But wait a minute, he's going to be with them for a good while, so he'll probably find out who they are ...'

I trailed off, as a result of getting my brain cells tied in knots with all the possibilities.

'Hmmm ...' said Aileen, looking round all of us again. 'Next question: why has nobody heard from the kidnappers?'

Silence. Furrowed brows. She tried again.

'I mean, no ransom note asking for money. No demands. Isn't that usually the reason for a person being kidnapped?'

Daphne used both hands to shake out her wild curls and said, 'Perhaps they did it because they wanted something from Daddy. You know, like, something he could deliver without needing to refer to anybody else ... or to force him to agree to do something or ... something like that.'

Not just a pretty face then, this Daphne. Aileen tapped her teeth with her pen, thoughtfully.

'Yeeees, that sounds very likely, considering. You would go along with that, wouldn't you, Kenny?'

I seized the opportunity to nod wisely. I was standing behind Aileen's chair, looking over her shoulder at her notes, part of which looked like a diagram of Mr Plank's organization. Actually, all it showed was Plank at the top, and two branches which Aileen had labelled West Plankers and East Plankers. Below each of these, she had written some of the names and other stuff we got from Debra Plank.

It was time for me to take charge.

'Absolutely,' I said. (Have you noticed that when someone is not sufficiently sure of themselves to give a definite *yes* they will happily say *absolutely*?) 'I think we need look no further than the East Plankers – or even the West ...'

I trailed off as my eye snagged on one of the names under West Plankers. I remembered hearing it from Debra. It was such an unusual name that you would notice when you heard it. But now it was reminding me of something else I had heard somewhere else.

Nick Pearson – that was where I heard it. As usual, he had got it wrong, but now Debra's version was correcting it. Not Blossom, but Absalom. Still a weird name for a sadistic tearaway.

I looked back at Aileen's notes. This Absalom (last name not known) was down as personal assistant to Vince Moorhouse. Vince Moorhouse was down as head of what Aileen had labelled the West Plankers. Debra had called him the managing director, but she didn't know the names of any other members of that organization, just these two – and only one name, Rod Simmons, in the East Plankers. However, she had been able to provide locations, or at least company names for both groups; Eastshire Eagle in the east (obviously), and the Ecological Recycling Company of Redditch for the west.

So now I knew for sure who had done the nasty deed of kidnapping Mr Short Plank, thanks to Nick Pearson – none other than Vince Moorhouse, aka The Boss, assisted by two of his assistants. If I had really been interested in acting the private detective, I would have decided there and then that Redditch must be my first port of call.

The only other location of interest to be found on the diagram was Mr Gerald Plank's personal office in Leamington. No address though, and I didn't suppose I would be likely to find it listed in the phone book. I must have muttered this last thought out loud, because Daphne came up with an answer to that one as well.

'I know where it is. I went there, oh, a couple of months ago when Daddy first rented the office … he was having desks and all office stuff moved in.'

The rest of us all ditched whatever we were about to say and turned to look at her. Suddenly she had an attentive audience.

'It … it's upstairs above Chickory Chicks … you know, the fashion boutique a few doors along from Boots.'

'What?' said Petesy. 'You mean you have to go in through the shop to get to it?'

Daphne giggled. 'No, silly. There's a separate door … it's got a brass plate with Pitch, Putt, and Carruthers on it. That's the name of the solicitors on the first floor; I think they must own the building because Daddy rents his office from them. It's on the top floor, upstairs from the solicitors.'

There was a pause while we all digested that piece of information. Aileen was the first to get some thoughts moving forward. She spoke in the kind of slow and deliberate voice you use when you're trying to make sure you've got the exact end of the stick, with no room for any misunderstanding.

'Daphne, I don't suppose you would know where we could lay our hands on the key of your Dad's office, by any chance? Maybe your mother would know where to find …'

She trailed off. Daphne was shaking her head.

'No, I can't say I've ever seen the office key. It's like … the kind of thing Daddy would keep with him all the time, so Mummy wouldn't have it. The only key I've got is the one for the street entrance at the foot of the stairs.'

Seeing our looks of incomprehension, Daphne added, 'See, he gave it to Mummy so she and I could use the loo anytime we were in town, you know, instead of public ones which might not be hygienic … it's on the landing next door to the office. But it's no use for getting into the office, that needs a different key, but Mummy passed this one on to me because I've been doing more shopping.'

She produced a bunch of keys and dangled them like jingle bells. Suddenly, Redditch and Ecological Recycling Ltd was relegated to second choice. Now, if I had been the least bit interested in playing private detective, that office in Leamington would at that moment have taken over from Redditch as my first port of call.

'Daphne,' I said, 'how about taking that key off the ring and lending it to me for a day or two? Don't worry, I'll let you have it back.'

I wasn't sure I was going to use the key, but I knew from bitter experience that there was some possibility I could be manoeuvred into a position where I had no alternative. In fact, given enough rope, I'm quite capable of doing my own self-manoeuvring.

Kenny Madigan, forever his own worst enemy.

—CHAPTER EIGHT—

My desk in my office at Lone Harp Auto Repair is where I do my best thinking. Sitting there with the door open, I can catch glimpses of my three mechanics getting on with doing mechanic type things to the day's intake of cars under Senga's critical gaze, and assisted by The Bear, Stratford's local radio station.

Having exhausted the resources of the Daily Mirror, a process which took me a whole ten minutes (I reckoned it must be getting more intellectual), I turned my attention to some of the questions that had been simmering away on the back burner of my brain since the previous day, ever since they had been put there, first by Debra Plank, and later by Aileen with the help of Petesy and Daphne.

For instance, Short Plank's business premises in Leamington. Surely that office must hold the key to much of the mystery surrounding that alleged criminal master-mind. That metaphorical key brought to mind the real key Daphne had given me. I took it out of my pocket and placed it carefully on the desk. After a minute or so of failing to receive any telepathic messages from the lump of metal, I fired up some of my brain cells and took a proper look at it.

It was nothing special, just a bog-standard Yale-type key. Furthermore, I reminded myself, it couldn't provide access to anywhere useful. Not unless I happened to be caught short in Leamington town centre. That's what I tried to tell myself, but all the time I knew perfectly well that this key was capable of opening up greater possibilities. Thanks to my Auntie Ursula.

You see, my mother and father were both killed in a train crash when I was hardly more than a baby. Auntie Ursula was baby-sitting me when it happened, so she found herself more or less stuck with having to bring me up. She was married to Uncle Ron at the time, and they lived in Henley-in-Arden, about ten miles north of

Stratford. Well, I think Auntie Ursula needed me as much as I needed her, especially after Uncle Ron died of a heart attack when I was about seven years old.

So we became a single-aunt family, and Ursula did her best for me. Of course, she wanted me to have a good career in a safe job. But just in case, she passed on to me all the knowledge and expertise she possessed. Auntie Ursula's wisdom wasn't limited to her vast stock of (sometimes dodgy) proverbs and sayings – she had a few other abilities stashed away up her sleeve. For instance, it was from her that I inherited my kit of lock-picking tools – and she taught me the skills needed to use them. (Though, of course, I must be pretty rusty by now, and it would take a lot of practice to bring back my old expertise.) It seems that she and Uncle Ron had been a right pair of Bonnie and Clydes before they got lumbered with yours truly. Aunt Ursula insisted on them giving up their life of crime when they took me on. She was afraid I would be left alone in the world for a second time if she and Ron went to prison.

If you don't know much about the criminal mind, and criminal activity in general, you might be wondering what all of the above has to do with the situation at hand. Why, you might ask, would I find it useful to be in possession of a key, when I have a much more valuable possession – namely the ability to pick open virtually any of the assorted locked doors we see around us every day?

Well, the answer is; I would prefer not to be caught and confined a long age behind extremely sophisticated and un-pickable locks, just for exercising my skills. Although I am quite confident of my ability to deal with the lock that this key is designed to open, I would definitely not want to do so while standing exposed to the public view in a main street for anything up to, say – twenty minutes, given my lack of recent practice. Even at night in that area, there is constant movement of people to and from the nearby pubs and restaurants until very late – and after that, a loitering person in a street, well-lit or not, is definitely up to no good.

On the other hand, I could be almost comfortable with the idea of letting myself in through that street door with the proper key, prior to proceeding upstairs where I would be able to spend as long as necessary out of the public gaze, working on the lock of the door leading to Mr Plank's private office. As my Aunt Ursula would have said, it would be a way of moving the goalposts off the level playing field.

I nodded, though nobody was around to appreciate the nod, and put the key back in my pocket. I certainly hadn't decided to carry out any raid – no, that's not what I mean, not a raid, more of a fact-finding mission is what it would be – on the beating heart of the Plank empire. Not yet, anyway. But at least I could see how it could be done without any risk to speak of, if it should ever seem like something worth doing.

Of course there would be no point in doing anything about it today – not during daylight hours. It was the same situation as the street door, really. I would be doing something which carried a slight whiff of illegality, so it would be better done when the staff of the solicitors' office had finished their daily milling around on the stairs and landings of the building.

Besides, that was a side-issue. Getting into the Leamington office might help to satisfy my curiosity, but that would be nothing more than an indulgence. It was clear where my loyalty really lay. In fact, Debra Plank's interests pointed in the same direction as my own. She wanted her husband back (there's no accounting for the irrational whims of a woman). Well, now I knew who had taken him, though not where he had been taken; and it was in my best interest to point out to those who were holding Plank, that neither I nor my friend Petesy, represented any threat to the said Plank-holders. So we can safely be left out of the equation. Who could possibly disagree with that analysis of the situation?

I would simply explain that we (Petesy and I) have no axes needing ground; we are extremely happy for our fingers to remain well clear of any or all of Mr Vince Moorhouse's pies. I would go on to suggest that neither Petesy nor myself give a flying fuck about what plans these people might have in mind for Mr Plank. So why doesn't Mr Moorhouse leave us alone to just walk away.

The trouble is, at this juncture I part company with Debra Plank. She would want me to ride on a white horse to the rescue of her Gerry – wrest him from the clutches of the evil kidnappers and restore him to the grateful bosom of his family. And she cares bugger all for my safety.

Should I get myself another mug of coffee and drink it sitting here in the pleasant but boring safety of Lone Harp Auto? Or was there something else I could be getting on with? Then it occurred to me that Petesy was out on the forecourt making sure the used-car display was tarted up ready to delight the eyes of potential buyers. Once he was satisfied with that, he would be left exposed to the unaccountable reluctance of the great British public to go out viewing second-hand cars on Monday mornings. Which means he would be free to come inside and nag me to plan a Plank rescue mission – something to be avoided, from my point of view.

Following the line of least resistance, I went outside, and got into my car. What the hell, if past form was anything to go by, sooner or later somebody was going to stick my head in the lion's dinner; so I might as well cut out the middle-person and get on with it under my own steam. I pointed the steering wheel in the direction of Redditch.

'Christ, Stella, I'm damn glad you're not a copper ... you're a bloody sight better at CID work than most of the incompetent bastards who get paid for doing it.'

They are in Vince's office on the second floor of the Ecological Recycling Company building in Redditch. Vince sounds quite impressed with Stella's detective work in following up the Petesy Curtain lead. She is embarrassed by his comment, for several reasons, but goes on anyway to tell him about Petesy's boss, Kenny Madigan. However, she holds back much of the detail she got from Neil – partly because it seems like a good idea to keep something up her sleeve. Besides, some of that information couldn't have come from anywhere other than a police source.

'Goodness knows what Madigan's connection with Plank might be,' she slyly adds, 'but it seems to have developed quite recently.'

Vince doesn't hesitate to step into ownership of the consequent idea.

'Well, I've been thinking for some time that this Madigan (though I didn't know his name until now – thank you for that) ... Madigan is none other than Gerry Plank's partner in his new business venture, so the kidnap could be a put-up job.'

Privately, Vince is thinking that he has now got hold of something concrete with which to confront that cunning bastard Plank. He had expected that physical control of his former boss, in the sense of having him under lock and key, would give him the upper hand in his negotiations with the aforementioned cunning bastard.

Frustratingly, in spite of daily meetings, progress has been almost non-existent so far, with Plank acting as if he is still in control; both of them playing a waiting game; tacitly aware that violence to the person of Mr Plank would be counter-productive for many reasons.

Maybe, now that Vince is armed with a couple of names to throw into the fray, Plank might be induced to crumble. How can he use his new knowledge to apply even more pressure?

Vince is uncomfortably aware that time is running out for him as the pressure mounts. There is a limit to how long he can keep Short Plank hidden from the world, what with increasing numbers of players elbowing their way into the game of find the head honcho. Fortunately, so far only Absalom, Dirk, and Vince himself know who stole Plank and placed him in his present location. Correction; there is one other fly in the ointment, now revealed by Stella as Petesy Curtain, who was a witness to the presence of Moorhouse and Absalom at Plank's house on the night of the kidnapping. From Vince Moorhouse's point of view, it cannot possibly be a coincidence that Curtain should turn out to be Madigan's assistant. Moorhouse knows nothing of Nick Pearson.

He turns his attention back to Stella who is waiting with the eagerness of a faithful puppy-dog for further instructions.

'Right, then,' he tells her, 'I need to know more about both of these troublesome people, Madigan and whatsisname … Curtain, is it? I'm pretty sure I shall want to have a little talk with Mr Madigan before too long, so anything you can find out will be grist to my information mill. As for Curtain – he may well represent a direction in which we can apply some extra pressure. Elimination of the monkey often has what you might call a civilizing effect on the organ-grinder, if you see what I mean. Absalom will be happy to go to work on this Petesy Curtain, especially considering that this is the fellow who slipped through his fingers last time …'

Seeing the puzzled look on Stella's face, he clarifies: 'The slimy sod performed a very athletic back-flip over a fence and escaped into the night. Absalom regards that kind of underhand activity as tantamount to cheating.'

He continues briefing Stella.

'So anything you can find out about Curtain's habits and surroundings will be useful – especially information about where Absalom can catch up with him discreetly.'

Vince puts on what he thinks of as his engaging grin to add, 'I'm almost certain Absalom can manage a small amount of discretion when it's really necessary. Just keep me in the picture, won't you … you know the score – anything that might help us to find Mr Plank.'

Before she knows what is happening, Stella finds herself on the outside of the office door feeling as if she has been dismissed with a patronizing pat on the bottom. All right, so she has her orders. Something to do next. But how will she feel about setting somebody up to be a target for Fat Absalom, whom she has pegged as a sadistic psychopath, in spite of his always talking to her in an extremely courteous manner. She has no way of knowing that Absalom's mother has, throughout his childhood and adolescence, drummed into her son the need to be ever polite when addressing a woman. Unfortunately she never mentioned that he should also act in a courteous way towards women. Thus it was that while Absalom is politely calling Stella Ms Galloway, he is quite likely to be also leering at her chest or making a passing grab for her bottom.

Oh well, Petesy Curtain is probably just as unpleasant, what with being a hardened villain and all. One fewer criminal in the world is progress of a kind, isn't it?

She is fairly sure Vince really does not know what has happened to Plank. She is equally certain that Vince is not being completely frank with her, but believes most of his attention is concentrated on the power struggle with Simmons and his eastern gang. She has pieced together from random comments and scraps of information, a scenario of tit-for-tat strikes between the two territorial halves of Plank's decomposing organization.

Outside in the car-park, Stella lights up and sucks in a calming lungful of therapeutic smoke. She gets into her car and sets off to pursue her assigned task. At the edge of Stratford-on-Avon, on Alcester Road, she stops at a petrol station to buy a street map of the town. The address of Lone Harp Auto Repair, incorporating Madigan's Motors, in Anthony's Bridge Road – turns out to be quite close, on the same side of Stratford.

As she turns the corner out of Compass Road into Anthony's Bridge Road, she passes a grey Ford Mondeo, travelling in the opposite direction. The Mondeo is being driven by Kenny Madigan on his way to Redditch to visit the Ecological Recycling Company, which Stella has just left.

Stella drives on, oblivious, and stops on the forecourt of the garage, under the long banner that proclaims: **Madigan Motors has the Bargains YOU can Drive**. On the right, and extending round the side of the building there are two ranks of cars with prices displayed on their windscreens. Stella takes a walk around them, not really paying much attention to the cars. Nobody seems to be in attendance. She is actually covertly examining the garage and its surroundings, on the look-out for the kind of premises where a kidnapped person might be hidden away. Nothing seems a likely candidate – too much activity, too many people coming and going. If Madigan has got Plank stashed away, it must be somewhere else.

She turns her attention to the large vehicle door that yawns directly in front of the garage. Above it are painted the faded words **Lone Harp Auto Repair**. Through the door she can see and hear people busily tending vehicles in various stages of suspension and disassembly.

She steps over the threshold, wondering what it takes to attract the attention of such a dedicated workforce. No problem, as it turns out, since the moment she is inside she is assailed by what sounds like more attention than she needs – a voice raised in volume to overcome the din of power tools. It is a no-nonsense voice pitched somewhere between the aggression needed for dealing with the mechanics and the reassurance which is more useful with concerned customers; a voice which sounds somehow inappropriate for the message it conveys.

'Good morning, welcome to Lone Harp. How can we be of service?'

The accent at least, is a familiar one to Stella. It emanates from a smallish person under a mop of curly red hair who is standing behind a short length of scarred wooden counter just inside the door on the left. Stella is aware of herself lapsing into the slightly heavier (not in front of the English) version of her own accent when she replies.

'I've heard tell you do a good job here at a reasonable price. See, my car's about due for its MOT so … could you maybe do it next week sometime?'

'Aye, right ye are, hen. I'll just book you in, what day wid suit you best?'

Between questions and answers relating to the matter at hand, Stella and Senga exchange pleasantries beginning with, 'Where are you from? … Oh, aye, my granny used to live near there', and ranging to matters closer to Stella's agenda, such as, 'Actually, I'm thinking about changing my car … not right this minute, you know, maybe in two or three months. I was looking at some of your er … Madigan Motors cars out there but there's nobody around. Would Mr Madigan be available, d'ye think?'

'Hah,' Senga exclaims, 'Kenny Madigan's out at the moment. In fact, you've just missed him … but anyway, he's usually far too busy to pay much attention to the likes of us workers … now don't get me wrong, Kenny's a great bloke – it's just that he sometimes seems to be away wi' the fairies; you know, living in his own wee world. Mind you, I think this place runs just as well, or maybe even better when he's not here poking his nose in.'

'So there's nobody who can let me have a closer look at the cars?'

Stella tries to sound a bit crestfallen, adding, 'What about you?' and hoping for something else.

'Och, I've got my work cut out here what with keeping this bunch on their toes. I'll just fetch young Petesy out for you. You might find him a wee bit cabbage-looking behind the ears, but he's a real nice lad just the same. Petesy's the one who is really supposed to be in charge of Madigan Motors.'

Stella is quite pleased with this outcome. She agrees with Vince that it will be quite a good idea to start with the monkey and leave the organ grinder for later.

─CHAPTER NINE─────────────

Redditch is one of those new towns, like Milton Keynes and Telford. Like them, it seems to be composed of a network of roundabouts tied together by dual carriageway roads all bordered by nothing but greenery – with occasional glimpses of buildings cowering behind clumps of trees which have been planted for the purpose. It's the kind of place that stretches distance in such a way that you drive much further within its boundaries than you travelled to get there.

I eventually located the home of Ecological Recycling Limited. It was in a two-storey building in a row of similar structures, all purpose built as commercial/light industrial premises, and all proudly displaying company names and cute corporate logos, none of which I had ever heard of. Definitely not an environment that would lend itself to the concealment of a kidnapped person for more than an hour or so. Moorhouse and his minions must have some other more suitable hiding place at their disposal.

I deposited my car in the tree-studded employees' car-park and went in through the plate glass front door. Striding up confidently to the post-teenage blonde girl in charge of the reception desk, I put on my important face to say, 'Mr Kendall Madigan to see Vince Moorhouse.'

I would have to go through the whole ritual, it seemed.

'What is the scheduled timing of your appointment with Mr Moorhouse?'

'Well, as I don't actually have an appointment as such, I can't have a time for one ...' I began, but stopped in fascination at the rapid response of her body language.

In the blink of an eye, she had drawn in a deep breath, thereby multiplying the magnitude of her bust. The badge pinned high on her left breast went horizontal, enabling anyone who might be clinging to the ceiling to know she was called Mandy. In a voice dripping exasperation, she spoke.

'Mr Moorhouse *never* concerns himself with the comings and goings of sales representatives. He is much too highly occupied with importance – and in any case, I am invariably notified of his impending visitors considerably prior of their visitations.'

'Look, I have not made my way here on any manner of Ecological Recycling mission,' I said, as if infected with some flavour of her speech patterns, and wondered what the hell I meant by that. 'Just tell him I'm here – all right? Vince will be very disappointed in you if you become instrumental in preventing him from meeting me.'

With sullen reluctance, Mandy picked up her telephone and tapped in four digits. After a pause, she said, 'This is Mandy-in-Reception. I am extremely regretful to disturb. However, I have here a ... gentleman here who persists that you will be inclined to welcome him with wide open arms, er ... Mr Moorhouse, sir.'

Pause.

'A Mr Cardigan, according to the person out of his own mouth ...'

I leaned forward over the desk, frantically hissing, 'It's Madigan, tell him it's Kenny Madigan.'

Mandy's voice was forging on.

'One moment, sir, I am receiving further information from the person ... it seems that he has revised his name to Penny Madigan. Shall I send him on his way with a flea? ... No? ... Very well. Thank you, Mr Moorhouse, sir.'

A rather deflated Mandy put down the receiver and turned her attention back towards me. A spider traversing her desk at that moment would be in a position to read her name.

'I have secured on your behalf, an interview with our Mr Moorhouse. I shall now conduct you to his place of business. Follow.'

I trotted after her rhythmic rear and tapping heels towards, and then up, a fancy open-tread staircase. Along the way I attempted conversation.

'This Vince Moorhouse – is he the top man of this, ah ... Ecological Thingy Company then?'

The words of her reply floated back to me, not necessarily in the order she uttered them.

'Mr Moorhouse is not in any way Ecological ... at least Recycling is merely one of his many multifarious business interests where he tends to inhabit this double office suite facility for himself ... including one or other close associate who is not always invariably the identical close associate we are almost with him now.'

That mouthful had indeed conveyed us past several glass-walled office areas populated with computers and their screen-minders. I inferred that we were now most of the way to what I presumed to be one of the aforementioned office facilities. Bloody hell, I was even thinking in Mandy-speak.

My escort rapped on the frosted-glass panel in a door of pale wood, flung the door open, and announced, 'Mr Milligan at your service, Mr Moorhouse, sir.'

I stepped inside. I looked at the man behind the desk. He gazed back at me with calculating eyes. A moment passed. He inclined his head to indicate a chair on my side of the desk. I took a seat. Through the now-closed door, I could hear Mandy's heels clicking off down the corridor. Vincent Moorhouse and I carried out a silent appraisal of each other.

His expensive-looking business suit matched his pale-grey eyes and the slight greying that crept round the edges of his neatly trimmed darkish hair, conveying an overall impression of greyness. This was no unassuming or retiring or ageing kind of grey quality. The grey of this man was assertive, suggesting authority with a hint of menace thrown in, though the menace probably sprang from my imagination which was conscious of his recent activities. A scarlet tie contributed the only slash of colour. He was obviously tall, even though seated in a leather swivel chair.

The overall impression was of someone who knew he was in control.

I was the one who broke the first silence.

'It's Madigan,' I said, 'Kenny Madigan.'

'Yes,' he said.

It sounded more like the end of a conversation. I couldn't think of anything sensible to say just at that particular moment. Usually, in a situation like that, my reaction is to say something which is far from sensible, but for once I scraped up the wit to keep my mouth shut.

(Just as well really, since the only conversational offering to arrive in my head at that moment, came courtesy of my Auntie

Ursula who once gave me a book of cartoons by someone called James Thurber. One of these cartoons was of a colossal grey animal with a huge mouth, standing impassive and immovable while a woman confronted it with the angry demand, 'What have you done with Doctor Millmoss?' Maybe it was the grey motif, but I felt an irrational temptation to demand of Vince Moorhouse, 'What have you done with Gerald Plank?'

That train of thought must have occupied my brain long enough to build up the Sahara of silence between the two of us, resulting in Moorhouse being the one who was sucked into filling the speech vacuum this time. He opened his mouth. I hoped he wasn't going to hiss, 'We meet at last, Mr Madigan.'

What he actually said was:

'Nice to meet you, Madigan. I've heard so much about you from Gerry Plank.'

Smooth start, I thought. Two short sentences – two lies. But smooth all the same, especially with that patronizing use of my last name to establish himself as a public schoolboy type (and therefore superior). Not to be outdone, I came back with a lie of my own.

'Yes, poor old Gerry; he's told me all about you, likewise,' I couldn't bring myself to throw in a Moorhouse at this point. 'I wish I knew where Gerry is right now.'

So far, so good. I reckoned I was one up in spite of the condescending form of address; I knew he was lying but he didn't know I was. I would have done better to remember one of Auntie Ursula's favourite sayings – smug as a bug goes before a fall.

'I like a man who gets straight down to business,' said Vince Moorhouse. 'You're absolutely right, Gerry's freedom has got to be our top priority. We really must pool our resources, you and I.'

He paused and favoured me with a look of such sincerity I was expecting the tears to start welling up in his eyes. However, he pulled himself together and continued.

'I'm sure you will be pleased to hear that I have already made some progress towards that end. It turns out that the villain of the piece is none other than that fucking treacherous bastard Simmons. As I am sure you are aware, he is – and has been for several years … Christ knows what he thinks he is now … my Eastern Region counterpart in Gerry's organization, and a notably slimy piece of work to boot … ah, excuse me.'

That last remark was in response to the ringing of the telephone on Moorhouse's desk. He picked it up.

'Yes?'

The reply was reduced to a wordless squawk by the time it reached my ears.

'So he's told you nothing at all?'

Wordless squawk.

'You've tried everything ... and he's still not talking?'

Wordless squawk.

'Don't waste any more time. Dispose of him.'

Moorhouse put the receiver down without waiting for any more squawks. The cold grey eyes swung round to fix on me. They remained unblinking as he told me, 'Some people have a misplaced sense of loyalty. Simmons isn't worth it.'

But I wasn't listening. That "Dispose of him" was still echoing around my brain. A lump of ice had formed in my stomach. I told myself he was just trying to scare the living daylights out of me. Then I admitted that he had succeeded.

I licked my lips and changed the subject.

'Have you made any progress towards finding out where they're holding Gerry?'

Regretful face, sad shake of head.

'Afraid not, old chap – but here's where you might be able to help.'

Vince leaned forward confidentially.

'Simmons has no particular reason to suspect you of any private agenda. So, why don't you go over to Leicester, introduce yourself, and offer to help him track down the bastards who have kidnapped the boss? That way, you and your chap – er, Curtain, isn't it? – might be accepted into the fold sufficiently for you to do a bit of digging without them suspecting anything. What do you think?'

He leaned back in his executive chair to await my approval of his masterly plan. I nodded to show I was mulling it over and tried to look as non-committal as I could.

'What about your own people?' I asked. 'Haven't they been able to find out where uh, Gerry is being held?'

He shook his head and put on a more-in-sorrow-than-in-anger expression.

'God knows we've tried ... but these people just won't see

reason. Simmons is too intent on pursuing his feud with me, as well as being too pig-headed to co-operate. He's already murdered one of my best men and put another two in the hospital. Fortunately, he hasn't managed to strike at me or my personal team yet.'

This is the lion's mouth he wants to send my head into, I thought, making an instant decision to stay well clear of the vicious Simmons and his merry men. Realizing that Vince was still talking, I dragged my attention and my stomach back to the present.

'You must meet the aforementioned personal staff by the way; there's Dirk Mills, who handles everything technical; and Stella – she's mostly assigned to gathering information and following up rumours and such. Then there is my strong-arm man, Absalom Higgens – I always think his parents must be a strange couple to land him with that name. Absalom rather enjoys handling unavoidable chores which most other people would find too unpleasant.'

'Aren't any members of your team around today,' I asked, and cheekily added, 'or are they all away on their annual holidays?'

That won me a big grin and a good view of a row of off-white teeth. I could tell the thought that was lurking just behind the teeth; it was, 'What a prat'. Well, I wouldn't want him thinking of me as any kind of threat.

'As it happens, at this moment,' Vince looked at his watch for effect, 'Absalom is fully occupied making life difficult for our friend Simmons and his cohorts ... that was him on the phone, by the way. The others have various tasks to get on with elsewhere,' he said, 'otherwise, there might be one, or even two of them occupying the other office or one of the spare desks outside.'

'So you don't have the use of Mr Plank's own personal office in ...'

I stopped without mentioning Leamington, suddenly aware that Moorhouse might not be privy to Plank's new office. Lamely I completed the sentence.

'... wherever it is.'

Silence for a moment, while he registered my clumsy attempted correction. The pale-grey eyes drilled straight through mine, probing my brain as if trying to read what I didn't want him to know. Then he put an unconvincing grin on his smarmy face and said, 'If you knew Gerry as well as I do, you would be aware that he has always preferred to work from his office at home ... and if I may say so, Gerry would be rather displeased to hear of that attempt of yours to extract information from me.'

'Right,' he went on smoothly, getting to his feet to indicate our meeting was at an end, 'I won't keep you any longer ... I'm sure you must have many other irons in the fire. Keep in touch and let me know if you come across any relevant information. I'll give you the private number of this office.'

He jotted it down on a yellow Post-it note which he gave to me; then held out his hand for shaking purposes.

'I expect you can find your own way out. Don't forget, I know where to find you, should the need arise.'

With that hardly veiled threat ringing in my ears, I tucked his phone number into my hip pocket and retraced my steps to the clean open air via Mandy-in-Reception. The threat itself didn't bother me (or so I told myself). What got on my wick even more was his infuriatingly patronizing attitude. But that's your public school product ... or at least one unacceptable face of him.

—CHAPTER TEN————————————

Driving slowly back towards Stratford, I reviewed my meeting with the arch-kidnapper. As far as practical purposes were concerned, such as finding out any clue as to where Mr Short Plank was being kept, it achieved nothing at all. On the other hand, I had now met the perpetrator and could only conclude that this Vince Moorhouse was an extremely dangerous and ambitious man – I thought it inevitable that he would sooner or later have made a bid to take over Plank's organization regardless. The current crisis merely made it sooner rather than later.

The strongest message I took away from my meeting with Moorhouse, was the threat to my personal well-being. Somehow, I had no doubts as to his ability to 'dispose' of me, or his readiness to do so at the least provocation.

I didn't feel much like going back to work. Instead, remembering that Monday was Aileen's day off this week on account of a swap with one of her work-mates, I went home expecting to find her painting or grouting or hoovering or doing one of the thousand other things that you would never believe necessary in a brand new house. Sure enough, there she was on her knees, in an old pair of shorts and a T-shirt, hair tied back, scrubbing and scraping at the gleaming ceramic-tiled kitchen floor. She looked up when I arrived.

'You'd think the builders would avoid spattering everything with plaster ...' she said, breathing hard, 'or at least lay the floor tiles *after* the plastering is finished.'

She stood up, and stretched. I made a grab for her, confirming in the process that she was not wearing a bra. I said, 'Let's go upstairs and check the bedroom floor for plaster.'

For some reason, the sight of Aileen slightly sweaty, out of breath, and dressed like that really turns me on.

'Look out,' she said, 'I'm very dirty.'

'Oh, good,' I replied, pulling her closer and sliding my hands round her back and down under the elastic waist of her shorts.

'I meant *really* dirty,' she said, but at the same time she giggled and rubbed herself against my sprouting erection. So we didn't bother going upstairs; the living-room carpet was quite comfortable, as it happened.

After the second burst of love-making, with Aileen still kneeling astride me (yes, but I was on top the first time round) and her cute little breasts still jiggling independently of each other, she said, 'That was great, I've really missed having sex the last few nights.'

'Well, it's your own fault,' I told her, 'you're the one who refuses to do it with Petesy just through the wall, in case he hears. I wouldn't care at all, especially as he and Daphne were hard at it themselves the other night.'

'Yeah, I know,' she agreed, 'but I would be really inhibited. And you know how much noise I'm liable to make.'

Well, yes. That's one of the things I love about Aileen.

Anyway, we stayed in that position while I told her about my visit to Redditch and we had a laugh about Mandy-in-Reception (more jiggling). But of course Vince Moorhouse had the starring role. Aileen made me recount the conversation word for word, as far as I could remember it – and my memory is extremely good for these kind of things.

As she pointed out, 'So you didn't actually find out any useful information, apart from Absalom's last name, and that's a pretty useless fact. And you gave away the fact that Plank has a new office, you pillock; I bet Moorhouse had no idea. Am I right? I am.'

I ignored the pillock remark, though I had to admit to myself, that it was justified this time.

'Yes, if you put it that way,' I replied. 'But look at it this way: I've made contact with the opposition, had a chance to size him up. You know …'

'Well, it seems to me that most of what was going on was nothing to do with what you and Moorhen were actually saying to each other.'

'Moorhouse,' I corrected her, but she ignored me and went on.

'You sat there knowing that he was responsible for kidnapping Plank and has got him hidden away somewhere, but there was no point in you mentioning it. Right?'

'I suppose so.'

'And *he* knew that *you* knew that he was the kidnapper and Plank-keeper.'

I protested, 'Well, he probably thinks I suspect him, but he can't be sure.'

Aileen shook her head at me. 'Yes he *can* be sure ... he knows Nick Pearson saw and heard him and his minion on the night of the kidnapping, though he doesn't know Nick Pearson told you – but he thinks Nick Pearson was Petesy and he can be certain that Petesy would put you in the picture. Am I right? I am again.'

'You are dead right,' I admitted, having picked my way through Aileen's spaghetti logic.

'That's why he's been after Petesy, and sent somebody to his flat – it must have been that Stella he mentioned ...' Aileen's voice trailed off. She stood up quite suddenly.

'Come on,' she said. 'Get some clothes on. I'm going to have a quick shower and then we'll get my case notes out and review *The Mystery of the Missing Mobster.*'

So there I was, lying abandoned and naked except for my socks (I didn't have time) on the carpet – all limp in more than one respect. Case notes indeed!

Aileen's version of a quick shower took longer than you might expect, probably because of being inseparable from a quick choice of skirt and sweater, a quick hair arrangement, and a quick make-up job.

Forty-five minutes later, she appeared, smiling and carrying her notebook.

'Let's see what advantages we've got on our side,' she said, leading me to our brand new dining room table, where she sat down. I watched over her shoulder (we've only got one dining chair so far) while she turned to a blank sheet and wrote:

1. Vince Moorhouse (M) and his gang think Kenny (K) is Plank's new partner. This suggests that Plank (P) is still not telling the truth to his Plankers – or they don't believe his denials. Either way, they cannot trust each other.
2. M mentioned a minion called Stella (S). She must be the one who raided Petesy's flat.
3. S must be S Galloway, the policewoman who was sent in by

Neil to work undercover at finding out the truth about the kidnapping and where they have got P hidden away.

4. M still does not trust S enough to tell her that he has got P, or where, otherwise she would have passed it on to Neil and he would have raided the place.
5. Nobody knows exactly what P's new business venture is, but M must think K knows because he believes that K is the new partner.
6. Who the flipping heck is the real new partner, if there is one?
7. K and Petesy are still in danger from the M mob because of them knowing that he (M) has got P. But he probably feels secure enough to wait and see what happens before doing anything serious to K or Petesy.
8. M will now be trying to find out about P's new office. Perhaps he'll threaten or even torture him to find out.

'Flipping heck,' I read aloud, incredulous. Nobody has said flipping heck since World War II.

Apart from that and the alphabet soup, I was pretty bloody impressed. I've said it before and I'll say it again: my Aileen has got a brain like a steel trap.

'You haven't said what we should do next,' I pointed out, when I had digested it all.

'Well,' she said, 'it's not a plan of action, as such, just a summary of the things we know for sure, but might not have realized we can be sure of. It should help us to make a plan of action.'

'Oh, no,' I groaned, 'not more bureaucracy. Why don't we just play it by ear? For instance, do you think I should go and see this Simmons character? I mean, he's like the Moorhouse of the East Plankers. Maybe …'

'No, no, Kenny, that's exactly what Moorhouse would like you to do. Simmons is just a red herring. Besides, that might turn out to double your danger; you could end up with both Planker lieutenants after your blood.'

I nodded my agreement. I never had any intention of going to see Simmons anyway, but I knew Aileen would probably object to my first suggestion, whatever it might be.

'All right then, I think I'll go and take a look at this office Plank has in Leamington. I'll do it tonight, before Moorhouse has time to catch up with its existence. Who knows, there might be some answers to be found there ... especially the nature of his new high-tech business. What do you think?'

Aileen considered it. I waited almost a whole minute for the verdict. When it came, I couldn't actually tell if it had been worth waiting for.

'Good idea, that sounds a reasonable thing to do. Plank himself is probably not going to be in a position to turn up there for a while, what with being currently imprisoned by his own mates ... and while you've got his office at your mercy, try to find out what other enterprises Moorhouse and the West Plankers are responsible for – the ones that seem to be proper legitimate businesses that is, as well as the bent ones. There might be some clue in there to suggest where they're hiding Plank.'

I nodded dumbly. It was all good stuff, though nothing I wouldn't have done anyway, without Aileen's advice. But she hadn't finished.

'And if you get any time to spare, you could think about our dinner party, and what courses we could serve to our friends – it'll be our first real occasion in our new house.'

Kenny Madigan, a mere leaf that gets blown around in the tide.

Petesy comes out of the recesses of the garage. Spying the waiting Stella, he goes into an embarrassed apology which ends, '... I'm not used to having a customer turn up on a Monday morning, but now here I am so how can I help you? Senga tells me you may be in the market for one of our hand-picked used cars ... er, sorry again. I'm Petesy, by the way.'

He stops talking and remembers to smile while he flicks a business card out of the breast pocket of his jacket and offers it to Stella. He cannot know that her handbag already contains one she took from his flat.

'I'm sure we have the ideal car for you, if you'll just come this way.' Petesy starts herding Stella towards the double row of vehicles, all his attention concentrated on her.

' Stella,' she tells him. 'Are you the person who hand-picks the cars, then?'

'Absolutely, I certainly am,' Petesy replies, trying to impress, but immediately feels guilty about such an emphatic lie. He points to the

Madigan Motors banner and adds, 'With some advice and assistance from my boss, Mr Madigan, of course. Now I'd like you to have a good look at this Ford Focus. It could well be a worthy replacement for your present transport.'

Petesy nods towards Stella's VW. He opens the driver's door of the Focus. Stella takes a cursory look and asks, 'That Mr Madigan you mentioned … would that be a Mr Kenny Madigan, by any chance?'

'Yes, that's right.' Petesy sounds pleased. 'Do you know Kenny?'

'No,' admits Stella. 'I'm new in the area, but a friend – somebody I work with – told me that Kenny Madigan can get his hands on all kinds of er … stuff, you know if you're a friend of his.'

Well, it's worth a try, she thinks. Petesy is looking at her in surprise.

'Sounds as if your friend is having you on. These days it seems to take Kenny all his time to get his hands on a set of new tyres for a customer, what with moving into the new house and everything. Sit in the driver's seat, you'll be amazed at how comfortable … yes that's right. Isn't that a great driving position? And the all-round visibility … have you just moved to Stratford?'

Stella feels herself losing the will to go on. She is bored by this car stuff, and can't believe she could ever get excited about being chatted up by this Petesy character. It is already obvious to her that he is harmless; his boss, Madigan, must be the brains of the outfit. She pretends to be surprised at the lateness of the hour.

'Oh, is that the time? I almost forgot, I have to be in Redditch in fifteen minutes … I'll come back when I've got more time.'

She makes her escape.

He puts his lunchtime sandwich, unopened, on the table, and turns to his visitor.

'I've made my decision,' he says. 'You're in. Welcome to the new world.'

He smiles and holds out his hand. Vince grasps it warmly.

'Thanks,' he says. 'Looks like it's the old firm back together again.'

Vince reflects on the dramatic change in his boss – all apparently brought about by a week of solitary confinement.

Gerald Plank leans back in his chair.

'All I can tell you right now is that it's a sure-fire guaranteed way for us to become extremely rich … oh, by the way, I've decided to call it the Cerberus project, just for the sake of giving it a handle.'

Devious bastard, thinks Vince, that's his way of showing he's my equal when it comes to a classical education – and at the same time emphasizing that the project now has three heads.

Aloud, he takes the opportunity to impress Gerry with his knowledge of the Cerberus project.

'Ah yes … on the subject of your other partner … I feel you should be aware that I have already made the acquaintance of Kenny Madigan.'

Plank controls his expression. No surprise; no puzzlement is permitted to show on his face.

'You *have* been busy,' is his only comment. He continues quickly: 'Look, Vince, why don't you sit down. We need to work out our moves … including how we can each rely on the other's continued co-operation, goodwill, what have you. We must be able to trust each other.'

'I couldn't agree more,' says Vince, taking a seat at the table opposite his boss.

'Good! Here's what I propose. I'll stay locked in here for the next day or so – that's your guarantee of my good intentions. Besides, it's reasonably comfortable considering its nature. Anyway, I've got to be somewhere, and if I appear anywhere else, everyone will know that my kidnapping is over. However, I do need to make some arrangements, so I would appreciate having my phone returned.'

His raised eyebrows bring a nod from Vince.

Gerry Plank carries on, 'In the meantime, you don't get to know all the details, not until the enterprise gets started – that's *my* guarantee of security. The next thing I need to do is finalize the arrangements with the person who will be responsible for the, er, overseas end of the operation. So I will set up that meeting – you, me, and uh, Madigan – with the foreign connection. OK?'

'Hang on a minute,' Vince protests. 'Is this foreign connection a fourth partner who has suddenly entered the picture? Talk about dilution of profits—'

'Steady on,' Gerry interrupts. 'The Dutchman is not a partner. He is a paid employee, that's all. We need somebody local to set up the overseas end.'

Vince is mollified. He says, 'Fair enough, Gerry. If you say we need him, then we need him. But here's a serious suggestion from me: once we get this thing off the ground, I suggest we grab the first opportunity to dump Kenny Madigan and his associate.'

'Agreed,' Gerry says, almost too eagerly. He doesn't know who the hell this Kenny Madigan is, but hating complications as he does, he welcomes any move towards simplification.

'Right,' says Vince, with some satisfaction, 'that's something Absalom's talents will be well suited for ...'

Apparently as an afterthought, he adds, 'Oh, by the way, Madigan seems to think that you've got another office. Where do you think he could have got such an idea?'

Plank shrugs, a what-do-I-care gesture. 'Haven't a clue.'

Vince Moorhouse departs in good spirits, feeling he has achieved the prime objective of his bold action in seizing his boss.

Alone once more, Gerald Plank starts to get that feeling of being back in control. At some time in the future, there will surely be a chance to eliminate the insufferable Vince Moorhouse – but wait until Moorhouse has got rid of this other interloper Kenny Madigan, not to mention his nameless associate.

Whoever they might be.

—CHAPTER ELEVEN—

I t all came flooding back, just like riding a bike. Even though I was entering premises in the interests of the owner, the police would still regard it as being in some mysterious way against the law – if they were ever to find out. That being the case, I owed it to myself to take all possible precautions to avoid being caught in the act. That meant dressing anonymously in black jeans and sweater, wearing rubber-soled shoes, and carrying no credit cards, driving licence, or any other identifying material. Just like the real professional criminal I used to be.

The other thing that goes with that is the professional criminal equipment. For example, there was my precious lock-picking equipment (inherited from Auntie Ursula), flashlight with adjustable beam, another light attached to a headband for hands-free operation, my black gloves of thin skin-like leather, and a few other items you don't need to know about. All of this equipment goes neatly into compartments in a black bag which looks like a smart soft briefcase. A feature of this briefcase is its ability to double its thickness by the use of a couple of zips. This can be handy if you are likely to be leaving premises carrying more items (such as documents, files, CD-ROMs, floppy disks, etc) than when you arrived.

I left my car in a street parallel to the main shopping street that contained my target; no parking problems in Leamington in the evening. It was about eight when I walked along the thinly peopled pavements and up to the door which sported Pitch, Putt, and Carruthers' brass plate. I thought it would be late enough for all the lawyers to have gone home to their families, while still light enough at this time of year to allow me another half-hour of daylight – enough for me to get my bearings in an unfamiliar office before dark. Needless to say, I would not even consider switching on the main lighting, no matter how small the apparent risk.

Confidently, I strode up to the street door and inserted Daphne's key. Within five seconds I was inside, at the foot of a flight of stairs, with the door closing behind me.

Enough daylight filtered down from a landing window to guide me up the stairs. I passed several first-floor doors, all either labelled with the solicitors' name or marked private. I headed for the next flight of stairs, which led to another landing containing just three doors. I had no trouble working out which one which would lead to Plank's office. One was adorned with the letters WC, while another proclaimed itself as *Carruthers and Putt – Records Store* in faded black lettering. Must have been labelled before Pitch came on the scene. The unmarked door on the left had to be the one.

The daylight from the landing window was enough for me to work by. I made myself comfortable, kneeling on the carpet, to tackle the lock. It was a fairly standard Yale type – nothing special, but my skills were somewhat rusty on account of lack of practice. So what should have been maybe a five-minute job ended up taking at least twenty minutes. However, in the end, the door swung open to reveal Gerald Plank's nerve-centre: the heart of his lucrative new business.

Absalom watches from a bus stop across the street as Kenny Madigan uses a key to let himself through a door between a fashion boutique and a travel agency. He immediately calls a number which is hot-keyed into his mobile phone. His boss answers almost instantly, and listens to the terse message.

Vince Moorhouse merely grunts an acknowledgement while his brain goes into overdrive. Thoughtfully, he takes a bunch of keys from his pocket. Gerry Plank's bunch of keys. It includes the key of Gerry Plank's Mercedes, in which Vince abducted its owner. It also includes a number of other keys, which until now, Vince has ignored on the assumption that they are designed to open doors in the Plank family home.

'Stay where you are,' he finally says into the phone. 'Tell me again your exact position – I'll join you as soon as I can.'

At that moment, Vince is relaxing with a nearly full pint glass in his local pub in Henley-in-Arden. He leaves without another sip. At this time of the evening, it should take no more than thirty minutes to get to Leamington.

✻

It was a big office with two windows on the left wall, which looked out towards the back of the building. I reckoned five or six people could work in this room without getting in each other's way. Not that there were facilities for that many. Two large wooden desks were positioned more or less centrally, in such a way that the windows were behind their swivel chairs. The wall opposite the door was lined with wood/metal tables from the rightmost corner right up to the green door marked EMERGENCY EXIT, which took up the last metre of that wall. To my right, when I looked behind the door, I could see a row of steel filing cabinets in mixed olive green and pale grey, obviously second-hand, and a bulky machine – a photocopier, I suppose. Against the wall facing the desks, there were several cupboards of the type normally used to store stationery and office equipment. The floor was covered wall-to-wall with coarse hairy corded carpeting.

Each of the two desks held a computer screen. Just what you would expect these days. What I would not have expected, however, was the line-up of four more computer screens with their attendant keyboards and mice on the tables against the back wall. They didn't look like work-stations, being too bunched together for that, and all angled towards the single chair that inhabited that side of the room.

No point just standing there admiring the view. I closed the door and advanced into the room. Where to begin? An amateur burglar would be inclined to take a stab here and there; open a filing cabinet at random, rifle through one of the desks, have a poke through one of the cupboards. Don't get me wrong – these days I also am no more than an amateur. But the difference is that I have experience in the field, which is how I know that an organized and rational approach is essential. Normally, you can't be sure of being able to work without interruption, so you have to assess which are the most likely places to find whatever it is you are looking for – and that is where you turn your attention first. It sounds so obvious when you say it like that, but you'd be surprised.

First, just out of curiosity, I went over to take a closer look at the main bunch of computers; Christ knows why, I'm no expert. Still, it seemed odd, even to me. They were all plugged in to electrical sockets and nothing else. I mean, you'd think they would be connected to each other, but it looked like they were all independent and so were the two machines on the desks. Well, to hell with the damn computers, let's get on with the purpose of my visit. The desks were my obvious starting point, even though I hadn't a clue as to what I was looking for. Maybe I would know it when I saw it.

The nearest desk was an immediate dead loss. All the drawers were empty except for the inevitable few ball-points of the transparent type that seem to breed in neglected corners. I moved over to the other desk. Right away, it felt more promising. For a start, it was locked. Always a good sign, that – it indicates how somebody thinks he (or she) has something which somebody else would want to take away from them. In fact it seems to me that a good solid lock is like a red rag to a burglar. You might as well put up a big sign to tell the world 'Here be stuff worth nicking'.

The lock on this desk had a nice solid look. Very deceptive, as it took me about ten seconds to get it open. Undamaged of course – I prefer not to leave footprints or any other sign that I have passed this way. The drawers here were quite well filled. The top two shallow ones contained the usual accumulated office clutter such as pencils, markers, erasers, scissors, calculators. Also lots of boxes all different shapes containing paper clips, staples, and rubber bands. There was even one little box with a length of coiled wire attached. I couldn't see how to open that last one, which had the words Portable 2.5 inch Enclosure printed on the lid.

Anyway, I didn't have all night. Well, I probably did, really, but who needs to waste time on Short Plank's knick-knacks and executive toys, no matter how intriguing they might look. What I was hoping to find was information, ideally in the form of a nice envelope folder which would contain sheets of nicely printed paper listing details of all Plank's secrets, businesses, associates, enemies, and plans for the future. Yeah, and why not just win the lottery while I'm about it – that would be just as likely.

I would even settle for a bunch of those computer diskette things with all his records saved on them. I have found these devices very useful a couple of times in the past. It's amazing how people are dead careful about access to their computers, using secret passwords and whatnot; yet they copy their files on to diskettes or CD-ROMs and leave the copies lying around for anyone to pick up. Not that I can do much with computers myself (though I'm learning), but I know somebody – my mate Steve in fact – who has all the expertise I'm ever likely to need.

So I moved on to the deep bottom drawer of the desk, which turned out to be equipped with rails for hanging file-folders. There would have been room for far more than the twenty or so that were present in their depressing shade of olive green. Of that number, most were inhabited by files, to judge from the hand-printed identification tabs sprouting from them. Prominent among the names I could see on the tabs were some I recognized – Moorhouse, Simmons, Ecological Recycling, Eastshire Eagle, for instance.

I was reaching for the one with Vince Moorhouse's name on it when the door opened. For a micro-second, I contemplated dropping out of sight under the desk. Too late. He had seen me. I froze.

He advanced on me. His face twisted into a smile. At that moment it seemed like the most sinister smile I had ever seen. His right hand came forward.

I cringed.

He spoke.

'You must be Vince Moorhouse. Pleased to meet you ... Doug Mellis at your service.'

Still unable to speak, I managed to rise to a half crouching position and shake the offered hand. My new friend burbled on.

'Had a call from Gerry today. He told me about you joining the enterprise ... so it would seem I've got three bosses now. Anyway, Gerry says the way is clear and I should get on with checking all the systems and start setting up the first three er ... scams, I suppose you would have to call them.'

He went over to the bank of computers on the tables against the wall and started switching things on. As he did so, the computer screen in front of me also came alive in spite of having no obvious connection with anything else, but I paid no attention to it – I had more pressing questions on my mind.

'Uh, er ... Doug,' I said, 'just so I can begin to catch up with things, how far have you progressed with the preparations, to date that is?'

'Right,' he replied. 'As you can see, I've got this Fire-Wire LAN all set up and running ...'

'Wait a minute,' I interrupted. 'Are you trying to tell me you're providing the technical expertise for this operation. I mean, I don't want to seem insulting or anything but ...'

I trailed off hoping he would catch my drift. What I meant was that he looked the very opposite of a hi-tech whiz kid. For one thing, they're not usually in their sixties with a fringe of grey hair surrounding a mainly bald scalp.

'If it will put your mind at rest, I can assure you that thirty years in the computer industry doing just about everything that's possible with computers is quite an adequate apprenticeship. OK? And then they dump you on a trumped-up ... well, they called it involuntary early retirement and seemed to think they were letting me off lightly with no prosecution or ...'

He sounded quite miffed, but at least it wasn't with me. I made some sympathetic noises, and got him back to the subject.

'So we have the wireless LAN, as I said. One of these systems is set up as a server to maintain all our information and provide organized data sets to meet the parameters of whatever criteria we define. As I expect you know, Gerry wants to initiate a complete cycle every two or three weeks, so in a way it's like starting up a whole new business enterprise every time.'

I nodded, pretending to understand the jargon. Doug burbled on.

'So all the data is held there and backed up regularly ... oh, except Gerry's own personal data, of course. He's very secretive about that – keeps it on a two-and-a-half-inch hard disk in an external enclosure that plugs into to his USB port. He always unplugs it and either locks it away or takes it with him when he leaves.'

Something in there rang a loud bell. Surreptitiously, I slid the top drawer of the desk halfway open. It still said **Portable 2.5 inch Enclosure** on the lid of that innocent looking box. At that point, Doug was walking across the room towards the filing cabinets. While he rummaged in one of the cabinets, I slipped the box with its attached cable out of the drawer and into my leather bag which was propped against the desk beside my left foot.

When Doug turned away from the filing cabinet, he was holding a folder which he put down on the desk in front of me on his way back to the computer wall.

'I've provided you with copies of most of the stuff I've produced so far. See what you think.'

'Thanks,' I said, putting the folder into my bag, which gave me an opportunity to make sure the 2.5 inch device was neatly stowed away. I closed the zip on top of the bag. Meanwhile, my colleague was once again seated at his cluster of computers.

'Look at your screen,' he said.

I looked. It was showing me a colour movie in which something seemed familiar. A man walked across a room. With a shock I realized it was me – in this office. When I first came in.

I watched myself stand for a moment while I surveyed the room, went to look at the computers, and sat down at the other desk ... and so on.

I sat with my mouth open. Doug grinned at me. The same story was unfolding on one of his screens.

'Easy to see it was your first time here,' he said, 'Gerry must have only recently given you the key.'

He pointed to one of the cupboards – a tall one nearest the corner of the room with a high shelf on which there was a row of those heavy binders made of thick cardboard, all apparently empty.

'The camera is inside one of these,' he told me. 'It shoots through the thumb hole in the spine of the binder ... activated by any movement in the room ... writes to a file in the server. Wireless technology.'

I began to consider the implications. What comes next? I tried to remember. We both watched as I moved to the other desk, the one where I was now sitting. Christ, I thought, suddenly knowing what came next. I stopped watching and started thinking feverishly, while Doug Mellis continued to look at his monitor, where I could be seen picking the lock on the desk. I could almost hear the pieces clicking together in his head.

He cut the picture. His chair swivelled. His face managed an expression composed of half indignation and half rage.

'You fucking ... you shit ... you're not him, not Moorhouse, are you? Who the fuck are you?'

I threw off the guilt feelings he seemed to expect me to have. I mean, I'm not like a bank that has to pretend to be trustworthy. I shrugged and said, 'Tough luck, Doug, seems you've fallen among thieves ... sounds like a case of the cat calling the dog's arse hairy.'

Well, there was nothing serious to be said. An uneasy silence fell. It seemed as if Doug couldn't think of a way to follow up his moment of revelation. He could hardly threaten to call the police.

Meanwhile I was trying to whip my brain cells into a creative frenzy, but they were failing to come up with a cunning plan of action.

Not that they got much more time to concentrate on cunning plans.

Not with that sound of heavy footsteps on the stairs. Then just outside the door.

Which burst open.

—CHAPTER TWELVE—————————

Vince turns the corner and immediately spots Absalom who is trying to merge seamlessly into the background. Somehow, even though his bulk is occupying a high percentage of the inside of a bus shelter, he completely fails to look as if he is waiting for a bus.

The arrival of Vince does nothing to help in that respect, since even in casual wear, Vince has the air of a man who has not stepped aboard a bus since World War II. But what the hell; the great British public is not noted for its powers of observation.

Vince peers across the street towards the building Absalom has pointed out.

'He's still in there, I take it?' he asks.

'Yeah,' Absalom grunts confirmation. 'Ain't took my eyes off of that door since he went through it.'

'All right, then,' says Vince, 'I didn't leave my pint unimbibed in order to stand here like a cigar-store Indian. Why don't we go and visit Mr Kenny Madigan?'

Under his breath he adds, mainly to himself, 'Perhaps we'll find out at last what he and our own dear Gerry are really up to. Come on.'

Vince takes a step in the direction of their destination, only to be halted by Absalom's meaty hand on his arm.

'Hang on, boss. There's another bloke also went in there as well – after Madigan was in for a while. Had 'is own key, just like Madigan.'

'OK, though I suppose there must be more than one possible destination in the building. What kind of bloke is this?'

'Old bloke … wrinkly. Looked harmless.'

'Good. No threat to us, then, wherever he was heading. Let's get on with it.'

The street door opens with the second key Vince tries. They proceed up the stairs, making no particular effort to keep the noise down.

*

I am paralysed. I reckon so is Doug Mellis, as a very large and very ugly man erupts into the office. He is followed at a more nonchalant rate by somebody I recognize – the unspeakable Vince Moorhouse. He is not surprised to see me there.

'Ah, Madigan. Thank you for showing me the way. My guess is that you and our esteemed colleague, Gerry, are planning to cut me out of the equation. A forlorn hope now, I think you will find. Why don't you introduce me to your mysterious companion?'

I say nothing, having sussed that this was a rhetorical question.

Moorhouse gestures an all-encompassing wave which takes in the whole office set-up, before continuing.

'I hope you will initiate me into all the mysteries of my new business.'

He turns to his large companion. 'Absalom.'

I have already worked out who the fat bloke is, so I am not too surprised when I see that his hand is suddenly holding a gun and it is pointing in my general direction – mine and Doug's.

Scared shitless, certainly. But not surprised.

When Absalom speaks, it is in a voice that is rough, but unusually high given his physique. Neither Nick Pearson nor Petesy have mentioned the wimpy voice.

'You two – on your feet and get over there against the wall, an' don't make no sudden moves,' he squeaks.

Doug stands up facing the gunman with his hands in the air. I move very carefully and deliberately, away from the desk to stand to the right of Doug, more or less against the recommended wall. I don't know why I think it a good idea, but I bring my black bag, which I put on the floor at my feet so I can raise my hands. As an attempted distraction, I say something. Anything.

'Twice in the same day, Vince. We can't go on meeting like this.'

An idiot remark, but one which makes a bigger impression than I expected. No effect at all on Vince or Absalom, but Doug becomes quite animated. He bursts out with, 'Vince! You must be the real Vince Moorhouse. Oh, thank God you've arrived.'

He points at me, quite rudely (lucky I'm not easily offended).

'This lying bastard here has been pretending to be you and he's got …'

I don't much like the way Doug's outburst is heading, so I am actually pleased to hear Absalom's encouraging interruption.

'Both you bastards keep your fucking mouths shut or I'll make dog meat of youse.'

I am inclined to take the dog meat threat seriously. So I continue to keep quiet, but Doug still seems to think the Seventh Cavalry has arrived. He insists, and that just winds Absalom up a bit more.

'No, look, I'm serious. I really mean it, Vince.'

'Shut it.'

Absalom's face shows that he is just getting more annoyed, but looks like he's preparing to issue nothing more than another volley of threats. However, Doug can't leave it alone.

'Watch this. I can prove it. Here, let me show you,' he says.

And makes his big mistake.

He suddenly whips round to reach for the controls of his computer system – a keyboard or a mouse, I'll never know which.

Before he can touch anything, a loud flat crack briefly fills the air – a gunshot from Absalom's revolver. Doug crashes back into the table he has been standing in front of. At the same time, I involuntarily flinch from the sound and feel something move at my back. It's the release bar on the green emergency exit. Absalom and Vince seem almost hypnotized as they watch Doug's slow-motion descent to the floor. I push hard on the bar at my back.

The door swings outwards, away from me. Without even thinking about it, I decide to accept Fate's offer of an escape route, pausing only to bend down and grab my black bag. Which is just as well considering the bullet that whistles over my head a microsecond before I register the crack of a second shot.

Then I'm out of there, crashing down the rickety metal staircase which seems too loosely attached to the rear of the building. Hoping the two gangsters get in each other's way and trip over Doug's body on their way round the desks to my exit. I don't stop running to find out – not until I thread my way through the jumble of backyards and out of an alley to an adjacent street from where I can get back to my car. As calmly as I can manage, I drive a few streets away before stopping to search for the bug which must have been placed on my car earlier in the day while I was having my meeting with Vince in his office at Ecological Recycling Ltd.

There it was – a disk about the size of a ten pence piece, clinging magnetically to the bodywork and almost completely hidden under one end of the rear number plate. I transferred it to the next nearest parked car, a mean-looking black Range Rover. Maybe the owner of a vehicle like that would like to meet some new friends. I'm not much of an expert on these things, but I think it was probably one of those dead simple types of bug which sends out a radio signal to a receiver which can tell what direction the signal is coming from.

But who cares? I proceeded to break the speed limit back to Stratford with my bag of treasure and a terrific sense of relief.

Now I would have to stop pretending I could stand back and treat this whole situation as if it had nothing to do with me. Not now that I had been a witness to what I reckoned was probably a murder. I mean I'm not a doctor, as they say, but Doug Mellis's fall to the floor had a certain air of finality about it.

Besides, I bet Absalom doesn't often miss the target at that range.

'You're a fucking stupid git, Absalom.'

'Right, boss.'

'These people are not like the Simmons thugs you've been playing with of late. Now we've missed out on all the interesting tales this pathetic old sod might have been able to tell us.'

'He was reachin' for somethin', boss … could have been his gun … moved too fast.'

'Somehow I don't think so, Absalom. Check him over, will you.'

Pause …

'He's dog meat, boss.'

'I do realize that, Absalom – the lesson for you to carry away from here is that he is unarmed dog meat. Get me his wallet and anything else in his pockets that might help us to find out his purpose and function. I'm beginning to suspect he was a computer consultant brought in by our own dear Gerry and his runaway friend, Kenny Madigan.'

'Right. Here you go, boss.'

'Thank you, Absalom. Now I'm going to leave you to do one of your discreet removal jobs on our friend here. Wait until later, when hardly anyone is about, then use that fire escape door which Madigan was kind enough to point out. Lucky you missed him really; I wouldn't want Plank finding out we had wasted his new partner – which means we would prefer Mr Madigan to remain alive for – well, for another few days anyway.'

'Are you leavin' now, boss?'

'Uh, yes. I shall get on the phone to summon Dirk and Stella. I'm rather curious as to the contents of that big black bag Madigan was so anxious to save. So we are going to have to see what we can find in his house, and maybe in his car. '

'Right, boss.'

On my way home, as the adrenaline gradually drained out of my system, I was thinking about dragging my limp-rag body to bed. So it came as something of a shock to find Aileen and Petesy proposing we go out and have something to eat.

'Nothing flash,' Petesy said. 'Why don't you just dump that bag here and we'll go out for a pub meal or ... how about Pizza Express?'

'That's a good idea,' Aileen agreed, 'I like the lasagne there ... and Kenny can tell us all about his adventures in Leamington.'

'OK,' I said wearily but resigned to it, 'but the bag comes along as well. The stuff in here – well let's just say I'm not letting it out of my possession for a minute before I've even found out what I've got here. I'll tell you all about it once I can sit down and rest my weary bones.'

So it ended up with me once again being dragged off to some place I hadn't intended to go, at somebody else's whim (although later on I was glad I went along). As I picked up my wallet and mobile phone, I realized I felt quite hungry. There were just the three of us, as Daphne was staying with her mother at Aunt Rachel's house that night.

Still, over our pizzas, I did at least manage to pin their ears back with my story and the new information I had gained at great personal danger. Trouble was, Petesy – and even Aileen to some extent – seemed to think I was exaggerating the peril I had personally been in.

As if I would. In point of cold sober fact, I was actually doing the opposite of exaggeration, as my story missed out some details (murder for a start) which I preferred Aileen not to know about for the moment. The main thing I tried to get across was how dangerous Vince Moorhouse was. Absalom was bad enough, but he was only a moronic thug: Moorhouse was emerging as the most callous and ruthless character I had ever met.

I also told of things like Absalom brandishing a gun. For the moment, I avoided mention of Absalom firing the gun and bringing Doug Mellis's life (probably) to a premature end. They did get to hear quite a lot about Plank's Leamington office, Mellis turning up out of the blue, the whole computer set-up, and the goodies I had put in my bag. We decided to wait until we got back home before reading the contents of the folder Doug had given me. We were all intrigued by what he had called 'copies of most of the stuff I've produced so far'.

Petesy was full of comments, and jumping in with all kinds of wild speculation all the way through my story. On the other hand, Aileen kept quiet – thinking, I decided. And so she was. When I had finished (and Petesy had exhausted his far-fetched ideas), she said, 'That must mean that Short Plank isn't a kidnapped prisoner any longer ... I mean if he was able to make a phone call to this Mellis person ...'

'Yeah,' I said, 'but Vince Moorhouse might have forced him to make the call.'

'No,' she insisted, 'it sounds as if the West Plankers knew nothing at all about Mellis before they met him in that office – not if you're telling it the way it was.'

I nodded, catching up. I took a swig from my glass of red wine while I went chasing after the implications of that.

'You're dead right, love – as usual. I suppose that might be significant, but I can't see what—'

Aileen broke in impatiently.

'Don't you see? If he could phone that Mellis person, he could also phone other people.'

'Yes, of course, obviously. Stands to reason.' I agreed, 'but we have no way of knowing who else he might have talked to on the phone.'

'What about his wife, silly? If you were in that kind of situation, the first thing you would do when you got the chance would be to call me so I could stop worrying about you – in your case, you would be in bloody big trouble if you didn't.'

That last bit was definitely true, though it didn't detract from the brilliance of Aileen's idea.

'Right,' she concluded. 'So maybe we should ask Short Plank's wife about her phone call.'

I turned that and other things over in my mind on the way home. We walked back from the restaurant, Aileen and I holding hands.

The other two at least were in good spirits, thanks to the beautiful late-summer night blending with Pizza Express house red and the sensation of being comfortably full.

It was Aileen who raised the alarm when we got to our front door.

'Oh no. I must have forgotten to make sure the door was locked when we left.'

It swung open. I grabbed Aileen to prevent her stepping across the threshold.

'Don't go in,' I told her, 'I checked the door was locked when we went out ... and we didn't leave any lights on, but the lights are on now. They might still be inside.'

It was quite dark outside our house. The sparse street lights were casting black shadows all around us. I told Aileen to wait about three houses back along the street. Then Petesy and I banged on the door, rang the bell, shouted, and generally kicked up a bit of a commotion, before joining her where we could peek round a corner at our door. Nothing. By this time faces had appeared at several windows in the vicinity, which was just what I wanted – no criminal likes to do his (or her) dirty work in the public gaze.

I was not really surprised when nothing continued to happen. So after a few minutes we approached the house again. Petesy and I went in carefully, checking each room for intruders or signs of them. Meanwhile Aileen was doing what I had asked her to do – staying in the deep shadow just outside the front door and watching for any activity further along the street in either direction.

Needless to say, the house was devoid of intruders; later we found that the contents of various drawers had been disturbed.

Soon, Aileen came in and reported, 'You were right, Kenny ... three of them – just three silhouettes really – like the three bears ... a big one first, followed by a medium-sized one, and then a little one trotting along behind. They strolled out from behind one of those unfinished houses down the road, where the builders are still working ... I'm not sure but I think the little one could have been a woman. They went off the other way like thieves in the night.'

'Yeah,' I said, 'they wouldn't be stupid enough to park close to their objective.'

We bolted the back and front doors. I sighed with relief: I'd had a hell of a day. It was all stress and pressure, except for my cosy interlude with Aileen on the carpet.

I did a mental recap. There was my trip to Redditch to meet Moorhouse; my visit to Plank's office in Leamington; the ill-fated Doug Mellis; my second meeting with Moorhouse; Absalom, fastest gun in the West Plankers; a narrow escape from being shot; and then my day has to go and end up with a break-in at our new house. It's not surprising I should be so knackered.

Petesy went off up to bed grumbling about having to sleep by himself. Aileen parked herself on the sofa.

I sat down beside her with a groan and put my black bag down between my feet. There were two more things I had to do, but one of them would be better left until the morning. The other, well it wasn't urgent at all but I wanted to do it before submerging into a well-deserved night's sleep. I took my mobile out of my pocket.

I heard at least five rings before Neil's voice barked an irritated 'Hello'. Good, I'm always happy to annoy the police. I hoped I was disturbing a session of marital arts (though I wish Sally no ill-will, only Neil).

'Hello, Neil. Sorry to disturb you at this time of night.'

I have to admit that I didn't sound very sincere, even to me.

'Oh, it's you, Kenny. What the bloody hell do you think you're doing bothering me at … half past eleven?'

'I'm just keeping you up to date with developments, like I said I would. So here goes – nothing to report,' I told him (I can't resist winding him up). 'I was wondering if you have any news for me, as such … like: have you found the elusive Mr Plank yet?'

''Fraid not. The whole thing has gone quiet … not a thing, not even a whisper. Sorry.'

Neil had regained some composure now, so I thought it was time to kick his crutches away.

'Glad to hear you've got the gangster population screwed down so tight, Neil. By the way, I think your undercover wonder-woman burgled my house tonight … when we have cops like that, who needs villains?'

I cut it off right there, and put my phone down with a grim grin.

Aileen said, 'Oh, I should have got you to check that they're still OK for the concert next week … never mind, I'll talk to Sally in the morning. Let's go up to bed – we need to have a serious talk.'

As you know, I was ready for sleep, but if Aileen had come up with some new slant on the Plank business, it would definitely be worth listening to.

If I could stay awake long enough.

Once we had got ourselves settled in, lying on our backs with the light out – our usual serious discussion position – I waited to hear what was on Aileen's mind.

'The dining-room furniture will be delivered next week,' she said.

I couldn't see what that had to do with me being in mortal danger from Moorhouse, so I just grunted to show I'd heard.

'So,' she continued, 'we need to plan our first dinner party ... I mean, the guest list is easy, but the menu is a real problem. What on earth are we going to feed them?'

Can you believe it? Here's me the target of a ruthless gangster and his hit man, and there's my woman deciding to join the chattering classes. I decided to humour her.

'Look, Aileen, I'll help you plan the menu if you like. It can't be that hard ... I mean you do great dinners for the two of us. Just multiply it up for eight people. No need to get your knickers in a flat spin over the simple matter of what to give them to eat'.

'Oh, it's not as easy as that, Kenny. For instance, Sally and Neil are both vegetarians – but I think they're different kinds of vegetarian. You know, one is a vegan or something. Do you think they would both eat Quorn fillets?'

'There's no such thing,' I protested. 'No quorn has ever even sniffed a bone, so it couldn't be filleted. Isn't quorn that fake steak stuff you tried on us last year? Remember, love, I didn't stop farting for a week.'

'I'll never forget it,' she said. 'That was a really unpleasant week. I suppose I could slip you a real steak, for the convenience and comfort of the human race.'

Luckily, I detected the grin in her voice before I could say anything. It was one of Aileen's attempts at humour. I offered another idea.

'You know how these vegetarian people are always going on about how their stuff tastes just like real meat. So give them proper steak or pork and tell them it's veggie food. It's not as if it could do them any harm.'

'I couldn't do that,' Aileen said firmly. 'They would know, and never trust me again ... anyway, Sally has given me some suggestions ...'

'That's good,' I said. 'If they invite us back, we can give them some suggestions about our dietary requirements. How we must eat lots of meat every day.'

After a thoughtful silence, I went on, 'Look, that's all right, love. I'm sure we can make allowances for a couple of vegetarians. The rest should be easy enough – for instance, Steve is dead easy to please.'

'Of course he is ... he's your best friend,' she said. 'It's Sheila who is the fly in the woodpile there. She has to have a low-fat diet, and no salt.'

This special diet business was getting right up my wick.

'Oh, for Christ's sake, what the hell is that about?' I asked.

'It's for health reasons in Sheila's case,' Aileen said, ' – and she's still avoiding beef because of the mad cow thing.'

'Bloody hell,' I said. This was a particular hobby horse in my bonnet. 'The whole sodding population is fifty times healthier than it's been any time in the past, and nearly everybody lives longer as well. But the less disease they have, the more health scares they invent. That's what you call a paradigm.'

Aileen felt the need to correct me. 'You mean a parallax, don't you?'

'Whatever,' I admitted, and changed the subject.

'What about Senga, then? She would eat a scabby horse. In fact, she probably has ... she buys burgers at that dodgy stand near the garage.'

'Well ...' Aileen said, 'didn't you know; she won't touch vegetables or fruit – except potatoes. Apart from that, Senga's great, but don't forget she's got a new partner now, Andy. Senga tells me Andy won't eat anything that swims or flies.'

'Well, that rules out ducks on both counts,' I pointed out. 'Is there a name for that? I mean, is it an official eating fashion as such, like vegan?'

'I don't think so. Not yet anyhow. I expect sooner or later they'll get around to forming a society and opening special restaurants. Goodness knows what they could call themselves.'

'What about calling it a Nof-Nof diet – No Fins-No Feathers?'

But Aileen wasn't listening to me any more. She was still trying to solve the problem.

'What about chickens?' she said. 'They've got feathers but they can't really fly, can they? And they definitely can't swim; I remember some of my dad's chickens getting drowned.'

I had to agree.

'Yeah, right love, that puts them one step below penguins.'

It was then that Aileen had her inspiration. She's got this Rottweiler brain that circles round a problem and then comes at it sideways when it thinks she's given up.

'There's only one answer, if we want to give them anything better than a plate of yoghurt,' she said.

'What's that, love?'

'Chinese.'

'Chinese?' I repeated.

She elaborated. 'Takeaway,' she said.

'Takeaway …' I began. Then I got it. In a Chinese takeaway, you can order all different dishes; veggie things for the veggies, and so on like that, a dish suitable for each fussy eater.

'That's brilliant,' I told Aileen.

As I was sinking into sleep, I thought of a snag, but in view of the lateness, I decided to keep quiet about it.

What occurred to me was this: you know what you see when you open up the packs of Chinese food, especially if you've ordered about a dozen different things, as we would be doing. They all look exactly the same – right? This is usually resolved by everyone tasting all of them, and each person ends up eating bits of whatever they like the taste of.

It might turn out to be the best fun I've had for years.

─CHAPTER THIRTEEN─────────

I slept like a boiled egg. In fact, I slept on beyond my usual waking-up time in the morning. I lay there absorbing the morning very gradually, while Aileen was tarting herself up ready to go to work. She brought me a mug of coffee. I said, 'Thank you, gorgeous,' and tried to drag her back into bed. It's always worth a try, though I know I don't have much chance, because Aileen has this horror of being late for work. So it's very hard to derail her morning routine at the best of times – and bloody impossible when Petesy can be heard moving around in his room just through the wall.

'Oh, never mind,' I said, firmly putting the lid on my thoughts of nookie. 'There's something I need to do first thing anyway.'

I leapt out of bed. It was already after half past seven. My mate Steve leaves home in time to be in his office by ten to nine, which means getting to his place before eight-thirty if I want to catch him before work.

Steve and I have been pretty close friends since we first met in school around the age of seven and we stayed close through our growing-up years. However, our friendship changed somewhat after he married Sheila and saddled himself with a bleeding great mortgage and a house in one of those expensive streets not far off Banbury Road. For some reason Sheila used to regard me as a bad influence on Steve, so our long nights at the snooker club and trips to Villa Park for the home games, became things of the past. Even our get-togethers in the pub had got further apart.

My mate Steve has never done anything dodgy in his life; unless you count working in the head office of a big insurance company, where he's steadily moving up the management climbing frame. Still, he's always been interested to hear about what I've been getting up to, even through my less law-abiding, more dodgy period.

Anyway, just last year our relationship changed again because I was able to help out (at considerable danger to myself) in some difficulties that Sheila's sister and her husband had got themselves into. So Aileen and I were now close friends with Steve and Sheila. Best of all in the current circumstances was the fact that both of them – especially Sheila, surprisingly – were so pro-Kenny that they would do almost anything for me, and no questions asked.

In this instance I was interested not only in using my friends' house as a safe-keeping place for my black bag and its contents, but also in picking Steve's brains for his expertise. Steve is quite an expert with computers – not to the extent of writing programs, I don't think; but he uses a computer all the time at work, and he's got one he fools around with at home. Databases and desktops are right up his street.

I didn't really think anyone would go to the trouble of following my car at the crack of dawn, but I took the usual precautions just the same. The last thing I want is for my friends to be in danger because of my lack of vigilance. By eight o'clock I was seated opposite Steve at his kitchen table, both of us wolfing down toast and coffee.

Well, Steve could hardly refuse to help me out, I knew that, but I was in a bigger hurry than he was probably prepared for. So it sounded as if some extra persuasion would be required when he said, 'All right, Kenny. Leave it with me ... I don't know when I'll be able to get around to—'

'Oh, come off it, Steve,' Sheila broke in from where she was standing over by the toaster. 'Have you lost your friendship gene ... after all Kenny has done for us ... and you've been complaining about things being too quiet at work lately? Here's a chance to do something useful. It must be better than sitting in your office playing solitaire on your computer like some of those boring old gits you work with.'

I carefully kept my mouth shut, other people's domestic bickering being such a minefield, but my brain cells were on their feet, silently cheering for Sheila.

Steve sighed and admitted, 'You're quite right, my dear.'

He turned back to me.

'OK, Kenny, looks like you get the VIP treatment. Let's have it ... I suppose it's a bunch of diskettes you've nicked from some poor sod of a villain, like the last time.'

I tactfully refrained from pointing out that the villain he had just referred to had been his own brother-in-law.

'Something like that,' I said. 'Not diskettes though ... I'm not sure what it is exactly, I thought you might be able to tell me.'

I actually did have some inkling of what I had, but I generally find that people enjoy parading their knowledge in front of those they consider more ignorant. What my Auntie Ursula would have called throwing good pearls after bad swine, or some such.

I opened my black bag and took out Gerald Plank's little box with its attached length of cable. Steve's eyes lit up.

'Ah yes,' he said, picking it up more carefully than I had put it down, 'this is a hard disk enclosure ... it holds the kind of extra-miniaturized hard disks you get in laptops. Very useful for keeping all your data available regardless of what computer happens to be at hand. I've read about these, but this is the first one I've seen.'

He uncoiled the cable and examined the end.

'Yeah, great, it'll fit any USB port. I expect it will plug and play in my PC at work – Windows XP has drivers for all kinds of hardware interfaces.'

I tried to ignore his hi-tech ramblings.

'Could we meet up somewhere at lunchtime?' I asked. 'So you can tell me all about what's on this ... er, thingy.'

'Christ,' he said, 'you really are in a tearing hurry, aren't you? Well, I don't know. Do you realize the disk in this ... thingy, as you call it might be capable of storing anything up to, oh, eighty or a hundred gigabytes? – that's many times more data than is stored in all the books in the public library, including the pictures. Even if I knew what I was looking for, it would take more time than you're allowing.'

'All right,' I said, as if reluctantly giving in, 'I'll give you until tonight ... you must be able to let me have me some good stuff by that time, more than just a flavour ... and you can keep a hold of this thingy and squeeze the details out of it later. I want the dirt on whatever people and companies and other, er, organizations are stored on there – and I really do need it as fast as possible.'

We agreed that I would come over in the evening, probably with Aileen, which would make it more of a social occasion. I left my black bag in the safe hands of Sheila; it still contained the folder that Doug Mellis filled for me. I didn't want to risk losing that before I got time to examine its contents. When I had the chance I would come back here to read that stuff but I sure as hell was not going to risk carrying it around. I was pretty sure the contents were dynamite. Hopefully, it would reveal the details of Plank's new business venture.

But that could wait. It was definitely lower down the priority scale than all the other crap that was flying towards me from every direction known to man.

Gerald Plank paces back and forth in the sparsely furnished living-room of the house where he has been held against his will until yesterday – and now remains at his own suggestion. So long as he stays here he is safe. His next move is crucial. If he gets it right, he moves smoothly towards future triumph, dumping Moorhouse and his minions on the way.

His mobile phone is the key. He is somewhat surprised that Vince Moorhouse agreed so readily to let him have it back; which, of course, rings alarm bells, suggesting that the whole place may be bugged. So Vince expects to review his recorded phone conversations. Already, Plank has made two calls from this living-room.

One of these was to Debra, his wife, just to tell her he is safe although he does not know where he is, not to worry, and she would hear from him soon – oh, and love to Daphne. That call would have been expected. The other one was to Doug Mellis – no names, no specific details mentioned. Just giving him the green light to resume work on the unnamed arrangements. Oh, and by the way, there is now a new partner in the shape of Vince Moorhouse whom he (Mellis) will meet in due course.

Those two calls are the ones Plank wanted Moorhouse to hear. In fact, failure to make these particular calls would have been most suspicious.

What Short Plank is about to do now falls into a completely different category.

He goes into the bathroom. He turns on the shower, the cold water tap, and flushes the toilet. He taps a number into his phone from memory. Lucky I can tell from the display when it's answered, he thinks, as he has no chance of hearing a voice through the noise of rushing water.

No time is wasted on introduction. Serious communication begins as soon as his phone screen indicates that someone has answered.

'Don't speak a word, I can't hear anything you say. Just listen carefully ... and press the red button on that recording device if you're in your office – you might need to refer to it later. Here's what I want you to do ...'

The instructions are quite detailed, and go on for several minutes.

From Steve and Sheila's house, I headed in the direction of the garage. There was still real work to be done. For example, it being Tuesday, Mrs Torrance the book-keeper would be doing her stuff at Lone Harp. She comes in once or twice a week to keep the payroll and accounts up to date and juggle with the mysteries of VAT. None of which I feel any great urge to involve myself in, though Mrs Torrance has other ideas. I always insist that I trust her completely and don't pay much attention to her lectures on purchase ledgers and balance sheets. But there are always letters and forms and Christ knows what for me to sign in my capacity as proprietor of the business, and Mrs Torrance gets wild at me if I'm not on hand to do the necessary.

In the middle of this morass of mundane thoughts, an icy finger suddenly stirred up an excitable bunch of my brain cells. The enemy had been in our house the previous night. So what? Neither Aileen nor I is the kind of person who would feel violated just because somebody broke into their house. And in any case the intruders didn't find anything that could be of interest to them because there was nothing to find. Right?

Right! So they took nothing. There was no robbery as such. Right?

Right! But they could have *left* something behind. In fact, considering the recent form of this unsavoury mob, it would be quite surprising if they hadn't donated us at least one discreetly placed piece of miniature technology.

I switched destinations with a sharp left turn at the next roundabout.

Back home, I did some brain racking trying to remember what was said in the house the previous night and that morning. It was all pretty vague, so I decided to get on with the search; I would ask Aileen and Petesy when I got the chance – preferably in the small piece of desert which would become our back garden.

My first find jogged my memory. It was a little piece of plastic-covered hardware inside the ear-piece of our house phone in the hallway. There was an identical one in our bedroom extension. These were easy to find because we still had old-fashioned low-tech phones with actual receivers attached to the other part by a curly cord and ear-pieces that unscrew to reveal a space big enough for a dozen bugs. Anyway, it was the sight of these that reminded me of my late call to Neil the previous night – even though I had used my mobile for that.

I replayed that conversation in my head. I recalled telling Neil that one of his coppers had burgled my house. Could the bug in the hall phone have picked up a conversation in the living room? If so, I had betrayed Stella Galloway to the villains even though it was only my end of the conversation they could have eavesdropped on. Christ knows what they would do to her if they had. Later on in my house-frisking, any doubts were eliminated when I found the radio bug inside the sofa. The undercover copper's cover was blown for sure.

Lunchtime had come and gone by the time I finished my search. There was a fourth bug on the underside of our bed, and that was it; the two in the house phones to pick up both ends of telephone conversations, the one in the sofa to monitor general conversation, and the bedroom one. I wasn't sure about the spies in the phone, but decided the sofa and bed bugs must be the kind that would transmit what they heard to a voice-activated recording device within 500 metres or so. Probably in a car parked a couple of streets away. You can buy these things for a few pounds out of catalogues, or even more easily on the internet; though I can't imagine what legitimate reason anyone might have for using them.

The thought of Vince Moorhouse paying serious attention to Aileen and me discussing our dinner party arrangements diverted me for a few minutes. Maybe he could come up with some menu suggestions. But my amusement faded as soon as I thought about the possible fate of the undercover copper if Moorhouse listened to the recording of the living room tape.

I decided to leave the devices in their present hidy-holes for the time being. The use of this kind of installation as a liar device to mislead the opposition is an idea that appeals to me, though I have never heard of it actually working as intended.

OK, so it was now mid-afternoon, and I couldn't put Mrs Torrance off any longer. I went to the garage with only one pause on the way. That was when I stopped for a moment in Compass Road to call Neil on my mobile. I would never forgive myself if Absalom was allowed to do his worst on that poor policewoman because I failed to pass on the warning that her cover was blowing in the wind. Unfortunately, Neil was not available; out of the station, nobody knew when he would be back. So I tried his mobile number only to find that the bastard had it switched off. Oh well, I tried.

The first thing I saw when I drove on to the forecourt, was Petesy out at the roadside waving goodbye to a young lady in a VW Golf that looked about ready for trading in. No doubt a prospective customer, and Petesy's favourite kind – female. He can't help chatting them up. I parked, and got out of my car just in time to meet him coming back in.

'Looks like that one's got you going,' I remarked. 'Have you got her pleading with you to let her buy one of our crap old bangers yet?'

'Hard to tell at this stage,' he replied, as we walked together towards the workshop on our way to the office. 'That was Stella's second visit … she's been asking my advice on where to live around Stratford. She's from Scotland, somewhere. Isn't she cute? – Oh you didn't get a good look at her, did you?'

Stella? I thought. I didn't need a good look to work out who she is. Probably sent by Vince Moorhouse to check up on us.

'What's her last name?' I asked. 'Is it Galloway?'

'Dunno,' said Petesy. 'Ask Senga, she booked her in for a service, so it'll be in the book.'

'Never mind. I know who she is,' I said, suddenly realizing I could have warned her that her undercover game was shot to pieces – if only I had got there thirty seconds earlier. Wild thoughts of charging after her quickly melted down to asking Petesy, 'Where was she going … I mean, when she left here?'

Petesy shrugged. 'How would I know a thing like that? And why would you give a bugger anyway?'

I didn't want to tell him too much; Petesy isn't a good enough actor to conceal what he knows. I told him, 'Because if she's who I think she is, she's not what she seems, as such.'

I refrained from adding that, through no fault of my own, I had put her life in danger. Instead, I said, 'Well, you must have got her number. Didn't you? You can't help yourself ... I mean she's female and cute, according to you.'

'Yeah,' he said, 'but there's still Daphne. I'm being faithful to Daphne ... besides, Stella never actually got round to giving me her number somehow, although I did ask – just in case we found the perfect car for her, of course.'

'Of course.'

'Oh, by the way,' he added, 'Senga tells me we've had intruders in here last night. Nothing missing, but stuff has been moved around, especially in the office. She's arranged to have the locks changed. I didn't tell her I knew who it was.'

'Yeah, that was the right thing to do,' I agreed. They could search the garage as much as they liked; there was nothing there that any one would ever find.

Then I had to turn my attention to Mrs Torrance, who came out of the office at that moment to claim control of my ears and my cheque-signing hand for the rest of the afternoon. Except when I broke off to make a couple of phone calls to set up my arrangements for the coming evening.

─CHAPTER FOURTEEN─

By five-thirty, I was waiting for Aileen outside Jonathan Philips's shoe store. However, it was nearly ten to six before she appeared.

'These three sodding women,' she said, really annoyed. 'They were already in the shop over half an hour when we locked the doors at five-thirty, and they insisted on trying on nearly every shoe in the shop between them … felt like stabbing them with some of those new stilettos. Eventually they left without buying anything … just killing time before the theatre.'

'Relax, love,' I told her. 'You can dump that job anytime you like. You know that.'

'Yes, I know,' she admitted, 'but I quite enjoy working there. It's only the most egregious customers that get on my wick.'

I didn't bother to reply – though I might have if I had known what egregious means.

On the way to Leamington, I filled Aileen in on my day. The result of my visit to Steve and Sheila; my finding of the eaves-dropper bugs in our house (I had also remembered to warn Petesy about them before I left the garage); my realization that Neil's woman copper was in danger, and there seemed to be nothing we could do to help her. I finished up with our plans for the rest of the evening. Namely, to visit Mrs Debra Plank, still with her sister in Leamington, where we were currently bound; and after that to visit Steve to get his report on the hard disk I left with him.

I suppose I could have spoken to Debra Plank on the phone, but face to face is far more useful, especially when you need to make a quick assessment of the percentage of crap that is arriving in your ears. Not that I felt Mrs Plank was lying, any more than anyone else in her position, but it was a stone certainty that she would be holding something back. And Aileen is the best I have ever known at spotting when she is not hearing all of the truth, which is why I wanted her with me – that and her native woman-to-woman empathy.

Stella sits at one of the two desks in the office next door to the one occupied by Vince Moorhouse in the Ecological Recycling building at Redditch. She is making notes for her own benefit; writing down everything she has discovered about Kenny Madigan and Petesy Curtain. Which is not actually very much. She has not even managed to meet Madigan yet; seems to keep missing him. Petesy, on the other hand – she feels qualified to think of him by his first name now that they're getting acquainted – Petesy turns out to be quite a decent-seeming bloke. On the surface at least. Surely he is too naïve, not to mention too nice, to be a hardened criminal; he must be well under the influence of the dreadful Madigan.

Stella is uncomfortably aware that she has already committed various crimes in her undercover persona. Such as breaking and entering in the company of Vince and Dirk. At least they hadn't stolen anything (she conveniently forgets about her solo fact-finding mission to Petesy's apartment). And she helped Dirk to plant bugs in the Madigan house.

There is also the matter of that bent policeman Vince has put her in contact with. She writes down the number she memorized; Inspector Cornfoot can have it traced. Then she scores out the number with strong black ball-point furrows. It's confusing when you work for two opposing causes at the same time.

She is also having difficulty trying to trace a thread of logic through a complex chain of ramifications while being constantly distracted by the drone of voices from the adjoining office. The sound is tantalizingly just short of the level at which individual words can be distinguished. The voices are clearly those of Vince's cultured tones, and Absalom's shrill squeak. The fat man is being given instructions at considerable length and complexity. It occurs to Stella that if she puts her ear to a glass held against the partition wall that separates the two offices it might be possible to listen. She looks around. No glass – only the empty polystyrene cup which has held the machine-dispensed coffee she recently drank. She tried that on the wall. Nothing. Less than nothing; it seems to make the voices even less distinct. She throws it at the waste-bin and misses. It is about then that the door of Vince's office opens and somebody comes out.

Stella is back seated at the desk and looking innocent by the time the obnoxious Absalom crashes in through the door. He approaches the desk and looms over her. He leers at her, eyes never leaving her chest, and squeaks, 'Ms Galloway, the boss wants to talk to you right now.'

She nods but remains where she is. Better to move once this creep stops being in the way.

He repeats, 'Right now, Miss Stella – the boss is in a fucking terrible mood – be fucking careful – or he'll have yer guts for fucking garters.'

Absalom reaches a hand towards her. A remarkably small hand, she notices for the first time. As Stella cringes away, he grasps her hand and gently helps her to her feet. She pulls away from his grasp and makes a dash for the door. He doesn't take his eyes off her.

'Could be you an' I are gonna be seeing more of each other, my little darling,' he says, attempting a lower tone of voice than he can really handle. 'You'll learn to enjoy our time together. I know a place where we can be alone … nobody to disturb us, not even hear …'

Stella is already knocking and entering Vince Moorhouse's office before Absalom's sentence has the chance to lumber to a full stop.

Moorhouse seems in no mood for idle chit-chat. He waves Stella into a chair. From the top drawer of his desk he takes a small rectangular object which he holds up between finger and thumb in such a way that she can be in no doubt as to its nature. At last he speaks, still keeping the object at the focus of Stella's attention.

'I'm sure you know what this is.'

He goes on to tell her anyway.

'This tape contains all the input from the conversation bugs we planted in Madigan's house last night.'

I introduced Aileen to Mrs Debra Plank. This time we didn't get to sit in the posh drawing-room. In fact, the vibes our hostess was giving out suggested she hoped our visit would be too short to make it worthwhile sitting down. We did get past the door (probably to deprive any watching neighbours of their entertainment) and stood in the spacious entrance hall. There was no sign of her sister, Daphne's aunt Rachel.

'I'm so sorry you've had a wasted journey, Kenny. I've been meaning to call to let you know we don't really need your services any longer.'

I pretended I didn't understand what she was talking about, which was easy, as I didn't have a clue as to what was going on.

'Oh, why. What's happened?' I asked innocently.

'Gerry's fine. I've heard from him … and he says not to worry and he'll be, er … back home in, well … in due course I suppose, except he may still have to stay out of sight for a few days. Just while he gets some, er business matters sorted out – no big deal, he said.'

'Oh, so you haven't actually seen him. It was a telephone call. Was he using his own mobile phone?'

I was just playing for time. I could hardly ask exactly what he said to her; not straight out.

'What exactly did he say to you, Debra?'

That was Aileen asking the unaskable.

Mrs Plank turned towards Aileen.

'Well … just what I told you, he's fine and don't worry and …'

'Oh, isn't that just like a man?' Aileen broke in, her voice and manner full of sympathy. 'You'd think they would have learnt by this time that telling us not to worry is a sure recipe for driving us to distraction. Didn't he even let you know where he is?'

'Well, he would have, of course, but he doesn't actually know where it is – the place where he's being kept … where he's staying. I mean. It's away out in the depths of the country somewhere, but he doesn't know where it is … hasn't got the actual address …'

Debra had to stop talking at that point to let out a pent-up sob. Aileen put a comforting arm around her shoulders. What a bloody liberty, I thought, when she's just reduced this poor woman to tears.

'Come on Debra,' said Aileen, 'let's go and sit down. It looks as if you might still be in need of some help from Kenny.'

So we ended up in the posh drawing-room after all. Aileen and Debra sat side by side on a sofa, while I sank into the deep cushions of an oversized armchair.

'Look, Debra,' Aileen said, taking the woman's nearest hand in hers, 'you must face the possibility that Gerry was forced into saying what he said when he phoned you. God forbid, but he could still be in danger.'

She paused to let that sink in before continuing.

'Look, Kenny has already found out who was responsible for kidnapping your husband … it was that Vince Moorhouse … it's only a small further step to discover where he's being held.'

My mouth fell open. But I was too fascinated to interrupt. They would probably have ignored me anyway.

Aileen went on in that soft comforting tone, 'So any other information you might have could be a great help … even if it seems irrelevant or even, you know … silly.'

Debra was nodding and mopping up tears at the same time. I could have told her that none of that nonsense would be any help in getting Aileen off her back.

'Tell me all about the conversation when you spoke to, er, Gerry on the phone. You must have asked him where he was.'

Debra blew her nose, sucked in a deep breath and it all came tumbling out in a torrent.

'Of course. That was the first thing I asked him and he said he didn't know but all he could see from the windows was fields and woods and a road a good distance away with hardly any traffic so it must be a quiet country road and I said why couldn't he just walk out, I mean so what if the doors are locked surely he could get out of a window which he could easily break after all. He said the windows were all barred as if it was intended to hold somebody there against their will … he mentioned that the window bars looked new and they were cemented into solid stone walls so the house itself must be a good age and was probably not big enough to be a farmhouse but might have been a farmhand or gamekeeper's cottage or something of the sort.' She seemed to run out of steam at that point, and simply stopped.

Aileen said, 'It could be just about anywhere, then. No clues at all? What about the garden of this place? Did he mention the weather … like, was it the same as here?'

Debra shook her head.

'No, we never talked about the weather at all … but there is something; he said the garden was like a jungle. Not a tropical jungle or anything like that; just all overgrown … and from an upstairs window he could see a big board like an estate-agent's board but it was lying flat in the undergrowth as if it had been wrenched off its post and thrown down there. But that's no help either because he said if there was any writing on the board it must be on the hidden underside – either that or it was so faded as to be unreadable.'

She paused and brightened up, only to continue in a more cheerful vein.

'Anyway, Gerry's main message was that he and his kidnappers have come to an agreement, which involves Gerry agreeing to remain where he is for a few more days until certain arrangements can be made. So he got his phone back. And I'll have him back soon … well, after he's finished staying out of sight, but he did say that would only be for a few more days.'

'Well I really hope you're right about that,' said Aileen. 'Meanwhile, Kenny will keep on doing everything he can to help.'

'Oh … that reminds me,' said Debra, 'I told Gerry about you, Kenny. Just in case you happened to turn up. I wouldn't want him thinking you were the enemy.'

I wished she hadn't told him that. I wasn't sure I wanted Plank to think of me as being on his side, but there didn't seem to be any point in getting into a discussion about it.

We politely refused an offer of coffee on the grounds that we had to be on our way to meet someone else. As we were being ushered through the front door, Aileen had a go at bringing Debra back to the comfortable world of shopping. She looked at her elegantly clad feet and said, 'Love your taste in shoes. You must come round to Jonathan Philips when you're feeling better – we've just got the new season's designs in.'

'Oh, that reminds me,' said Debra, 'I had a visit from a policeman earlier today … that inspector, what's his name …?'

'Neil Cornfoot?' Aileen said, taking the change of subject in her stride. I was still trying to work out how the latest shoe designs could remind anyone of an over-qualified policeman. Maybe it was his name.

'That's the one,' Debra agreed. 'He wanted to know if there had been any contact by the kidnappers … like demands for ransom or such. I didn't tell him anything, especially not about the phone call … Gerry is always careful not to tell the police anything they don't need to know. Anyway, Daphne and I are going to move back to our own house at Lower Pebbington tomorrow; there's really no point in staying here now that the police know where I am.'

I nodded in agreement.

'That makes sense. I think Inspector Cornfoot's visit was just his unsubtle way of letting you know that your location is no longer a secret.'

Aileen and I managed to leave without any more interruptions.

It was time to head back towards Stratford to find out how Steve had progressed with his investigation of Mr Plank's personal computer files. Aileen was very quiet beside me in the car; thinking, I suppose, since her only comment was, 'What do you think he meant? You know, that bit about staying out of sight for a few more days.'

I shrugged and muttered something to the effect that I was buggered if I knew. Aileen wasn't the only one who was thinking – I was managing to squeeze in a bit of worry about Stella Galloway. However, we all know it was Neil who actually dropped her in the shit, as such.

He was the one who would have to shoulder the blame if something nasty happened to his undercover policewoman.

─CHAPTER FIFTEEN────────────

'Take this tape,' Vince Moorhouse tells her. 'Play it back and listen carefully to every iota of sound that it's picked up. We need to know everything we can find out about that devious bastard Madigan ... and his sidekicks.'

Stella is in her efficient impress-the-boss mode. 'Right,' she says crisply, reaching for the tape. She peers at it and asks, 'Does this include stuff picked up by the phone bugs as well?'

'No,' comes the reply, 'the phone bugs alert Dirk when a call starts ... then he can listen to the call in real time. Your tape is just from the voice-activated devices in their sofa and the bedroom. However, it is probably the most important one; the things people say in ordinary conversation in off-guard moments usually tell us a hell of a lot more than what they say in telephone calls.'

Having impressed Stella with the vital importance of her assignment, Vince now rewards her with a look that says: this is serious and important and I'm trusting you completely.

'All right, Stella? Let me have your summary first thing in the morning ... just the relevant stuff, no more than one side of a sheet of A4. I'll probably have another tape ready for you by then – Dirk will make the next changeover first thing in the morning, so long as the bug is still active.'

'Right, boss ... by the way, is there any news of Mr Plank?'

Vince shakes his head sadly.

'Not so much as a whisper,' he tells her. 'That bastard Simmons has a lot to answer for... actually, I'm glad you asked me that, Stella, it reminds me that I need to keep my senior staff in the picture.'

He favours her with a confidential smile, and she basks in it a little. Vince leans forward and continues, 'Actually, this is what I've just been discussing with Absalom. Simmons's people have ... er, taken out one of our collection operatives in Coventry, and we've been working out how best to strike back. That's Absalom's speciality … the kind of thing he does best, so it's his assigned task for today. That tape is yours. Off you go and get on with it.'

Stella waits until she gets back to her rented two-room apartment in Alcester before playing the tape. Although the tape recorder's voice-activation saves Stella having to waste a lot of time listening to blank tape, it introduces various types of confusion.

For example, what sounds to the listener like a continuous conversation may consist of a number of separate remarks which were made minutes or even hours apart; at other times the recorder springs to life merely to capture the clinking of glasses or coffee mugs – even the occasional cough or incoherent mutter.

So Stella has to replay sections of tape several times just to discover that someone has spotted the intruders leaving the street; that nothing seems to have been stolen; that the American hot one with green jalapeños is probably the best kind of pizza to order at Pizza Express; and that Petesy (she recognizes his voice) is knackered and is going up to his bed wishing Daphne was here with him instead of back at Aunt Rachel's with her mother for the night.

All very well, she thinks, but so far she has heard nothing useful – or even interesting. She moves on through more disconnected sounds. Then she's into a section which hangs together well enough to make narrative sense. A telephone call. This is more the kind of thing she was hoping for. She listens until the call ends. Stops the recording.

Stella leans back in her chair. She fumbles a cigarette out of the pack, lights it, and sucks in a calming lungful of smoke. Some heavy thinking is called for. She slots her cigarette into a groove in the ashtray, an action which brings to her notice the previously lit cigarette already burning there. Angrily, she stubs out the new one. She rewinds the tape to the start of the telephone call.

The voice must be Kenny Madigan's.

'Hello, Neil. Sorry to disturb you at this time of night.'

Distant mutter.

'I'm just keeping you up to date with developments, like I said I would. So here goes – nothing to report. I was wondering if you have any news for me, as such … like: haven't you found the elusive Mr Plank yet?'

Distant mutter

'Glad to hear you've got the gangster population screwed down so

tight, Neil. By the way, I think your undercover wonder-woman burgled my house tonight … when we have cops like that, who needs villains?'

Bleep.

That must be Madigan pressing the hang-up button. Bloody hell. Thank Christ he used a mobile. If he had used the house phone, Dirk would already have heard the conversation, both ends of it in fact – and Stella would have been dealt with one way or another by this time.

She shudders, trying not to imagine Ugly Absalom's methods of dealing with spies. The thought causes her to generate a thunder cloud of tobacco smoke over her head.

Although still shaking, Stella consigns her own narrow escape to the immutable past and turns to consider the implications of what she has just heard. She opens her notepad, intending to enumerate and analyse the various possibilities and combinations of possibilities (with a mental note to burn the page afterwards).

Meanwhile, the tape is running on, spewing out yet more fuel for Stella's confusion. Immediately after the end of the phone call – a woman's voice.

'Oh, I should have got you to check that they're still OK for the concert next week … never mind, I'll talk to Sally in the morning. Let's go up to bed.'

Kenny's girlfriend, she assumes. What's her name? Eileen … something like that. Who cares.

The ensuing conversation, a load of rubbish about a dinner party, goes right over Stella's head. It doesn't make any sense in the current context. Lucky there wasn't a simultaneous conversation on the living-room bug; that would have made it even worse.

Stella is trying to get her head round the chilling knowledge that these people – these known criminals – are on what sounds like familiar terms with her police boss. More than familiar, in fact. It sounds as if they are close friends. She shuts off the tape, crushes out the cigarette burning on the ashtray, lights a new one out of her Silk Cut packet, and readies the notepad at a clean, unsullied page.

It's about to become extremely sullied, Stella thinks. She is plagued by such symbolic thoughts which protrude at distracting tangents from her central concerns.

She writes: *cover blown*, and stops to think about that. On reflection she scores out *blown* and substitutes: *half blown*. It seems probable that her cover remains intact within the Moorhouse organization, thanks to her lucky interception of the tape; it's only Madigan, and presumably Petesy Curtain, who know who she is ... on second thoughts maybe not Petesy (whom she rather likes) as he would have let something slip if he was in on the secret – considering his evident naïvety. Just Madigan then, the still-unknown quantity. Madigan and Vince are at loggerheads, so there seems little risk of their exchanging notes on poor little Stella. OK, maybe she can still live with her cover cracked but not necessarily smithereened. Not yet anyway.

Just as well, really, considering that a fully smashed cover would have to be reported back to Inspector Cornfoot. Stella jots down a new line in her notepad: *Inspector Bastard Cornfoot.*

What to think of him? He might be a good conscientious copper with a direct line to the secrets of the crime world via some kind of hold over Kenny Madigan.

Yeah, right – and politicians might keep their promises.

Face it, girl, she tells herself. The butter-wouldn't-melt Inspector Bastard Cornfoot has got to be firmly in the pocket of master criminal Madigan.

But what is to be done about it? Can she keep herself fireproof while she goes about gathering evidence which will put Inspector Bastard Cornfoot away where bent cops belong?

Looks as if I'm on my own from here on, she decides. It is time for her to live up to the letter of her last annual appraisal, which had been perhaps a little too free with the terms *imaginative*, and *resourceful*. She is aware of, but prefers to ignore, the fact that this glowing testimonial has arisen largely because her DCI back in Ayrshire hoped she would exhibit these qualities in his bed, when his campaign to entice her there reached its inevitable successful conclusion. There is no record as to the extent to which his aspirations were fulfilled – Stella's current 350-mile-distant assignment in Stratford could argue either way.

Our arrival at Steve and Sheila's place threw Sheila into a catering frenzy, as soon as she had established our not-eaten-yet condition. Aileen went off to help her examine the contents of the freezer, while Steve produced cans of lager for the two of us. I immediately sat down at one end of the sofa to open mine, and took a grateful swig.

'Not like that, Kenny,' Steve protested. 'You must know better by this time ... you've got to wait till I bring the glasses. Sheila will go berserk if she comes in here and finds you drinking out of the can.'

He was kind of joking, but only kind of. Sheila was dead serious when she included drinking-straight-from-the-can in a wide range of banned actions. She called them low-life practices, which were to be considered inappropriate in the genteel environment of her executive home. I gave in gracefully and poured the rest of my lager into the glass Steve handed me.

'What have you found out?' I asked, when Steve sat down facing me across the coffee table. I was impatient to get on to the main business of the evening. He must have had it all ready and waiting, because he opened the door of a cabinet-type piece of furniture beside his chair, reached in, and pulled out a brown folder which was thin enough to be held shut by a large paper clip. Can't be much paperwork in there, I thought, feeling a bit disappointed what with Steve having wittered on about the vast amounts of data that could be stored in one of these disk-in-a-box things.

'Look for yourself,' said Steve. He skimmed the file across to me. I flipped it open. It contained about a dozen A4 sheets, at a rough guess.

'Doesn't seem to be very much here.' I suppose I must have sounded a bit ungrateful, but Steve was used to me by this time, so he wasn't bothered.

'I've just printed out what I think you'd be interested in,' he told me. 'You don't know how lucky you are – I was the one who had to wade through every week's collections from every shop for every protection collector in every town for the past two years ... not to mention every night's takings for every prostitute in the Midlands in every ...'

'OK, OK,' I said. 'I get the idea, mountains of stuff which is there just to provide raw material as input for the accountants. Right?'

Steve nodded.

'There's also the details of sales and other transactions and even stock inventories for all the companies listed on the first two pages you've got there. Their complete accounts are on the disk too, but I've only given you a few key figures for each. I think these are the legitimate enterprises which your Mr Plank controls in addition to his fine range of rackets.'

I looked up in surprise.

'I don't remember mentioning any Mr Plank to you. Is his name in there? I thought he would have used an alias, or made sure everything was attributed to somebody else who would get it in the neck anytime something went pear-shaped.'

Steve put on that irritating smug look of his.

'Give me bloody credit for a small amount of brain, Kenny. It didn't take a lot of inspiration to come up with the Plank name; haven't you noticed it in the papers recently? You're actually quite right ... his name doesn't figure. The people responsible, according to these records, are called Moorhouse and Simmons. Just the two of them – but it's been set up to look quite obvious that they're the ones pulling all the strings.'

In that instant, I was struck by a blinding ray of understanding. Here was the real motive for Short Plank being kidnapped. I had never been really convinced by the previously-advertised reasons – the ones about the struggle to be his successor and access to his new business venture. Or so I now told myself with hindsight.

All the time, it had been what Aunt Ursula would have called a mystery wrapped up in an enema.

I was still pondering this revelation when we were summoned to Sheila's dining-table to get stuck into some hastily prepared chicken Kiev with mashed potatoes. Sheila was quite apologetic at serving guests with prepared meals from Marks & Spencer. If only she'd realized we would be too busy to eat earlier ... blah ... blah. Aileen and I really enjoyed it though.

Making light conversation while we ate, I mentioned that the disk-in-a-box had been languishing in a drawer in Plank's office: that Daphne, his daughter, had given me a key, in the hope that it would help me to find out where her dad was hidden. I didn't bother to explain that her key was for the street door of the office building, as I wanted Steve and Sheila to understand that I had not done illegal things.

'Wasn't it a bit careless of him,' I suggested, 'to leave such dynamite information just lying there?'

Steve looked ready to agree, but Aileen, who knew a lot more about the circumstances, had to point out, 'I don't think so ... he left it locked in his desk so it couldn't be accessed by anyone using the computers. And remember, he must have expected to be back there the next day – he didn't know he was going to be kidnapped.'

She shrugged. 'It had to be somewhere, didn't it?'

As usual, my Aileen had put it in a perfect nutshell. I gave her knee a squeeze under the table.

When the rhubarb crumble and custard came to an end, I risked becoming a social outlaw by opening up my folder to take a good look at the important data Steve had squeezed out of that portable hard disk. I felt privileged when Sheila, far from complaining about inappropriate activities at the dinner-table, moved dishes around so we could spread out the sheets of A4.

The list of company names and addresses was interesting in itself. Most of them we had never heard of. A few were fairly familiar names, if only because they were regular advertisers in the local Midlands press.

'Look,' said Sheila, 'there's Grant and Mitchell, Bespoke Construction Engineers … we had them in to build our conservatory. No wonder it leaks.'

I looked for Ecological Recycling Ltd, and sure enough, there it was in the list. It occurred to me that I had no idea what the hell the company did, apart from providing a base for Vince Moorhouse and his personal staff. I mean, it's the kind of label that people find reassuring. With a name like that, it must be doing something really worthwhile for the environment. Boring, probably, but definitely worthwhile.

I asked Steve if he had noticed anything about Ecological Recycling; anything that might single it out as being different from the others in some way.

'Hang on a minute,' he said. He went to fetch his own black leather briefcase, opened it and took out a lined notepad which proved to contain page after page of dense pencil notes in the tiny capitals Steve uses instead of writing. With a slightly sheepish expression on his face, he said, 'Just my working notes. You can't keep all the information in your head when trying to pick your way through this much data.'

It's dead typical of Steve to try and make something look effortless when most people would be surprised it can be done at all.

He leafed through his notes.

'Nope. Nothing really – Ecological Wotsit is pretty much in the same boat as all the rest of these companies.'

Aileen was on to this like a rabbit up a tree.

'What do you mean, Steve, same boat? What kind of boat is that?'

'Well, for anyone who has shares in any of this lot, Shit Creek beckons … take a look at the print-outs I've given Kenny.'

'Steve, really.' That was Sheila's protest at the Shit Creek reference.

'Just tell us about it,' I said. I'm actually quite competent with figures, but I'll do anything rather than dig my way through a raft of financial balances, even when they're tarted up for me to digest – just ask Mrs Torrance, who does the garage accounts.

'OK. In a nutshell, every single one of these enterprises is within a cat's whisker of going belly up.'

'But …' I protested, 'weren't they being used to launder the money from all the organized crime activities? I mean, that would swell their profits … their revenue streams would be forced to absorb great wodges of dirty money they hadn't actually earned.'

Steve nodded wisely. Bloody annoyingly.

'Yes, that's how it has been until fairly recently. But within the last year all their accumulated profits from whatever sources, all their cash reserves, and even the loans they've raised from the banks to finance their expansion – all of these have been deliberately drained away.'

'Where to?' Aileen asked, playing up to Steve's sense of drama.

'Well, that depends how much of this data is available to whoever is asking. For instance, when the official receivers examine the company accounts carefully, they'll congratulate themselves on detecting the clever frauds perpetrated by these poor sods Moorhouse and Simmons. I reckon both of them will go to jail, the money will never be traced, and everyone will assume that the two guilty parties have salted it away in Switzerland.'

Aileen came in on cue.

'But in reality, the two Planker lieutenants are left without two beans to rub together?'

'Exactly, Aileen … you're really on the ball. Meanwhile, Gerald Plank, who engineered the whole thing strolls off into the sunset without a stain on his character – at least, not one that can be proved. Except by someone who has access to the accounting acrobatics on that disk of yours … by the way, Kenny, you should be aware that I've copied the whole thing on to two DVDs and backed it up on my work computer so I can be sure we have the data – just in case.'

'Oh, right. Just in case … what exactly do you mean by that, Steve … just in case of what?'

I was a bit taken aback. Steve is usually anxious to wash his hands of any tainted associations with me. Then I remembered to add, 'And what have you done with these DVDs of yours?'

He answered my last question first.

'Don't worry. They're in a safe place. I made the copy for several reasons: first, it's always a good idea to have a backup in case of technical problems; second, the information in there is such dynamite that somebody – quite a few somebodies – would stop at nothing to get that disk back from you … if those somebodies know or find out that they exist. Which means that you could be in *beaucoup* personal danger, by the way.

'Thirdly, I'm going to pass this information on to the authorities. There's no way I can ignore a fraud of this magnitude. It's a major disgrace to Midlands industry. I'll hold back for a while to allow you time to extricate yourself, or finish up whatever investigations you're involved in … in fact, it might be useful if you can find Plank within that time-frame – assuming you don't already know where he is. The Serious Fraud Office will appreciate knowing where to lay their hands on him.'

'Steve, you're a pompous git, you know that?' I said with a sigh. 'But I've got to admit you're right. How long have I got though?'

'Look, Kenny,' he said, 'I don't want to know any details about your activities, which we are all aware can be a bit shady at times even if you do usually come out smelling of roses. Just make sure you keep yourself fireproof … I'll give you until the end of the week before I blow the lid off. But that's it, today is Tuesday so – the deadline will be Friday. OK? Friday afternoon, so nothing can happen before the weekend.'

'That Serious Fraud Office you mentioned; is that a police thing, like the Fraud Squad?' Aileen asked.

'Something like that,' said Steve. 'It's actually the updated hi-tech successor to what they used to call the Fraud Squad.'

'More tea, anyone?' said Sheila brightly, brandishing the pot.

Aileen and I turned down the offer of further hospitality. We left carrying Steve's sheaf of printouts and the still unopened envelope that Doug Mellis gave me in the Leamington office. Everything else – the hard disk in a box and the other contents of my black bag – I left with Steve and Sheila for safe-keeping. Their door closed behind us with Steve's estimate of Gerald Plank's fraudulent fortune ringing in our ears.

'I can't be exact about it,' Steve had said, 'but Plank has definitely caused at least fourteen million pounds to vanish into thin air – that's just in the last twelve months – leaving a string of crippled business enterprises in his wake.'

─CHAPTER SIXTEEN─────

I made a detour from the short route home in order to park off the beaten track. That was so we could discuss the situation in private; what with our house being bugged, not to mention the probable presence of Petesy and Daphne who could no longer be trusted with incriminating information relating to Daphne's father. So Aileen and I sat in the twilit car-park at the start of the Greenway, a local walk that burrows into the heart of the countryside. The idea was to slot the new information in beside all the stuff we already knew, and to work out the implications for ourselves and our friends.

As always, Aileen put her finger straight on to what she thought would be the button of greatest relevance.

'I suppose your priority must be to find out where Mr Plank is hidden ... though according to Debra Plank it looks as if it has now become the place where he's hiding out. I mean, Steve thinks it will help the Serious Fraud Office if you can tell them where he is.'

'Why should I want to help the bloody fraud filth?' I pointed out. 'Actually, my best plan might be to warn Plank that he's about to be exposed to the police. Then he would have the chance to skip the country with his wife to enjoy the fruits, er ... leaving Moorhouse and Simmons to their fate. That would get me out of the shit with Moorhouse and his gang of thugs.'

'As usual, Kenny, you've grabbed hold of the wrong end of the brush. Moorhouse thinks you're in cahoots with Plank ... so if Plank disappears abroad, Moorhouse will concentrate on you even more. You'll be deeper in the ... in trouble than ever.'

Trust Aileen to go for the jugular of the problem.

I asked her, 'So what do you think I should do?'

'What I said – find Plank. Now why don't we check through Steve's list of Plank's failing business ventures. Maybe one of them is ... oh, an ostrich farm, or something out in the wilds of the country – some place that's got a house like the one Plank says he's in. He's not likely to be close enough to any of his businesses to recognize that level of detail; and it might amuse Moorhouse to imprison his former boss in a house which is his own property.'

If only I had ignored Aileen for once and left Plank to his own sad devices. But I was so used to her being right that I just assumed she would be right again, as usual. On the other hand, she wasn't wrong either. Of course, we followed her suggestion, and waded through the list by the light of the overhead map-reading lamps in my car.

No ostrich or any other kind of farms, but we did snag on to Mildew Swain & Co., the estate agents, who were one of the Plank enterprises presided over by Vince Moorhouse. We recognized the name because they had an office in Stratford. Finding it there brought back Aileen's memory of the fallen board at the kidnap house; according to Debra, her husband had said it was like an estate agent's board.

Could it be that the hidden side of that board carried the words Mildew Swain & Co?

I took my mobile phone from my pocket and summoned up Steve's number. He was not overjoyed to hear from me while getting ready for bed, but agreed to do a quick search in Plank's database.

'I'll connect your hard disk to my home system and see what I can find. Call you back. Give me fifteen minutes or so.'

'Right,' I said to Aileen, as I pressed the button that ended the call. 'We're going home now. I'm buggered if I'm going to avoid having normal conversations in our own house just because these obnoxious bastards have bugged it.'

So off we went. Luckily, neither Petesy nor Daphne were in residence. The first thing I did when we got in was to say a few insulting things about Vince Moorhouse in a loud voice. I hoped he would hear my opinion of his ancestry, his mother, his lack of testicles, and his generally cretinous nature. A completely futile exercise, I admit, but I was feeling more like my normal self by the time I shut up and smashed all the hidden bugs. To hell with trying to feed them false information. I couldn't think of anything that could usefully mislead them anyway.

'OK, love,' I said, 'while we wait for Steve to call back, why don't we take a look at the contents of that envelope Doug Mellis gave me – I suppose it was his last bequest – and I really ought to know what kind of new business Moorhouse thinks I'm going to be sharing with Mr Plank ... oh, Christ, I didn't mean to ...'

I trailed off with the dawning realization that my last bequest reference had blown the gaff. Aileen had not been aware until now, that Doug Mellis had bitten the dust. She was now standing as if paralysed, with that look in her eyes – the look you see in a World War II film when the heroine stares at the sky after hearing that her pilot boyfriend's plane has failed to limp home after the night raid on Dusseldorf. Not that she cared about Mellis as such; it was just the indication of how much danger I was in. The Short Plank affair was no longer just an interesting problem to Aileen – it had suddenly sprouted some big sharp teeth.

I carried on regardless, and slid the contents of the Mellis envelope on to the dining table, while Aileen was off on her sudden security mission – double-locking the front door and checking all the windows were firmly fastened. All this in spite of knowing that none of these precautions would delay our enemies for more than a couple of minutes if they decided to come in uninvited.

When Aileen came back to the table, I was able to display Gerald Plank's future business plan. A bit of an anti-climax actually, if I had been looking for some sensational headline-hogging crime of the century.

Quite interesting though, even if none of it was half as scary as the ongoing struggle between the rival factions of Plankers – a struggle which might well become even more lethal as a result of Gerald Plank dealing himself a cynical hand in the game.

What I showed Aileen consisted of several little bundles of printed sheets, obviously prototypes of mail-shot flyers designed to be sent out in their thousands. All were variations on the same theme. All were beautifully designed to look official. In fact, they bore a great resemblance to the prize draw packages which are a familiar feature of the junk mail delivered to addresses all over the country. Many of these prize draw mail-shots come from *Readers Digest*, *Which Magazine*, and similar companies which I suppose are quite respectable and operate well within the law, no matter how bloody annoying we find them.

Together, we pawed through the Short Plank bundles. A major difference was immediately apparent; these documents were easier to understand than the usual prize-draw kind. They didn't mince words – they came straight out with their message. The sample I was looking at said:

> *Congratulations Mrs Evans. You are the sole winner of the first prize: a cheque for £20,000.00 in cash.*

'That's the most obvious difference, right there.' I pointed out that up-front sentence to Aileen. 'The rest of it could be any of the usual prize draw stuff; personalized with the name of the recipient … and here comes the sting. See this other official-looking form.'
We read it together. It said:

> *Our Legal Department insists that we must guard against the possibility of fraud. Before we can pay out monies in excess of TWENTY THOUSAND POUNDS, we must be satisfied that you really are Mrs Evans, our major jackpot winner. This is for your own protection.*
>
> *To receive your guaranteed cheque for £20,000.00, return this Winner's Certification Declaration within seven days of receipt, duly authenticated. Just meet the three simple conditions listed below, and your cheque for £20,000.00 will be in your hands within three days of our receipt of the completed Declaration.*

The three conditions, with check boxes for the lucky winner to tick off, were:

> 1. *Affix your triangular £20,000.00 Winner sticker in the triangular space provided.*
> 2. *Sign your full name in the box marked £20,000.00 Winner's Signature.*
> 3. *Place this Winner's Certification Declaration in the addressed envelope provided, together with the administration fee of £29 (cash, cheques and postal orders accepted), and post it first class in the addressed envelope provided.*

The accompanying envelope was addressed in large print to a box number in Rotterdam – presumably an accommodation address which would disappear without trace before anybody could get round to questioning it. I reckon these kind of mail pick-up points can be rented by the month. Also, it reminded me of Doug Mellis's mention of 'the overseas end', and the Dutch name he mentioned, Jan van Whatever.

'They're not really asking for much,' said Aileen, 'only twenty-nine pounds.'

I was doing some mental arithmetic.

'Yes, but think about it,' I said. 'If they sent out, say, ten thousand of these … I suppose they would have to make sure each one goes to a different post code … but that's one reason why he needs a well-organized computer system, to maintain the lists of names and addresses. Anyway, if they got a five per cent response, that would bring in nearly fifteen thousand pounds. Easy money … and they do it all over again, maybe with a slight variation two or three weeks later.'

'Hmm, if you say so.'

Aileen sounded reluctant to agree, but went on to convince herself.

'I suppose enough people might be greedy enough to want to believe it … and even if you are suspicious, twenty-nine pounds doesn't seem too much to invest on the off-chance. You would be kicking yourself if you did nothing and then found out it was genuine … but wouldn't everybody just reply, saying take the administrative charges off my twenty thousand?'

'No, love,' I pointed out. 'Everybody knows about stupidly inflexible bureaucratic systems. We make allowances for adminis-trative idiocy all the time, and put the blame on badly designed computer systems.'

We couldn't resist going on to remark on just how sordid Short Plank's thinking had become. Somehow, this kind of fraud seems such a snivelling and cowardly crime compared to the more straightforward traditional stuff. Of course, the truth is that any move away from physical violence is a move in the right direction. At least until the criminals start killing each other – something which was already happening, and might well go on happening.

As I remarked to Aileen, it's only when the criminals start

murdering each other that the police begin to get serious about bringing in the guilty parties. Which seems to me to be a perverse way of going about it. Surely, if you leave them to get on with bumping each other off, you end up with a lot fewer villains to bring in, which would save the country a fortune. Not to mention honest taxpayers like me. However, as my Auntie Ursula would have said, you can always rely on the good old British police force to rush in like a square pig in a round poke.

The telephone jabbed a welcome finger into our philosophical discourse. It was Steve calling back with word of a property with specifications that might make it suitable as a temporary prison. A listing on the books of Mildew Swain & Co described it as 'Sedge Cottage, a bijou residence enjoying a secluded location in open countryside far away from the madding crowd'. Its file record was annotated 'withdrawn from availability'.

'Talk about comprehensive records,' Steve said, 'I even managed to cross-reference this cottage to an invoice which led me to a job record in the files of another of Moorhouse's West-Plank companies … a so-called security firm called Loxco. It seems they were contracted to "install rustproof hardened steel bars exterior to the windows of the property and equip both external doors with keyed deadlocks capable of being operated from either inside or outside". The job was completed last month.'

'Brilliant,' I said. 'Not much room for doubt as to its use. Let me have the address and directions.'

I wrote them down, thinking I now knew exactly what I would be doing the following morning. What I did not know was whether Gerald Plank would welcome his rescuer. Now that he regarded himself as being back in control of the situation, he might resent my interference.

To Steve, I said, 'Thanks, mate. Do you mind if I drop round your place in the morning … just for a minute to pick up something out of that black bag of mine? Something I might be needing tomorrow.'

I was not sure if my burgling tools – not to mention my breaking and entering skills – would be adequate to deal with the new locks in Sedge Cottage, but I was definitely going to give it my best shot.

Irst thing in the morning, as requested, Stella turns up at Ecological Recycling to find Vince Moorhouse already at his desk and apparently hard at work with several files open on his desk. As she knocks and enters, he looks up to greet her with a welcoming smile. Stella cannot recall ever having seen Vince in such a good mood. She hands him the prepared sheet of paper resulting from her study of the tape recording.

'Nothing worth the bother, I'm afraid.'

Vince looks, scans the few lines that are all she thought worth reporting, not including Kenny's call to Neil, of course, just coffee-making, Petesy going up to bed, and some near-surreal comments on the dietary habits of Aileen and Kenny's friends. Vince crumples the sheet into a ball and drops it in the waste bin.

He says, 'At least we know we haven't missed an opportunity … anyway, it seems we've been rumbled. Madigan has smashed the bugs … probably knew about them all the time. When Dirk picked up the new tape, he noticed very little had been used, so he played it. All it contained was a load of abuse directed at me by name, followed by nothing. Quite amusing really, though it serves as a reminder that we must never underestimate Madigan.'

Stella cannot help feeling some disappointment.

'So there's nothing much for me to do at the moment, then?'

'Don't you believe it,' Vince replies, looking at his watch. 'You won't be twiddling your thumbs too long. I shall be leaving here in about five minutes, and I bet you can't guess where I'm going.'

Stella puts an interested expression on her face to belie the sudden inexplicable butterflies in her stomach region. She shrugs and lets her raised eyebrows take the place of words.

'All right,' says Vince. 'You'd never guess anyway … I'm on my way to liberate Mr Gerald Plank, your boss and mine. How about that?'

'You've found him,' Stella gasps. 'Is he all right? How did you manage to get him out of Madigan's clutches? Are you sure it's safe for you to go, er … wherever it is?'

Vince throws up his hands, pretending to be overwhelmed by her over-eager questions. Actually, it has momentarily slipped his mind that Stella believes Madigan to be the kidnapper (whereas he knows Madigan is Plank's intended new partner). Smoothly, he takes the adjustment on board.

'All in good time,' he tells her. 'The main thing for you to be aware of right now, is that we are about to turn the tables on Mr Kenny Madigan and his egregious crew.'

Vince looks at his watch again.

'I'll fill you in briefly about what is about to happen. It is now nine-fifteen … within the next hour, our Mr Plank and I will leave the kidnap premises, bound for a safe destination. Meanwhile, you will be off on another mission – you and Absalom together, in your car with you driving. Right? … OK so far?'

Stella nods dumbly, still thinking about the release of Plank.

'You drive your car to Stratford, where Absalom will perform his assigned task with his usual efficiency. You will then drive your passengers to the former kidnap location which will by that time have been vacated by Mr Plank. Absalom knows the way.'

While telling Stella of her impending assignment, Vince has been placing his files carefully in a steel filing cabinet to the right of his desk. He now locks the cabinet and checks all three drawers to make certain they are securely locked.

He holds the door open for Stella, and exits behind her. He fills in the final details.

'Absalom already has his instructions … he's waiting for you in the car-park by your VW. He'll tell you all about the job while you're on the way. Come on, I'll walk out with you.'

Stella has no alternative. She is forced to trot on downstairs trying to keep up with her boss, when she desperately needs a chance to pass on this new information to her other boss, Neil, the detective inspector. Oh well, she thinks, maybe he knows already, what with him being in the pocket of at least one member of the local villain fraternity, namely Madigan.

*

I was in no particular hurry. When I went round to Steve and Sheila's house to get my burgling tools out of my black bag, I stopped to drink a coffee with Sheila. I also borrowed a couple of Steve's large-scale Ordnance Survey maps, which I studied over my coffee. Then I set off in a kind of south-westerly direction.

My leisurely drive took me across Worcestershire on quiet roads, past Evesham and through a group of small villages known as the Lenches. Then it was just anonymous open country with only the occasional isolated house or barn. On this network of local byways, each road I turned on to was narrower than the last, and more winding, until, as I neared my objective, I was mostly on the kind of lane where vehicles can only pass each other if one of them finds a wider piece of grass verge where it can pull over.

There must have been a local heavy shower in this area. Puddles still adorned the pot-holes, everything in the countryside was looking fresh and green, and the air hinted at a promise of sunshine to come later in the day.

Having previously pinpointed the house on Steve's map, I was able to avoid the direct approach. Instead, I parked on the verge on a road from which I could just make out the isolated shape of the cottage across a couple of fields. The gate I climbed over to reach the first field seemed to have received no maintenance in the last hundred years. Maybe it was a Grade II protected structure or something.

Walking across this field and then the next one, brought me in towards one side of the cottage, and at the same time enabled me to keep a clump of trees between it and me most of the way. I just had to put up with the heavy mud which becomes the main feature of the countryside whenever it gets wet.

In the end, I managed it all without dramatics. The place was pretty run-down and grotty-looking from the outside. I could see how the estate agent's efforts would be unlikely to bear fruit (a rare opportunity to acquire a country home with great potential). No sign of life; no movement. The whole place seemed as peaceful as a graveyard.

I made my stealthy way to the front of the house, keeping close to the wall and ducking below the level of the only window in this side, while being shredded by thorns of bramble (well-stocked cottage garden). When I peered round the corner to the front of the cottage, I could see there was a once gravelled but now weed-encrusted area just about large enough for two cars, or one car to turn around (the property benefits from ample parking space). A hundred yards of deeply rutted track led from the cottage towards the unpaved farm road that would be the normal means of access. This narrow track had apparently never enjoyed the benefit of gravel – nor any other attempt at a load-bearing surface (no noisy traffic to disturb the pastoral tranquillity).

Since no cars were presently occupying the parking area, I concluded that the current occupier had no visitors. That gave me the freedom to move to the front door, where I began to examine the locking arrangements. There were two locks attached to the door – a run-of-the-mill two-lever device, presumably the original lock; and a newer security deadlock. The big surprise for me came when I discovered that the deadlock was not engaged. The high-tech device was unlocked and the place was only secured by a lock which could be picked by a blindfold granny. Taking out my little pouch of burgling tools, I opened the simple thing in about twenty seconds, and was through, into a small but clean lobby (welcoming reception hall).

Still no sign of life. I was already beginning to suspect that the bird had flown, but nevertheless, I went around feeling foolish as I called out, 'Hello. Hello there, anyone at home.'

Soon I had to face the fact that I wouldn't be liberating Gerald Plank today. Nor was there any trace of his occupancy to be seen in the small living room. I quickly checked the few other rooms in the cottage (deceptively spacious family accommodation). The larger of the two bedrooms and the kitchen revealed traces of the recent presence of someone, but nothing to indicate the identity of that someone. A refrigerator which was much too large for the kitchen held half of a sliced loaf, a plastic carton half-full of milk, a lump of cheese, and several tins of various kinds of meat and fish products, the kind of stuff you would use to make sandwiches.

Now I felt like a train which has run out of track. What next? I went back to the front door and stood looking out. Only then did I notice something which had escaped my attention on the way in. That track leading away from the house was sporting fresh muddy puddle-riddled ruts, surely made by a set of wide car tyres. So it looked as if Plank must have been spirited away quite recently, maybe earlier that morning. I had probably just missed him.

Kenny Madigan, always the worm, never the early bird.

No point in hanging around here, I thought. I'm getting back to civilization. I really hadn't a clue about what to do next.

Stella feels overwhelmed by the crushing presence of Absalom at her side. It requires an effort of will to absorb the instructions he passes on. In fact, given Absalom's communication skills, it also requires an effort of intellect.

On arriving at Stratford, she pilots the car along the High Street, with some guidance from her escort, and makes the turn into Sheep Street. The most immediately eye-catching feature of this thoroughfare is the baleful presence of a traffic warden who is busily writing car registrations into her notebook.

'That's good,' Absalom squeaks, 'keep moving ... right past and go on round the block. By the time we get back, she'll have moved on and we'll have all the time we need. I spotted Gibbsie in position ... that's good as well.'

After their slow circuit, the warden is indeed gone, so Stella stops on the double yellow line right outside her destination. She gets out of the car, leaving the engine running, and walks into the shop which has the words Jonathan Philips Footwear above its stylishly dressed windows. The sales racks are an instant attraction, as Stella is always interested in looking at shoes (like most women in the civilized world). She rejects the attentions of the wrong sales assistant, before moving on round the rack where she comes face to face with the one she is looking for. Absalom's description would have been sufficient, even without the confirmation of the name badge which says AILEEN and FOOTWEAR CONSULTANT.

Stella holds up a shoe of an indeterminate hue. For some reason she doesn't understand, she tries to minimize her Scottish accent when she says, 'I'm not sure about this colour. It seems to be somewhere between taupe and terracotta ... do you think I could look at in daylight ... out at the door?'

Stella is aware that the sales assistant will have to accompany her to the doorway (just in case a customer runs away with a single left shoe – Kenny has been known to remark that it should only be necessary to take that precaution with one-legged customers who might hop away with a shoe).

In the doorway, she holds the shoe up to the light. Aileen comes forward to help her peer at it, to be roughly seized by two enormous men, and carried off to the car before she has time to utter a word. Stella scurries round to the driver's side and gets in while the muscle-men are stuffing the struggling Aileen into the back seat. Then Absalom is in the back beside Aileen, Gibbsie, the temporary help has vanished, and Stella is driving away feeling like the cow that leads her herd into the slaughterhouse.

Nobody in the street or the shoe store has noticed anything unusual. Even if they had, the only comment capable of fitting the bill would be 'It all happened so fast.'

In the back of the car, Aileen has finally remembered to yell and scream at the top of her voice. But it is too late now that she is inside the vehicle. Attempts at scratching and biting result only in vicious thumps and a backhand swipe across her face. Stella drives around the town's gyratory system and makes for the bridge leading to the south side of the river. Once across that, she will need further instructions. Absalom by this time has a blindfold tied round Aileen's head. From this point onward, he guides Stella with high-pitched orders limited to 'right', 'left' or 'straight on'.

Their destination is the cottage which has recently sheltered Gerald Plank, and which has even more recently been visited by Kenny.

Absalom produces a large bunch of keys and uses one of them to open the front door, through which he bundles Aileen with her blindfold still in place. He indicates to Stella that she should follow him inside. All three stand in the living room. Aileen is subdued, holding back the anger, blinking at her kidnappers in the restored brightness. Her face now sports a livid bruise incorporating some dried blood where Absalom's finger ring has torn the skin.

Absalom nods in satisfaction; hoping he will have the chance to come back and renew his acquaintance with this sullen bitch. He turns to Stella.

'You're supposed to stay here with her, Ms Galloway,' he grins at her before adding, 'for a couple of hours anyway. The boss has got something going on that a pretty little thing like you shouldn't know about … it might corrupt your innocent mind … I'll come back for you, don't worry.'

'That's not what the boss told me—' Stella began, but was interrupted.

'Tough shit, my pretty one,' said Absalom. 'You got yer phone with you?'

'Er … no, I left it in the car.'

But the hesitation is enough. He grabs her roughly round the waist, pinning one arm to her side. Once the first shock is past, her other arm flails uselessly at Absalom while he runs his free hand around her body for longer than is strictly necessary to locate the phone in a pocket of her denim jacket. Some people just enjoy their work too much. However, he finally plucks her phone away and puts it in his own pocket.

There is no pretence left. Abruptly, Stella understands that she is as much a prisoner here as Aileen. But is she Vince's prisoner or just Absalom's?

He treats Aileen to a calculating look. It would be nice to search that one for a phone … or anything else for that matter. But he hasn't time at the moment to give that task the attention it deserves. Later, when he gets back and can take the time to enjoy himself at leisure. Anyway, Aileen is dressed in a narrow skirt and short-sleeved blouse. No place to conceal a telephone – not unless she had reason to be creative about it. Which of course she didn't. Absalom allows himself a brief moment of running his eager hands over her anyway – a taste of things to come, he promises himself.

With a yellow-toothed smile he stands back to survey the pair.

'You'll have a great time with me … later on … we'll not be disturbed the whole night. I like some enthusiasm in my women, by the way; it helps them not to become dog meat.'

He can't resist a more than slightly manic giggle when he adds, 'Maybe that should be bitch meat.'

His prospective victims don't even notice the semantic inconsistencies; they are intent on keeping their expressions as impassive as they can manage.

It is with some regret that Absalom tears himself away and waves a cheerful goodbye to the two women. They hear the front door being locked, twice.

Driving away from the cottage, Absalom uses his own mobile phone to report back to Vince.

'Hi, boss. It's me. All done an' dusted. Both o' them bitches is nice and cosy in their dream cottage.'

'That's good. I was starting to think there was some hitch. You better hurry back now; there's plenty of work to be done.'

Moorhouse is being careful about what he says and how he says it, Gerry Plank being within earshot and no doubt eager for any morsel he might manage to overhear. Otherwise Vince would be quizzing his minion a bit more closely, given Absalom's history in the sex crimes department. Not to mention his general attitude to women.

It is as if that goon knows exactly what his boss is thinking.

'Never laid a finger on 'em, boss,' he says. 'Not so much as a fucking finger.'

Moorhouse cuts the connection with a grunt of satisfaction at the completion of another building block in his plan – the successful snatching of the girlfriend must guarantee that Plank's partner, Madigan, will now do as he is told, as much at his beck and call as Absalom, if somewhat less willing.

In addition, the imprisonment of Stella relieves his mind somewhat. Not that he has any specific cause for suspicion; it's just that a slight unease always nibbles at the edges of his mind when she is around. There is a nagging feeling that Stella is just a bit too good to be true, or to be trusted. What the hell, she is dispensable; willing assistants are a dime a dozen. When your arrangements are moving so nicely towards a crucial turning point, you have to make sure you have eliminated all possible wild cards, no matter how unlikely.

CHAPTER EIGHTEEN

I couldn't think what to do next, so I headed back towards Stratford and my desk at the Lone Harp Auto Repairs garage. That's where I tend to go anytime I feel the need to do some serious thinking.

By the time I got there, most of the morning had swirled down the drain. But it was good to see life carrying on as normal. On the forecourt, Petesy was doing his usual fussing over the cars in the Madigan Motors line-up. There were no customers or browsers around, so I hauled him in to the office for a chat. It seemed only fair to let him pass on the news to Daphne about her father being no longer a kidnap victim; no doubt she would run to Debra with the news. I was assuming that Plank was still incommunicado and not yet in a position to talk to his nearest and dearest.

'So there it is for what it's worth.' I held out my hands in a who-knows-what-it-all-means gesture as I finished my report. 'I haven't a bloody clue whether it makes the situation better or worse. We'll just have to wait and see what happens.'

'OK, thanks,' said Petesy. 'At least it's something to tell her. I just hope it all gets sorted out before Daphne goes back to college. She would never be able to concentrate on her studies if her dad was still in danger.'

Which just goes to show that everybody has their own personal slant on everything that happens. I was glad I had decided not to mention that Daphne's dear daddy was in all probability heading towards a long spell in prison if Steve carried through his intention to involve the Serious Fraud Office (which I was sure he would). For a moment I wondered vaguely if there was a matching Trivial Fraud Office, staffed by junior coppers. Aloud, I just said, 'This must be what Plank meant when he called his wife and said he might have to drop out of sight for a few days to sort out some business matters. I seem to remember he explained to Debra that it was no big deal.'

But then he *would* say that, wouldn't he, I added mentally but not out loud. Having done my duty, I packed Petesy off, back to his used car line-up. A love-struck calf was definitely the last thing I needed around me when I was trying to think.

I got myself a coffee and sat down at my desk with office door closed, and started trying to analyse the situation I found myself in. It seemed I was definitely wasting my time when I went to find that cottage where Plank was languishing, presumably until this morning. Why not just sit back, relax, and think of England; let nature and the Fraud Squad take their course. So what would come of it all?

Well, the police would be after Gerald Plank, once they checked out the information from Steve, though surely that would take an unpredictable length of time, given the mysterious and slow ways in which the authorities move. (Mental note: We, Steve and I, that is, need to work up a convincing story to account for how the files happened to come into our possession. Well just me really, since all Steve can say is that he got them from me.)

Meanwhile, Moorhouse would carry on with his policy of horning in on Plank's new enterprise. As far as I knew, he still believed that I was Plank's new partner. I supposed he thought Doug Mellis was just the computer guy who set up the system in the Leamington office under my supervision.

And then I was thinking of Short Plank's reaction. My thoughts were going something like this: considering that he is a lot smarter than his nickname suggests, he will be anxious to make sure his hard-disk-in-a-box is safe. He might even want to move it to a safer place if he gets the chance – I don't know where. Assuming he can ditch Vince Moorhouse long enough ... because he wouldn't ... but then what happens when he doesn't find ... Jesus Bloody Christ.

I jumped to my feet, knocking over the polystyrene cup which was still half-full of tepid coffee. I left it soaking into the pile of job sheets on my desk and charged out through the garage, leaving Senga and a couple of startled mechanics staring after me.

Fortunately, Sheila was at home. Unfortunately though, I might have been a bit – well, not rude exactly, but maybe kind of brusque in turning down her offer of coffee and a lunchtime prawn cocktail or something similar. I just grabbed the disk box and left in a rush. In Leamington, I parked illegally on a double yellow in a street near the one in which the office was located. As before, I had no problem getting into the building, as I still had Daphne's key. So I was straight up the stairs like a dog on fire and past the entrance to Pitch, Putt, and Carruthers' offices, from which several well-dressed legal types of both sexes were emerging. They paid no notice to me.

Mercifully, on the next floor up, there was no obvious sign of life. I was taking quite a big risk now, by using my lock-picking tools inside an occupied building in broad daylight; they can put you away just for possessing these kind of instruments; and here was I sweating while I muttered curses and twiddled at the lock on the door to Gerald Plank's office. It didn't take as long this time, no doubt because of my recent experience of this very lock, though it still seemed like forever before I finally got safely inside.

The large room looked exactly as it had on my previous visit. No sign that a brutal and stupid murder was done there just a couple of days ago. I went straight for the desk drawer. It was still unlocked, of course, so I slipped the disk box complete with its cable back where I had found it, as near as I could remember. Then it only remained to put my lock-pickers into reverse for a moment in order to leave the drawer looking innocent and unviolated.

As I breathed a big sigh of relief, I couldn't help having a speculative look round the office, you know, just wondering if there was anything else I could ... no, I decided, better not tempt fate. It probably wouldn't be that long before the police would be all over the place like an ugly rash. They would investigate the computer set-up, check out Plank's database, and find plenty of evidence of his proposed new scam. Why should I interfere with evidence? Why not just leave well alone and get out of here before anything else happens?

So that's what I did. I left the office, pulling the door firmly shut to make sure the Yale-type lock engaged. I trotted casually down the stairs without a care in the world, and out into the street, where I arrived just a moment too soon to hold the door open for an approaching man who was still a few steps away, fiddling with his key-ring.

I did a double-take, and watched as this business-suited character selected the right key and inserted it in the lock. He was not a tall man, nor was he bound for Pitch, Putt, and Carruthers. I had recently seen a photograph of him at Daphne's Aunt Rachel's house. Short Plank, for sure.

He didn't spare me a passing glance. Not that he would have recognized me anyway. I was pretty sure Mr Plank had never heard of me until Debra went and informed him that a certain Kenny Madigan was trying to rescue him. I would have greatly preferred if he had no knowledge of my existence.

I decided not to go straight back to my car just yet. Maybe I would collect a parking ticket, which is something I really hate. But what the hell. I crossed the street and joined the shopping classes admiring the SALE goods in the display windows of the local stores. I chose a window which reflected a good view of the door leading to the office I had just left.

Ten minutes later, Plank was back on the street, now clutching a brown-paper-covered package. I followed, staying on the other side of the street. He didn't go far before stopping outside the post office to drop a letter into the big red pillar box. I didn't get a good look at the envelope, but it had a quite bulky look. The next thing he did was to disappear inside the post office. I followed him in and developed an interest in the huge array of forms available from a wall-rack of pigeon-holes to the left of the cashier positions. Meanwhile, Plank stood in the queue waiting for the attention of one of the counter clerks.

I managed to hear enough of the exchange when he placed his package on the scale, asking for it to be sent first-class recorded delivery. No, it was not going abroad. My sideways glance showed me that he had put it in a manila envelope and taped the folded-in ends to make a neat parcel. It was quite a bit thicker than the disk box it must contain, so I reckoned he had bound it up in bubble-wrap for protection from the ravages of the Royal Mail. There was no chance for me to find out the address; but if I were to make a wild guess, my money would be on his own country abode at Lower Pebbington, where Debra would by now be back in residence. In fact, now I thought about it, he probably told her to go back there when he made that phone call.

After the post office, I couldn't keep up with Plank. I followed him to a multi-storey car-park where he got into a black Mercedes

– presumably his own car that he was taken away in when they kidnapped him. I briefly cursed my Mondeo for being too far away for me to follow him.

Anyway, on the way back to Stratford, I was able to enjoy a feeling of some satisfaction at having replaced the disk where I had found it. I wasn't quite sure why it was important that Plank shouldn't know it had been interfered with, but surely the whole situation was already so tortuous that any further complications could make it as hard to understand as that book about time by Stephen Hawking.

Plank, I was sure, didn't know about the murder of Doug Mellis, so he must have believed his new business partnership was still on. Vince Moorhouse thought that I was the Plank partner, that was why he had forced himself in as a third partner. What I was wondering now, was how much detail Plank had filled in for Moorhouse concerning the scams he and Mellis were setting up.

I concluded that it didn't matter. The most important fact here was that Moorhouse would undoubtedly object to sharing the proceeds three ways (despite being unable to contribute anything to the partnership). He would be going all out to dump me any way he could, and would be intent on eliminating me whatever I might do.

Even Plank himself might resent my unjustified involvement sufficiently to take action against me. Meanwhile, I would need to be constantly on my guard to prevent Vince Moorhouse gaining any advantage that might let him think he had some power over me. I couldn't see how he could influence me in any way. After all, I knew more about what was going on than he did.

So it really all boiled down to quite a simple situation, I decided. There were only a few players who mattered, and I knew roughly where they all were and what they were doing. With a bit of care and luck, I could sit back and watch the power struggle between Plank and Moorhouse.

Kenny Madigan, citizen of his very own fool's paradise.

Oh, I had to correct myself there. One area of mystery was left – Plank's man in Antwerp. Was he a full partner or just a well-paid employee? He would certainly need to be well paid, considering the amounts of money that would pass through his hands.

✻

From the window of what must be intended as the living-room, they watch Absalom drive away in Stella's car. Once it is lost to view, Aileen and Stella turn to face each other. There is a long glare-filled silence while their rage spreads its wings wide before coming to roost, focused on each other. Betrayal gives Aileen overwhelmingly the greater justification for her target selection. Thus, hands on hips and squinting slightly through her black and yellowing eye, she is the first to translate body language into furious speech.

'You damned bloody shitty bugger, Stella Galloway ... here you are, supposed to be upholding the forces of law and order and whatnot and how Neil could pick you to go into a dangerous mission and betray decent law-abiding members of the public I just simply cannot imagine and I'll tell him about your perfidious conduct as soon as I get the chance ... and then you have the bloody gall to go and break into my house well, let me tell you your boss is married to my best friend and he'll believe her when she lets him know what a bloody bitchy bitch has kidnapped his wife's best friend and I hope your mate that monster moronic gorilla comes back and beats the shit out of you ...'

Aileen is not yet running down, but she does have to pause at that point in order to breathe. Stella hastily grabs the opportunity to get into the conversation.

'Shut up the fuck!' she yells. 'You know as well as I do that he's going to do a hell of a lot more than beat the shit out of the both of us!'

That has the unexpected effect of stopping Aileen in her tracks. Her mouth opens, and instead of continuing her tirade, she says, 'You mean *shut the fuck up*, don't you? You made a mistake and said *shut up the fuck*. The correct phrase is *shut the fuck up* ... you should at least get it right even when you're mad enough or crude enough to use that kind of uncouth street language.'

Silence for several beats. Then Stella says, 'It doesn'ae matter – you know what I mean.'

'Well, that's just bloody typical,' says Aileen. 'You've got to care about getting things right. That's what life is about. You might as well have said *up fuck the shut*.'

Stella takes a deep breath and starts to feel the floor under her feet.

'Sorry. You're right, I did mean to say *shut the fuck up*.'

She breaks into an unplanned grin; mainly because it is very difficult to maintain hostility towards someone who has fallen into the same leaky boat in a shark-infested ocean, especially when you are at least partly to blame for that someone's presence in the boat.

Suddenly the two women are able to talk rationally – not yet about their state of imprisonment. First there is the need for what politicians call a *frank* exchange of information when they really mean a *selective* exchange of carefully chosen information. At the end of which, Stella begins to understand how few true facts Vince Moorhouse has allowed her, especially in relation to Kenny Madigan and who kidnapped Gerald Plank.

Everything Aileen tells her has sufficient ring of truth to convince Stella; Aileen just doesn't include all the truth. For example she sees no need to mention Plank's sinking industrial empire, and only hints vaguely at his plans to hoover large quantities of cash out of the pockets of gullible members of the public. Stella is somewhat ashamed at her own inability to make any appreciable contribution to the pool of information. She ends up feeling dirty – as if she has been temping for the bad guys. Which is actually what she has been doing, she admits to herself.

Stella reaches into a pocket of her business-style jacket where she keeps her currently open packet of cigarettes.

'Oh, bugger it!' she exclaims. 'I've only got three left in this packet. My new pack is in the car.'

However, she lights one of the precious three with her disposable lighter and takes a few ragged but calming drags, while Aileen looks on in silent disapproval.

The next stage comes when the two women get down to considering what options might be available to them in their current predicament, Aileen is at first insistent that Kenny will arrive to set them free; he will know right away that she is being held in the cottage that has previously sheltered Gerald Plank.

'Yeah, right enough,' Stella says, 'but how long will it take till he realizes you've been snatched away? I mean, it was all done so fast and discreetly I bet the people in your shoe shop have no idea what happened. They must be thinking you just took it into your head to walk out. They'll be trying to guess why, and coming up with everything from forgetting to turn off the gas to a family emergency or pregnancy.'

'Well,' begins Aileen, 'they know I would never ...'

She trails off, sounding and feeling doubtful. Stella piles on more persuasion.

'And, by the way, even after he realizes you're in trouble, your precious Kenny might not be able to get us out of here. It must be just as hard to break in as it is to break out, you know.'

Feeling she has won that argument, Stella presses on, 'What I think we should do is prepare as well as we can to repel Absalom ... because he will definitely be coming back; he's been grabbing at my boobs for weeks and he scares the shit out of me. That bloody gorilla gives me the dry boak, so he does. The only thing that's been stopping him was Vince, and it kind of looks like I've suddenly become the flavour of last month for him. So like I said, we need to be ready to deal with that Absalom when he gets back here. Have you any ideas how we could stop the bastard? What about trying to knock him out as he comes though the door?'

Aileen turns it over in her mind, trying to find some merit in Stella's suggestion.

'D'you mean we should look for something to bash him on the head with? So we just tell him to keep still so we can stand on a chair to get a good swing at him with a ... a broom handle or something. Come on, Stel ... that sounds pretty half-baked even for a police person. Why don't you just wave your warrant card or whatever and tell him he's under arrest? Then he'll give himself up and say "it's a fair cop, guv, I'll come quietly." Isn't that how it works?'

As we know, Aileen can be very scathing indeed. Stella certainly feels scathed.

—CHAPTER NINETEEN—

So it was back to the Lone Harp garage for me, where my faithful staff were hard at work clearing up after their day of gainful employment. Senga was too busy dealing with customers who were here to pick up their mended, serviced, and MOT'd vehicles, to have any time for me. Petesy, however, shot straight into the office behind me.

'Here's Aileen's handbag,' he said, holding it out. 'She must be worried, wondering where it's got to.'

I was a bit surprised.

'It's not like her to leave it anywhere,' I said. 'That handbag is sacred ... she normally never lets it out of her sight. Where did you get it?'

'There was a call from the Jonathan Philips ... the shoe shop. They were trying to call you. It seems Aileen must have left the store in such a tearing hurry this morning, that she forgot her handbag. I thought she would appreciate it if I went down there to collect it for her, so I went ...'

'Wait a minute,' I said, as something clammy started taking bites out of my stomach. 'What do you mean, she left in a hurry? Why would she leave right in the middle of ...'

Petesy shrugged. 'They thought either she felt sick or had a message from you ... some kind of emergency. They know she would never just walk out without a bloody good reason ... oh Christ.'

I was already dialling home on my mobile. While I listened to the ringing tone repeating far too many times, I told Petesy, 'Call the shoe shop ... in case she's gone back there – and find out what time she left.'

While he was doing that on his own mobile phone, I called everybody else I could think of – Aileen's dad, Sally, one or two other girlfriends, and even Steve and Sheila's number. Nobody had any news of her.

I forced myself to sit down. I made myself take deep slow breaths for what felt like ages to give my overheated brain cells a chance to calm down. Petesy was now trying to tell me something which I didn't take in a word of, though it sounded as if he had now followed me into anxiety overload.

'Sit down and shut the fuck up ... I'm thinking,' I told him.

Some moments of painful silence ensued, at the end of which I started to rummage through the pockets of my chinos. Eventually, I came up with what I was looking for – the grubby piece of paper bearing the number of Vince Moorhouse's office at Ecological Recycling Ltd.

I dialled, and spoke my name when I recognized the answering voice.

'Ah, Madigan,' said Moorhouse, in that maddening tone of false affability, 'so good to hear from you ... I was just about to give you a call. I expect you are a teensy bit worried as to the welfare of your lady friend.'

When this situation crops up in a TV drama or a movie, the poor sod whose woman or child has been kidnapped always reacts exactly the way the gloating kidnapper wants; that is, he shouts stupid (and useless) things like you filthy swine and you'll never get away with this and I'll make you pay for this if it's the last thing I ever do. I think it must be one of the rules for writers. Anyway, I was certainly not going to give him the satisfaction. I just kind of grunted, 'Yeah?'

'You and I must stand shoulder to shoulder at this meeting tonight, old chap,' he told me. 'I expect Gerry has already told you about it – just the interested parties in the new business venture. That means, Gerry, you, me and the Dutchman, van Tongerloo, whom I have not yet met ... by the way, have you made his acquaintance?'

'Er ... no, I've not actually met him,' I admitted, but felt this was a bit inadequate, so I added quickly, 'not face to face, but we've talked on the phone a few times. You know, what with setting up ...'

'OK, OK,' Moorhouse broke in. 'You answered the question; I don't need all the sordid details.'

A moment of silence. Christ, I thought, he's a lot more wound up – not to mention more insecure – than he makes out. Sounds like there's more at stake than he wants me to know.

Then he was all composed and speaking again.

'You must understand, Madigan, that I am not inclined to take chances, any more than I have to. My safety precaution in this instance, *vis-à-vis* your lady companion, Eileen, is designed to ensure—'

'Aileen,' I corrected, but he ploughed on regardless.

'... to ensure that I shall not find myself alone and isolated in the event of any hypothetical treacherous behaviour on the part of any one of our partners. I want your technical expertise working on my behalf. Not that I believe for a moment that Gerry would ... well let's just call it an insurance policy on my peace of mind.'

It seemed I was expected to know what was going on, whereas I was actually in Shit Creek country without a rudder. Moorhouse apparently had me down as the computer brain behind Plank's new business. I hadn't a clue about the meeting Plank would have invited me to if I had really been his new partner. I tried to extract some information from Moorhouse without revealing my ignorance.

'So what do you think Gerry is up to ... he hasn't said anything to me?' (Nothing but the truth there.)

'Listen carefully, Madigan. All I need is for you to turn up in the car-park here at ten ... just as Gerry instructed – and don't let them blind me with computer science when we meet the Dutchman and anyone else that Gerry might see fit to wheel out. I want you acting as my technical adviser in this affair. I must say Gerry is playing his cards quite uncharacteristically close to his chest this time.'

This was more stuff I didn't need to know about, since I had no intention of sticking my head into the lion's den by turning up at Redditch. My brain cells had not been idle, and as a result I was sure Moorhouse had Aileen stashed away in that cottage where he had kept Plank. Nobody knew I had found the place.

I could easily have her out of there long before it was time for that meeting.

So as far as I was concerned Moorhouse could go and ... but for the moment I should concentrate on acting the part of the worried guy whose girlfriend was in peril.

'Looks like I haven't got much choice,' I said, in a voice that indicated I was resigned to helping the bastard Moorhouse. I added, 'But how do I know you'll let Aileen go unharmed?'

'You don't, Madigan. You'll just have to hope I mean what I say – and trust that I can keep Absalom on his leash.'

The phone went dead.

I turned to Petesy, who I now realized had been fiddling with his mobile during my Moorhouse conversation.

'What's going on here?' I asked, maybe a bit more sharply than I intended.

'I was only checking that Daphne is all right,' he replied, with a hurt expression on his face. 'See, we text each other all the time so I know she was fine an hour ago, and then just now I sent her a … well, a kind of intimate message, and she texted me straight back, so—'

'Right,' I told him, 'switch that damn thing off for a while … we've got things to do. We have to get Aileen out of that bloody prison cottage before it gets dark. Let's go.'

I wanted to do some quiet thinking, so Petesy drove us in the Renault he was using while his own car was shut away round the back of the Lone Harp garage. As we got under way, I filled him in on the story of the cottage; how Aileen and I had tracked it down, and how I had already gone there in vain. As I remarked, 'Thank goodness it's only September and still light until after eight … it would be sheer hell trying to approach that place in the dark—'

… and stopped dead as that thought gave birth to another one. What if the baddies had left somebody there to guard the prisoner? That sadistic bastard Absalom, for instance. If he was there I would prefer some dark. Quite a lot of dark.

But no, surely I was being paranoid – they wouldn't need a jailer for one harmless little female, especially as they had no way of knowing that I was aware of the location of their jailhouse.

Knowing the way didn't help us get there any sooner, and I found myself fretting and cursing that bunch of West Wankers (I was in no mood to think in Aileen's sanitized language) for choosing such an out-of-the-way place for their version of a safe house. Petesy knew better than to try starting up any conversation with me, simply turning left or right without comment when I told him. Eventually we got on to the narrow twisty road and found the gateway into a field with its rotting gate near where I had parked before. It didn't feel as if it had been only that morning – more as if a week had passed.

At first we took plenty of care to remain out of sight of the cottage windows. Knowing the layout, I led the way to a position where we could check for cars parked in front of the place. It was all clear. That was enough for me.

'Thank God,' I said. 'We can give up this cloak and dagger act, let's just get there as fast as we can.'

So we went across the next field at full tilt, heading for the front side of the cottage, and more specifically the front door, where we arrived out of breath, or at least I did. First we hammered on the door with our fists, then the windows.

Nothing. No sign of life at all. My worst fears were confirmed. They must have tied and gagged her, or chloroformed her. We would break in – if we could break in – to find poor Aileen flat out upstairs on a bed, bound and gagged and unable to move a muscle. Christ, if that bastard Absalom had a woman at his mercy – and on a bed at that, I bet he wouldn't hesitate …

I forced these thoughts out of my mind and put my brain cells to work on the problem of getting into the place. Meanwhile, Petesy, who never knows when to stop a useless course of action, was off round the building peering into all the downstairs windows. I could hear him banging on them and shouting at each one.

I was planning how we could bring the car round here – a couple of miles, maybe on the tortuous country roads – maybe we could use it to pull out some of those window bars. If we could find a length of rope or a chain or … My train of thought was interrupted by an over-excited shout from Petesy.

'Kenny. This way … round the back. Come on.'

I groaned a bit, and dragged myself through the same bushes and the same thorns that I had first impaled myself on earlier in the day. And there was Petesy standing staring at the back door – which was sagging off its hinges to reveal a gap big enough for a person to squeeze their body through. Which we duly did with our own bodies.

The cottage was empty. No trace of Aileen. Just as empty as on my last visit when it was Plank who turned up missing. I was beginning to feel as if I was living in Goundhog Day, and I was destined to find this place empty every time. There were two beds in the upstairs bedrooms, neither of which featured an enraged struggling woman.

I didn't know whether to feel relief or get even more distracted with worry.

We stood in the living-room. Petesy, as usual allowed himself to be irrelevant, pointing out that it was really very comfortably furnished. I ignored that (apart from muttering something about him getting a job as an estate agent), and suggested we both sit down on the comfortable facilities to consider the situation. After a few minutes of concentrated thought we had come up with several possibilities:

> Someone got here before us, and stole Aileen away. (Who? Why? Simmons?)
> Someone got here before us, and rescued Aileen. (No.)
> Moorhouse's people took her somewhere else instead of here. (Where?)
> They brought her here, found the door broken, and took her elsewhere. (Ditto.)
> They left Aileen here and she escaped by her own efforts. (Unlikely.)

None of these had the ring of truth, or even plausibility. I couldn't think of any other possibilities. She might as well have been captured by aliens who took her away in a big flying saucer. As for how the back door got broken open, and by whom, it was not worth even speculating – although if I had to guess, I would have put it down to the feud between the East and West Plankers. Anyway, it was completely irrelevant at this point.

For lack of anything else to do, I got up and looked around once more. This time I went into the kitchen and checked the fridge. Milk – I was sure it had contained milk on my previous visit. Now there was none. I found the empty carton beside the sink. And now I noticed two glasses on the table; empty now but with traces of milk in them. A saucer, also on the table, had been used as an ashtray. Like all the best private detectives, I picked up the single cigarette end which was also in the saucer, and examined it carefully. A cork tip (well aren't they all tipped these days?) with more than a trace of lipstick on it. So there had been a woman here – and it was definitely not Aileen. She hated even the smell of cigarette smoke.

I walked back to the living-room where Petesy had been looking around. He held up something small in triumph, as if he had found the holy grail.

'Look, it's a cigarette butt with lipstick on it so it couldn't be Aileen.'

I managed a sickly grin.

There was no evidence to suggest that Aileen had ever been here at all. It looked as if they must have taken her somewhere else. In the absence of any definite information, I would have to assume that she was still firmly in the clutches of the megalomaniac Moorhouse. He was the one calling the shots.

For me that had to mean doing exactly as I was told until I knew for certain that Aileen was safe – which is easy to say, but not quite so easy to put into practice. I said as much out loud, mostly to get it straight in my own mind, but at the same time needing the uncritical agreement of Petesy, who was not up-to-date on all fronts as I had not really kept him in the picture for various reasons.

'I'm going to have to turn up for this meeting tonight. Right?'

Petesy nodded.

'Now, Vince Moorhouse thinks I'm Plank's other business partner, the computer expert who has set up the systems to make the new scams work. Not only that, but Moorhouse – or Shithouse, as I prefer to think of him – he is holding Aileen over my head so I will back him up against Plank.'

Petesy nodded again, his brow furrowing with the mental effort of keeping up.

'Right. But Mr Plank, on the other hand, doesn't know me from Adam … correction; he's heard my name – when Debra told him on the phone that I had been working on her behalf to free him from his kidnappers. But Plank has never seen me face to face. Are you still with me?'

Petesy looked a bit less convinced, but nodded just the same.

'So when I waltz into this meeting with a joyful cry of "Good to see you again, Gerry, old mate", there's a good chance that all hell will break loose. I can't predict the result, but whatever happens is very unlikely to be good for my health. The only consolation I can come up with, is that nobody will have anything to gain by holding on to Aileen any longer, because they will all very quickly realize that I can no longer deliver anything that anyone wants. I mean, I never could, but they didn't know that.'

Well summed up, I thought. I looked Petesy in the eye.

'What do you think?'

He scratched his head, and said, 'That mad bastard Absalom might still have Aileen in his clutches. He would think she was in a position to deliver something he wants.'

'Look, Petesy,' I said seriously, 'when I want your opinion I'll ask for it. Right?'

'But you just …'

'Right?' I insisted.

'Right,' he agreed.

'So I'll just have to go there and hope things develop in some way that I can turn to my advantage. After all, I've been in worse situations than this before … and come out on top. Haven't I?'

All I wanted was a bit of encouragement – moral support if you like. Petesy has had first-hand knowledge and a certain amount of experience of some of the situations I was referring to there.

'Have you?' he said, as if I had just told him something unbelievable. This is the bloke who hero-worships me, according to Aileen …

… whose name whisked my brain cells right back to the deadly serious matter of her predicament. She was almost certainly relying on me to ride to her rescue on my white horse. I couldn't let her down.

Whatever the outcome, I would grab the bull in the china shop by the horns.

—CHAPTER TWENTY——————————

Stella feels responsible. How could she not, when she has been instrumental in bringing danger down on the head of a member of the public? The very public that she is supposed to protect. In someone with Stella's sense of responsibility, the frustration generated by her failure comes out as aggression.

'Look, you … Aileen, or whatever your name is, I'm the professional here. You're just a member of the public, and it's my job to provide leadership and er … lead you. To safety.'

'Well it's the least you could do,' says Aileen, 'considering how you're the deceitful dorothy who provided the leadership that led us both straight into this stupid plight … and then all your so-called leadership can come up with is useless suggestions about waiting for that sadistic big bastard to come back and then bashing him with a broom.'

To be fair, Stella thinks (though she hates being fair in this instance), she's right except that I never mentioned a broom. Anyway, I'm not English, so I would have called it a brush. Och, I'll give her a chance.

'All right then, little Miss Smartass … what's your brilliant suggestion?'

'Well,' says Aileen, 'you can do what you like, but I'm going to look for a way we can break out of this dump. Nobody's going to keep me where I don't want to be. Come on – we've got a better chance if we work on it together.'

Privately, Aileen is having doubts about Kenny being able to turn up to save her. Maybe they've snatched him too – to extract information under the threat of harming her. Besides, there is still Stella's point about it being just as hard to break in as out. These sophisticated locks might be beyond Kenny's ability to crack. So she'd better be deadly serious about finding her own way out.

The two women start with a complete survey of the cottage, paying special attention to the windows and doors. The windows are all sash type. They open fairly easily, giving access to the steel bars with which they are equipped.

Stella wonders if it would be possible to lever two adjacent bars apart to make a wider gap that they could squeeze through. Aileen chokes back a sarcastic remark to the effect that such an attempt would only break the broom handle and then what would they hit the big bastard with.

The front and back doors each have two locks, an old ordinary one, and a strong-looking high-tech affair. The doors themselves are of stout wooden construction that give the impression of having been there for a hundred years and being on their toes, ready to fill the same gaps for the next hundred.

With sinking hearts, the girls turn their attention to the cupboards, of which there are several. Those upstairs are very nearly empty, containing only minor pieces of useless junk such as old hairbrushes, empty picture frames, and tattered paperback books. The kitchen cabinets, on the other hand, are well supplied with cheap cooking pans, glasses, crockery, and cutlery in a variety of non-matching designs. A larger kitchen cupboard shelters an ironing board, steam iron, a vacuum cleaner which should have been junked many years ago. And a near-bald specimen of the brush species that causes Aileen to point out to Stella, 'There's your broom … better start practising.'

The inevitable cupboard under the stairs is no better. It seems to be reserved for gardening tools, notably an ancient rusty push mower. The other contents are equally ancient. They include garden shears, a rake, blunt secateurs, a spade without a handle, and several rustic-looking implements whose purposes and methods of use are anybody's guess.

That is it. In desultory slow motion, Aileen and Stella pour the contents of the milk carton out of the fridge into two glasses and sit down opposite each other at the kitchen table. Stella's chin is supported by both hands which are supported by her elbows which are supported by the table. She sees no point in mentioning that there is no way out, short of the arrival of Kenny or some other knight in shining bulldozer. Bugger it let's have the only consolation available, she thinks, lighting up her second-last cigarette.

Aileen too, has lost heart. She finds herself alternating gulps of milk with wild speculations about putative methods of subduing the big bastard Absalom. The only significant difference between her and Stella now, is that while the latter's gaze is directed down towards the surface of the table, Aileen stares unseeing through the wisping smoke from Stella's cigarette into the straight-ahead distance. This is an important and significant difference, as it turns out.

Gloom and doom have taken over as the predominant mood. They remain under its baleful spell for an indeterminate length of time, occasionally stirring themselves to imbibe a sip or gulp of milk. The break comes when Aileen drinks her last mouthful of milk, leaving the glass empty. An event that marks the end of something – even if only her drink.

Her eyes come back into focus, to find themselves seeing the back door through Stella's final cloud of smoke; a door which leads from the kitchen out to the garden – or would, for anyone with the ability to get it open. It is a stout door, as we have already remarked. Now Aileen notes that it is also an old door, definitely a much older design than the front door; probably an antique.

In the absence of anything constructive to do, she examines it idly, noticing the old-fashioned ring-shaped handle, independent of the locks, which turns to lift a latch, all in black-painted wrought iron. The rest of the door furniture is in keeping, including the black nail-heads with which the door is studded. There are three hinges, which of course, are in black wrought iron, being long strap-type hinges which extend across the kitchen side of the door, tapering as they go, to come almost to a point about twenty-five centimetres in from the hinged edge of the door.

Nice feature, those hinges, thinks Aileen, noticing that they are attached to the door by black dome-head screws – three to each hinge.

Aileen is suddenly alert. She replays that last thought.

They are attached to the door by black dome-head screws – three to each hinge …

When that security firm was hired to make the house impregnable, they were thinking in terms of making it virtually impossible for anyone to break in. Nobody ever mentioned that it might be used as a prison and would be used to prevent someone leaving.

It will not be an easy job without a screwdriver (and hard enough even with one unless it be powered), but both of them are filled with new hope. The screws must have been in place for God knows how many years and the knives from the kitchen drawer are not up to the job, swiftly becoming twisted parodies of their former selves with no discernible effect on the screws.

Aileen solves the first problem with the old garden shears. Opened out, there is a sufficient edge near one of its tips to fit into the slots in the screw-heads – and the considerable leverage generated by the length of the opened-out implement is just about enough to turn a screw a minuscule degree before the shears' grip slips. With many a slip and much swearing (mainly by Stella) they eventually manage about three turns of each screw. It takes them more than an hour to get this far.

'Right,' says Aileen, still panting from the effort, 'maybe we can get something under the edge of the hinges and lever them up off the door.'

This time it is Stella who comes up with the goods.

'I know what we can use for that.'

She is off, to return almost immediately with the handle-less spade from the cupboard under the stairs. They both try, but its blade does not quite fit under the edge of any of the hinges.

Again, Stella, 'It's like a hammer and chisel, only we're missing the hammer. Just hold it there for a minute.'

This time she brings the steam iron. A few bashes are enough to drive the business end of the spade under the centre hinge, where it lodges tightly. Aileen is delighted.

'This is the most interesting use I've ever seen for an iron. Now all we need is another kind of lever. Watch this … your favourite weapon is about to find its true vocation at last.'

She fetches the bald broom, inserts the handle end of its stick into the empty socket of the spade, and they both apply their whole weight to levering the hinge away from the door.

Success is accompanied by a loud splintering noise – and a wild cheer from the sweating pair.

Now it's simply a matter of going through the same procedure for the top hinge. Then, rather than suffer all over again for the bottom one, they try using the spade and broom handle combo to prise the hinge side of the back door away from the frame. The door twists partly open, distorting its remaining hinge – and they are free. Free to leave their prison, at least.

Aileen and Stella hug each other briefly, all enmity forgotten. They squeeze through the gap opened up by the door, which now leans at an impossible-looking angle. Standing there in the jungly back garden of the cottage they hesitate, not yet ready to choose any specific point of the compass over any other.

No sign of civilization is visible in any direction. The day's light is already beginning to fade from a mercifully benign sky.

But it is still perfectly superbly wondrous to two people drawing deep breaths of free air to flush the captivity out of their lungs. The night, no matter how dark, no matter what terrors the imagination might conjure up in an unfamiliar countryside – nothing could be quite as disturbing as the menace of a promised encounter with the awful Absalom.

'What now?' Aileen wonders aloud, thereby ending some minutes of euphoria. Stella groans; she now has to face her new circumstances.

'Well, I've got to assume that my undercover role is over, so there's no point in trying to get back in with Moorhouse. My natural instinct is to run to the police – that's what I am, after all – but I can see the problems in that.'

Aileen is surprised.

'What do you mean? What problems?'

'It's my guv'nor, Inspector Friggin' Bastard Neil Cornfoot.'

'Sounds as if you don't get on very well with my friend's husband,' Aileen remarks carefully.

'It isn't just that we never really took to each other,' says Stella. 'I mean, it's that too, but ...'

She stops in confusion as she realizes that Aileen is a friend of the man in question. Not only that, but her own reason for losing confidence in Neil had been his excessive familiarity with Kenny Madigan (whom she had then believed to be a master criminal) which had threatened to expose her to Moorhouse. There is no way she can explain to Aileen about the telephone bug, the taped conversations, and so on. Anyway she has not yet had time to review her judgement of the Bastard Inspector in the light of what she has recently learned from Aileen.

Finding herself standing silent with her mouth still open, Stella has to choose a new ending for the sentence that still hangs in the air, unfinished.

'... I'm just not ready enough yet to start trusting him all over again ... what I mean is, I don't think we should run straight to the police – the real police, the other police. I mean, later on, yes, of course, but not right now ... not without giving it a lot of thought first.'

My God, she thinks. That was more than a bit garbled, but I think I managed to express the idea that I'm not prepared to run greetin' to Inspector Bastard Cornfoot.

Aileen agrees readily. This suits her quite well, as she would prefer to avoid any police interference in whatever Kenny might be up to. Neil can come in at the right time and sweep up the pieces. But the right time is not yet. For once, Aileen has got it wrong, not that she would have been able to point Neil in the right direction to prevent disaster.

There is just one big priority for Aileen – at the first possible opportunity she must get word to Kenny. To let him know that she is now safe.

They decide not to leave by the track that leads away from the front door of the cottage. Anyone arriving by car will come that way; and when Absalom arrives, it will certainly be by car. So instead of taking the obvious route, they set off at right angles to the orientation of the house, mainly because Aileen has the idea that they may come across a road over that way. And it's roughly north, judging by the rosy glow that points out where the sun has sunk. She remembers from the estate agent's description that this place is a good bit further south than Stratford.

CHAPTER TWENTY-ONE

I checked my watch. OK, still plenty of time. Petesy and I were in the car on our way back to civilization. Petesy was driving. My stomach was still churning in time to the scenes being presented by my imagination – scenes in which Aileen was at the mercy of Moorhouse and his murderous minions, especially that mad bastard Absalom. I switched on my phone and tried again in case Aileen had washed up somewhere safe. Nothing. Maybe it was actually better when she was a prisoner in that cottage. If she ever actually was there: at least I knew where she was then. Well, I thought I did.

I was uncertain about everything – even whether to leave the phone switched on. I mean, I definitely wanted to hear from Aileen if and when she got the chance to call me. On the other hand, I didn't want to be available to Moorhouse. Yes, I know I wasn't being logical, but I had an invitation to this meeting he was organizing for later in the evening, and I was not going to be put off. In the end, I left it on.

I continued to sit there lost in thought for Christ knows how long. It was the sight of a road sign that brought me back to life. **Tewkesbury**, it said in big black lettering on a white background.

'What the bloody hell are we doing in Tewkesbury?' I demanded. 'This is nowhere near our route home.'

'Oh, sorry,' Petesy said. 'I didn't recognize the names of any other places on the signposts of these country roads. So I made for the only place which I know where it is … you should have said when I took the first wrong turning.'

'Yes, but … oh never mind. Just get us out of here and point the steering wheel towards Evesham.'

'OK, OK,' he said, sounding a bit aggrieved. 'You don't have to get your knickers all twisted … I know the way from here.'

I sighed and left him to get on with it. I worked out that on leaving the cottage, he must have taken us off in completely the wrong direction. My memory of the map told me that we would soon pass not too far from the area we intended to leave behind – within a few miles of the cottage as the crow flies.

As we got back into open country, we could see that the sun had set, and even though the sky to our left had turned a deep red, it was now dark enough to make Petesy switch the headlights on.

You might have thought that Petesy's directional dyslexia would have caused him enough embarrassment to keep his mouth modestly shut for the rest of the journey, but no, that's not how it works for our boy. We were still in the middle of nowhere when he suddenly said, 'I'm bloody starving. I've just realized I haven't eaten a thing since lunchtime. We could stop somewhere and get a bite.'

'All right, if you must,' I agreed, as it came to me that I hadn't eaten since breakfast, and I couldn't even remember if I'd had anything then. Strange that my stomach should feel so active in the circumstances. Maybe some food would help my digestive system to settle down.

Petesy was sounding a bit more cheerful.

'Good,' he said. 'There's a place ahead, on the Evesham road, not far after the junction where we turn on to it. I think it's called The Jolly Muncher or something like that – a combination of country pub, burger joint, and transport caff. Just what we need.'

Doesn't sound like anything I need, I thought. But tactfully I kept my mouth shut.

Sure enough, a few miles further on, a garishly-lit oasis loomed up out of the darkness. Petesy slowed down and turned in. Our headlights swept across the lightly populated car-park to settle on a space beside a Range Rover which had just arrived and was disgorging its occupants.

My heart skipped a beat. One of the Range Rover's passengers was briefly lit up as she jumped out, and there was …

But no, it was just some girl who looked a bit like Aileen. Bloody hell, I must be in a serious state of anxiety to keep thinking I see her in the most unlikely places. My stomach took the opportunity to shift up a gear in its churning. When we went inside, I caught myself looking around to see if there was anyone here who looked like my lost woman.

On Petesy's recommendation, I had a greasy burger with a slice of plastic cheese in a cotton-wool bun. Not that I felt any pangs of hunger; I just thought something substantial would help to jam the mechanism which was convulsing my guts. It didn't seem to be helping; not at first anyway. Thank goodness it wasn't my brain that was revolving, otherwise I wouldn't have been able to make plans for my meeting later that night.

While we ate, I explained to Petesy how to get to the Ecological Recycling company's office in Redditch.

'Just so you don't have to be too desperate about keeping up when you're following me there,' I told him, and went on to give him the benefit of some of my thinking.

'See, I'm a bit puzzled about this meeting I'm supposed to go to. That slimy bastard Moorhouse never said it would be in the offices. He just told me to meet him in the car-park outside the office. Now, I suppose that might mean the place is locked up for the night, he has the keys, and we all go in together, and lock ourselves in. Right?'

Petesy nodded as if he understood. I moved on.

'On the other hand, it could mean that the meeting is somewhere else, and we're all going to get in a car – or maybe two cars – to go there. And that's where you come in. You take up your position near that car-park ... there's a good spot about fifty metres up the road from the entrance, where you'll be partially screened by some trees but you'll still be able to see any vehicle that comes out of the car-park.'

Petesy's brow furrowed.

'So I'm supposed to follow. But what if there's more than one car ... and they go different ways ... which one should I follow?'

'You don't need to invent difficulties,' I explained patiently. 'You'll just have to deal with the unexpected when it happens. It's not something we can expect, that's why it's called unexpected ... anyway, I'll give you time to get into position and then you call me on my mobile before I go in. Is your phone fully charged?'

'Of course,' he assured me. 'I keep it topped up constantly so I can be sure I'll always be able to talk to Daphne—'

I cut him off.

'That's good. If things get really hairy for me, I want you to make an emergency call to Neil Cornfoot, and get him to charge to the rescue with a million cops.'

'But how can I tell if you're getting hairy?' he protested.

'All in good time,' I said. 'Remember I'll have to somehow brazen it out with Moorhouse who thinks I'm Plank's partner ... and Plank himself, who doesn't know me from Adam. Let's go ... take me back to the garage to get my car, and then we're off into the fray.'

At last I was beginning to feel completely committed to this dodgy meeting, if only for Aileen's sake. I sat quietly in Petesy's car all the way to Stratford, trying to compose myself mentally – and failing to compose my wrenching guts. Just in case I came to grief, I was trying to persuade myself into the belief that Aileen must have escaped from that cottage. It was not an easy thing to believe though.

And that bloody treacherous burger was still biting me back, which was no help at all.

I stopped by the roadside some distance away and waited for Petesy to take up his position. I must admit I fretted a bit while waiting, but who wouldn't? Eventually, my phone rang, and I was able to ask Petesy, 'Have you got a clear view of the entrance to the car-park?'

'Yes, I've got a pretty good view. There's one of those tall orangey street lights just beside the turn-in.'

'You're not sticking out like a spare rib at a wedding, are you?'

'Not at all, Kenny, I'm just one of several cars sprinkled along the edge of the pavement here.'

'Good. Well done ... oh, I meant to say you should park up past the place ... the office, that is, and turn round so you're facing back in this direction. They're bound to turn this way when ... if, they come out. Further up that road only takes you into an industrial estate.'

'It's OK. That's what I did.'

I let out a sigh of relief which didn't help me to relax at all.

'That's great, Petesy. You're a real mate.'

'Yeah,' he said, 'but it's a kind of long shot, isn't it? Them and you, all of you, going someplace else ... I mean, it's far more likely that the meeting is going to take place in that office, and where does that leave me? I'll tell you where – I'm left sitting here no use to man nor beast.'

I was a bit alarmed. I groaned aloud.

'Christ, Petesy, what a time you've picked to start using your brain. I'm not sure I can cope with you when you start thinking. In actual fact, your presence will be dead valuable even if you don't get to do a car chase.'

'How's that then? I can't see how I can help.'

'I'm just coming to that. Be quiet and listen. What you do is, when we've finished this conversation, you don't break the connection, and neither do I. So this line stays open. We both lock our keypads, right?'

'Right.'

'You keep your hands-free headset on so you can listen, and keep your mouth shut so you can't talk … stick some chewing-gum or something over the microphone bit and put the phone in your shirt pocket. I'll keep my phone in the inside pocket of my jacket, so with a bit of luck, you should be able to catch quite a lot of the conversation. So if something nasty happens to me, you'll have information to pass on to the cops.'

'Great. That's brilliant, Kenny,' he said. 'Why didn't you tell me about that stuff back at the caff?'

Actually, I hadn't really thought it through back then; I only worked it out on the way to Redditch.

'Oh, er … I wanted to keep you concentrating on one thing at a time, that's all.'

I moved quickly on.

'OK, lock your keypad now, to prevent any accidental button-pushing. I'm going in now. Good luck.'

I started the car. A glance at the clock told me it was time to be on my way.

Kenny Madigan, the intrepid flier takes off to do battle with the Red Baron.

─CHAPTER TWENTY-TWO─

My stomach was not behaving any better yet. It was still spinning around but now with the solid mass of that sodding burger as an immovable centrepiece. Well I would soon have plenty to take my mind off my minor discomforts.

No hesitating; I drove straight into the office car-park and went face-in to a slot near but not quite beside the several cars which were already there. I got out and walked slowly towards the knot of figures already congregated behind the bunch of cars, in a pool of yellow light cast by a mock-Victorian lamp standard.

Vince Moorhouse turned towards me and acted as if he was only now registering who was arriving. He addressed his companions.

'That's Kenny Madigan here now, right on time. This must be the full complement, surely.'

The last part of that remark was directed at Mr Short Plank, who turned his head to look at me as I came up to the group. That look continued longer than I would have thought necessary. I knew he was about to make some remark that would expose me as the fraud I was; and that was why I felt such a powerful need to open my big unnecessary mouth. I spoke directly to Plank.

'I thought Doug Mellis might be coming along.'

It was a weird thing to say, and pretty damn cheeky, considering Moorhouse and I both knew that Mellis was dead. However, it would let Plank know that I had knowledge of his plans for the future, regardless of whether he knew about Mellis's unfortunate demise.

Actually, in retrospect, maybe it was quite a clever thing I said there. And it brought a response from Plank.

'Mellis is not invited … he is the last person whose presence I would require at this meeting.'

It was only much later that I understood that comment. At the time, it was the voice that struck me, what with this being my first chance to hear it properly (the few words I overheard in the post office didn't count). He had an air of being quite well-educated, but not public school like Moorhouse – and you could hear an echo of Birmingham vowels in the background.

Even more interesting was the body language in this group of people. Any stranger who might have walked up out of the blue would be able to tell right away that Plank was the dominant member. The others were facing him. Moorhouse was one step closer to Plank than the two men who flanked him – fat Absalom and the other whom I took to be Dirk, Moorhouse's technical fixer.

I suppose you could say that Short Plank towered under the others.

Now he started to demonstrate being in charge. He checked his watch.

'Right,' he said decisively, 'time we were on our way. I don't like to keep people waiting.'

He turned to Moorhouse.

'Vince, we'll take my car, as it's black. We want to be as inconspicuous as possible. Your man will drive ... I'll sit in the front and direct him.'

So Absalom was the driver. I found myself in the back on the right side. Moorhouse was in the middle and Dirk against the left door. As we turned out of the car-park, Moorhouse asked, in a manner that seemed unusually tentative for him, 'Now that we're on our way, Gerry, surely you can let us have an inkling of where we're going to meet this van Tongerloo. There's no point in keeping us in suspense any longer.'

'All in good time, Vince, old chap. All in good time,' came the reply.

I guessed that Plank got some kind of kick out of mocking Moorhouse's public-school manner and speech. Nothing more was said. The silence inside the Mercedes was broken only by occasional muttered instructions to Absalom, which were limited to 'turn right here', 'left at the next corner', or 'straight on'. We were off in what I would have said was roughly south-easterly – a direction which was relatively unfamiliar to me, or at least the places are, once you get away from Leamington and its satellite villages.

Now that there was nothing else for me to do, I turned to

thinking about Plank, and why he had accepted my presence apparently without a second thought. If he remembered my name from the phone call to Debra, he could have guessed that I had infiltrated the Moorhouse mob, and might be on his side. Whatever the case, it was very much a mystery to me.

Then what about Moorhouse? He obviously didn't trust Plank, or anyone else for that matter. Witness how he brought along two of his personal staff, including a bodyguard, and had gone to a lot of trouble to capture Aileen, just to ensure my loyalty.

The thought of Aileen brought the persistent disturbance in my stomach back into focus. It had been rumbling on in the background while action and thoughts of action were taking place, but now it came to the fore. I wondered vaguely if I was developing an ulcer.

At least Plank's Mercedes was a nice smooth-running car. I leaned back in the comfortable seat, and tried to relax while still keeping an eye on our progress. Sooner or later, I would find out where Gerry Plank's secret route was leading us.

Petesy must have set out to follow us of course. But I had no way of knowing whether he was still on our tail, it being quite difficult to track a car in the dark, even through light traffic such as we were in that night.

Somehow, the relaxing failed to work for me. My stomach just kept on feeling worse and worse all the time. I spent most of the journey in a kind of tortured stupor, so I lost track of the route we took. Lucky there was no chit-chat going on that I might have had to contribute to.

Eventually, I was roused out of my daze by a change in the external world. Our wheels were no longer running on a paved road. We must be near our destination. The car had made a right turn, in through a gap in the wooded landscape. Absalom responded to Plank's urgent whisper of 'kill the lights', and we were plunged into an even deeper darkness.

The road must have been little more than a car-wide track through the woods. Inside, the five of us had become even more silent than before – too tense to change position or even fidget.

The black Mercedes rolled slowly along it, silent but for the occasional crack of a fallen twig. Absalom leaned forward anxiously, nose almost touching the windscreen as he concentrated on guiding the vehicle through the dark tree-framed tunnel with only the low-level illumination from the sidelights to guide him.

At the end of several minutes, I had the impression of the road opening out wider, as if we had reached some kind of woodland clearing, and then some minor visibility came back thanks to a half moon no longer screened by the trees. Plank tapped Absalom on the shoulder and ordered a stop. Then came the instruction to 'turn everything off', which our driver applied to the sidelights and the engine.

Short Plank opened his door and got out. For a brief moment, he turned back, leaned into the car, and whispered, 'Wait.'

A commanding finger somehow made it clear that this was a warning aimed specifically at Moorhouse.

Then the car door was firmly closed and Short Plank was away along the pale pathway that led up the hill to our left, his collar now turned up as if he needed protection from a shiver in spite of the mildness of the night air.

It was at that point that I knew I would be unable to contain my digestive situation for much longer. I broke the jagged silence in my need to share this information with my companions.

'I have to get out and puke,' I said, in a simple statement which merely irritated Moorhouse.

He snarled, 'Shut up, Madigan; sit still and try to act in a civilized manner. Gerry will be back in a few minutes with van Tongerloo.'

The only reply I could manage was a subdued whoop. I managed to hold back the dam, but it was a close thing. It did persuade Vince to change his mind, though. Nobody wants their boss's expensive Mercedes smelling of burger-inspired vomit which might well persist for months.

'For fuck's sake, get out of the car, Madigan, and be quick about it. Absalom, you go with him. Make sure he's not cooking up any funny business.'

At last, an instruction I could comply with. I did so with some alacrity, especially after that reference to cooking. However, as I opened the door, I managed enough presence of mind to slip my open-line mobile out of my pocket, and down the leathery gap between the horizontal and vertical seat cushions. With a bit of luck, Petesy would be able to catch any chat that might take place in the car during my absence.

Then I was away in a mad rush for the comfort of the trees. I managed to get myself behind the reassuringly solid trunk of the first big one before I was obliged to let go of the entire contents of my body. For some moments I didn't know if there was more to come. I stood there hunched forward with my feet well back and my head resting on the cool bark, feeling wretched, feeble, and helpless. I don't know whether my performance was sufficient to persuade the gingerly lurking Absalom that my dedicated throwing up was more than simply an adjunct to some cunning double-cross. It certainly had me well persuaded.

At first I thought the noise was my insides reaching for new depths of disruption. It was only when I opened my eyes and noticed that the night was lit up, that I realized the world had continued on its way without me. The noisy disintegration of our transport put my stomach back in context. It couldn't compete with earth-shattering chaos, and was immediately shamed back into normal behaviour.

I stayed behind my tree, my ears bombarded by further explosions, none of which quite matched the decibels of the first one. When the magnitude of the noises tailed off a bit, I looked out. Plank's Mercedes was ablaze with much fizzing and crackling. Somewhere within that inferno must have been the blackened bodies of Vince Moorhouse and his faithful sidekick, Dirk.

My own blackened body would have been in there beside them – as well as Absalom's larger and more deserving one, of course – if Plank's brutal plan had claimed all the victims he must have intended.

At first I couldn't tell what had happened to Absalom. Then a movement on the ground only a few feet away caught my eye. The huge bastard must have been blown off his feet by the blast. He didn't have the benefit of the protection provided by my trusty tree. I watched by the light of the blaze, as he struggled first to his knees, and then stood up, a dark shape silhouetted against flames. Even without visible detail, I could tell he was shaky and confused.

If only Moorhouse had trusted me enough to let me spew my guts up without a chaperon, Absalom would now be dog meat. Well, more like burnt toast really.

My first thought was one of regret that I could detect no signs of injury.

My first thought was swiftly followed by my second thought, which was to the effect that there was no longer any need for me to remain in the vicinity of Absalom. No sooner thought than done; I was haring it away through the trees in the direction from which the car arrived. I stayed just within the edge of the wood until I was sure I had left the conflagration some distance behind. I could tell by the reduction in the level of illumination.

When I passed a point where there was a bend in the track, I lost the remains of the light and found it was no longer possible to thread my way through the undergrowth. Even so, I persevered at a slower pace until I tripped and went full length into an extremely scratchy clump of brambles. That persuaded me to leave the cover of the trees and follow the less demanding vehicle track.

No sooner had I started making progress along the road, than I heard pounding footsteps behind me and hastily had to make friends with another tree. I stood still behind it while a large black shapeless shape that had to be Absalom, charged past at a brisk trot. A big rat was leaving a burning ship. Very sensibly, he had no wish to be found hanging about near the scene of a spectacular multiple murder, especially as this particular rat was a criminal well known to the police. He probably had an impressive record of serious mayhem under his belt.

Once Absalom was out of earshot, I warily got back on track on the dirt road. The rut I followed brought me within sight and sound of a real road in ten minutes or so according to the luminous hands of my watch – a bit under half a mile then, given that my walking speed was hampered by darkness and by dread. This was the time for me to wish I had kept my mobile phone in my pocket instead of leaving it to be blown up with the car. Now I had no means of asking Petesy to pick me up. Not that I could have told him where I was anyway. I would have had to hope that he had managed to keep up with the Mercedes. Actually, I still did have to hope Petesy was not far away, otherwise I would have a long walk ahead of me.

──CHAPTER TWENTY-THREE──

O ut on the main road – well, it wasn't very main, just a country road (I discovered later that it linked a string of villages before joining up with a proper A road), but it was straight and well maintained – I stood blinking in the feeble moonlight. In contrast with the deep dark of the woods, everything looked quite well-lit to my eyes, which enabled me to detect a lone shape on foot in the middle of the road some distance to my left. I turned in that direction, keeping to the grass verge where I would blend in with the forest shadowland. Although I was not moving very quickly, I soon found myself catching up with the mysterious figure. Which even then struck me as foolhardy, since the most likely candidate was Absalom. But I had to know.

As I came closer, I discovered two things: first, this person's movement resembled loitering with no particular intent, rather than walking, which implies a purpose. Secondly, his (definitely male) silhouette was nowhere near bulky enough to be Absalom's.

Realizing there was no menace in the situation, I moved to the middle of the road and called out, 'Petesy?'

He turned and came towards me.

'Kenny. There you are … what the hell is going on? The phone went dead … I didn't know if I should turn in at that road … I thought it looked like a private road to a house, or something. So I waited here – well down there actually … and nothing happened. The phone was still working then but nobody was saying anything until I heard just the one word, *wait*. I thought it sounded a bit like you, so I waited and—'

I broke into his monologue.

'Look, Petesy,' I said, 'you must have known something pretty drastic had happened when you heard the bang.'

'What bang. I never heard any bang. My mobile crackled a bit and went dead. I told you—'

'Not on the phone, you pillock, you must have heard the bang out there, in the night.' I waved an arm in the direction of the night, but as I did so I caught his baffled shake of head. I said, '... Oh never mind, it must have been muffled by the trees. I suppose you might not hear it through half a mile of forest.'

'Well, what was this big bang, then? Tell me what happened.'

'All in good time, Petesy. Just show me where you've left the car ... we can talk about all that stuff on the way home.'

'Er, I'm sorry Kenny ... I've lost the car.'

To be fair, he did look a bit embarrassed. I didn't lose my temper. I didn't yell at Petesy. I took it all very calmly and confined myself to staring at him until he had no alternative but to come up with some kind of explanation.

'See ... it was this enormous bloke. I was just sitting in the car waiting, like you told me ... and this huge bloke ran out of the woods. I thought it was a big bear at first, in the dark, but there aren't any bears here, in this country ... anyway it couldn't have been a bear because they can't talk. He yanked the door open and before I knew what was happening, I was being dragged out and he said "Out, mate, I need your car", and I was left dumped on the ground and he was driving away in the Renault. I had somebody interested in that car ... he's coming back for another look at it tomorrow and maybe a test drive ... and I was just wondering what to do next and then you arrived.'

I had to tell him to shut up again.

'Getting back to this big bloke who took the car,' I said, 'did he happen to mention dog meat by any chance?'

'Dog ... oh, bloody hell. Is that who it was? The bloke who threatened Daphne in her bed that night her dad got kidnapped ... works for that Moorhouse bloke? I never got a good look at him then.'

'The very bloke,' I agreed. 'But I think he's unemployed now.'

The lack of transport was a bit of a blow, but it could have been worse.

'All right, Petesy,' I said. 'Relax, and give me your mobile ... first, I'll call around and see if there's any news of Aileen. Then we'll get someone to come out and pick us up ... I suppose you can supply directions. I wasn't able to keep track of every turn and twist of the journey here.'

'Sorry Kenny. I haven't got my mobile any more … it went away in the car.' he said.

I suddenly came all over weak, and had to lean against a tree for support. My brain cells were telling each other that if this prat ever played the fool, the fool would definitely win.

'But you had the sodding phone in your pocket and the sodding hands-free head thing. It should have stayed with you instead of …'

I trailed into silence, overcome with the unutterable futility of life, the universe, and Petesy.

'Well, when the connection got lost, there didn't seem to be any point in keeping the headset on …' Petesy began.

Like I needed to listen to more of his bloody lame excuses. But he carried on regardless.

'… so after I finished talking to Daphne and Aileen, I put it down on the passenger seat. What can I say? Sorry.'

'It's no good being sorry now,' I began, before I digested what he had said.

'Wait a minute, Petesy. You spoke to Aileen? Where is she? Is she all right? How did she get away?'

'Yeah, she's fine. Says it's complicated, she'll tell us all about it when we get back. She's at home … oh, and she's got some police-woman with her, so it sounds as if she's got protection. I suppose your detective inspector mate must have arranged that.'

'Right,' I said, 'the policewoman must be your friend Stella the car buyer who isn't going to buy any car – even if you don't lose them all. Let's start walking … I haven't a clue where we are, but I know the Merc turned to the right to go up that track, so it must be this way.'

I set off at a brisk walk in the indicated direction, leaving Petesy to work out the Stella reference while catching up. Presently he told me, 'We should come to a main road in a couple of miles. We can try to get a lift.'

'No lift,' I said firmly, putting my foot down, 'the last thing we need is to be the subject of a police appeal for any information leading to the arrest of two men who were seen trying to hitch a lift near the scene of the vicious murders.'

'Murders? What murders?'

So I told Petesy how I had luckily avoided being blown up, and how unlucky it was that Absalom had missed being blown apart. His first reaction was not, as I expected, relief at my escape, but concern over Daphne's dad.

'Oh, yes,' I assured him. 'I'm quite sure Mr Short bloody Plank is still living and laughing. He got away too.'

I explained what had happened, and how it happened. Petesy thought about that for a while. Then he said, 'That doesn't necessarily mean that Daphne's dad was responsible for blowing up the car. I mean, maybe he got a lucky break too ... just like you did – you and that Absalom bloke.'

'Yeah, right,' I replied, 'and pigs can swim, as my Auntie Ursula would have pointed out.'

When we reached the T-junction with an A road, it was not too difficult to suss out roughly where we were, on account of the large sign that indicated Daventry was in one direction and Banbury in the other. We chose to walk towards Banbury, hoping to find a good old-fashioned phone box which would enable us to summon assistance. I was working out who would be the best person to call. Neil maybe. Or perhaps Steve would be a better choice as I didn't need a load of questions about how we came to be wherever it was that we were.

Traffic was light, as you would expect at that time of night. Petesy and I kept well in close to the verge whenever a vehicle passed. I was pretty certain we would not be noticed. Well, not until there was a loud and extended hiss of powerful air-brakes, and a huge articulated truck slid to a throbbing halt beside us.

A head bearing a heavily moustached face poked itself through the cab window above us and said something that reached our ears (well mine at least) as a meaningless garble.

'Sorry, mate, I didn't catch that,' I replied, noticing at the same time that the door of the cab was displaying an address in Limoges. I happen to know that Limoges is a place in France, so maybe this guy was speaking French. It certainly didn't seem to bear any relationship to English.

'No comprendi,' I shrewdly added.

The door opened. The head's owner climbed down and turned to face us. He addressed us as if we were retarded children, speaking very slowly and very loud. I still didn't get it. I turned to Petesy.

'What did he say?' I whispered. Don't ask me why I was whispering.

'I think he's asking us something about a key monster,' said Petesy.

'Don't be bloody stupid,' I hissed. 'That wouldn't make any sense – the last part sounded more like a mean stair to me.'

'Oh, of course, that explains the whole thing,' Petesy said, which surprised me, as he doesn't often go in for sarcasm.

Turning back to the Frenchman, who was waiting with an expectant expression, I raised my shoulders while spreading my hands sideways, palms up, and keeping my elbows bent and tucked in at my waist. I may not be able to speak French, but I can gesture in it. In case there was any doubt as to my meaning, I repeated, 'No comprendi'.

Our fellow European held up an index finger (no, not the middle one), said 'Attend ... er, moment,' and climbed back up to his cab. After a brief pause, he came back down bringing a sheet of paper which he handed to me while pointing to an address in the heading.

'Ah,' I nodded wisely, smiling, 'Kidderminster – of course. You've taken a very wrong turning somewhere.'

He grinned and nodded eagerly.

Anyway, that solved it, though it still took quite a bit of sign language and pidgin English (mostly from Petesy and me) before we got ourselves up into the cab and started directing our French friend towards his destination. His co-driver remained asleep throughout, in a bunk behind a curtain affair at the back of the cab.

From where we started out, the most direct route to Kidderminster would not normally involve a close approach to Stratford, but I'm sure Gaston didn't mind, since he wasn't aware of that fact. We introduced ourselves to him as Brian and Roger, though I can't remember which of us was which.

Petesy and I dismounted from Gaston's truck on Stratford's northern by-pass, which left us with less than a couple of miles to walk. We left him a pencilled map which would get him to Kidderminster.

All quite satisfactory, really, since I could think of no way in which Gaston would be likely to hear of the exploding Mercedes, or know that he had been anywhere near it if he did. He would definitely not understand any police appeal for a driver who might have picked up anyone near the scene. As my Aunt Ursula would have said, ignorance is twice blessed.

Back home at last, we entered a living-room which contained two seriously nail-bitten women. I headed straight for Aileen and held her tight without saying a word – and without a second glance at her companion. The companion was of course the elusive Stella Galloway.

Once we got the flavour of their story, I was glad to know that Aileen had at least had some company in her captivity. Especially the company of someone who was resourceful enough to get them out of there. Luckily, I didn't say that out loud – something I realized later on when I had digested the details.

Now that the excitement of a highly fraught day was at last over, we were all suddenly extremely knackered. The girls, who had hitched a lift to Stratford in a Tesco truck, had been expecting us to arrive complete with a car. So Petesy could have taken Stella home to her flat in Alcester. That was obviously impossible now. We didn't have so much as a roller skate between the lot of us.

Stella was assigned the bedroom and bed that Petesy had recently been sleeping in, and he was relegated to his sleeping bag on the floor of the dining area.

Aileen and I fell into our bed and were immediately asleep, but only after she had made me gargle with Listerine to fumigate the dragon breath that resulted from my earlier throwing up.

—CHAPTER TWENTY-FOUR——

'So where does that leave us?'
The question came from Aileen as she buttered another slice of toast. We were at the later end of a long late breakfast. Just three of us were still at the table: Aileen, Stella, and me. Petesy had just left on foot, bound for the garage with instructions to come back driving a Madigan Motors car with some time left on its tax disc. He would take us to Redditch where I had left my car in the Ecological Recycling Company's car-park the previous night. With luck, Stella would also be reunited with her VW in the same place, assuming that was where Absalom would have left it.

'What do you mean; where does that leave us?' I had to answer Aileen's question with one of my own. 'There must be about a thousand answers. Do you mean, you and me, or Stella, or where has Plank gone, or has Debra Plank heard from him, or – and this is a big one – what is Neil going to do about it now that Plank needs to be hunted down for murder? And can we take this chance to walk away unscathed?'

'Don't forget that big evil bastard Absalom,' Stella said, 'he must be wanted for murder as well. You were a witness to that, Kenny, in Plank's office at Leamington – the way you tell it, at least.'

For some reason, Stella didn't seem ready to believe me a hundred per cent yet. Already that morning we had, all four of us, pooled the information we had. Nobody had got so far as to start considering any of the consequences or implications. I suppose Aileen's question was an attempt to start that process.

Now she added, 'I didn't mean anything as complicated as that. All I meant was you and me, Kenny. It would be nice if we could slip back into our cosy lives in the shoe shop and garage and forget the whole Plank affair ... but I don't think we can do that. We would always feel there was some unfinished business that we never er ... finished.'

I scratched my head and said 'Hmmm', the only comment I could think of.

Aileen went on, 'We would never feel safe. Plank will definitely be out to eliminate you if he finds out you escaped being blown up. With no witnesses, he could get away with the car-bomb murders. He might even be slippery enough to avoid getting put away for fraud, which could take a long time even if it works and if they find him.'

'And Absalom,' Stella brought up her own obsession again, 'he'll likely be after you as well.'

I ignored Stella, as something had just occurred to me. I said, to nobody in particular, 'I've just realized why Short Plank accepted me so readily, to join the so-called meeting, even though he didn't know who I was – he didn't care. Everyone in the car except him was going to be blown up, so what the hell; what's one smithereen more or less – and even better if it gets rid of someone else who has been poking his nose where it is not welcome, according to his wife.'

'Yes,' said Aileen, 'and we can also see why he said Mellis was the last person he would want there; he was the useful Eustace Plank didn't want blown up ... but none of that matters any more. What is important is who Short Plank's best friend is. I mean, it seems likely that whoever was around to pick him up after the bombing is the same person who provided the kind of assistance a person needs when he wants to plant a bomb in a car and blow it up from a distance.'

Stella joined the brains trust, more sensibly this time.

'That sounds logical. Isn't it most likely that it was Plank's new partner in his junk-mail scam?'

'I don't think so,' I said. 'We know Doug Mellis – the late Doug Mellis – was the new partner. I think the car must have been done by, oh, maybe Simmons, the chief East Planker; or how about the Dutchman, van Tongerloo?'

'Wait a minute, Kenny.' Aileen again. 'What proof do we have that Mellis was the new partner? Didn't you just jump to that conclusion because he turned up at the office?'

Stella's turn again. My head was starting to feel as if it was watching a tennis match.

'Right, Vince Moorhouse thought Mellis was nothing more than the computer expert they brought in to set up the systems. Didn't he?'

I was quiet for a bit. Thinking. I was trying to remember exactly what Mellis had said to me that night in Plank's office, when he first arrived.

'*You must be Vince Moorhouse ... had a call from Gerry today. He told me about you joining the enterprise ... so it would seem I've got three bosses now ...*'

Three bosses, Mellis said. I didn't give it much thought at the time. I suppose I just went, oh, yes, Plank, and Moorhouse, and now me. But Mellis thought I was Moorhouse. So my assumed trio comes down to two – Plank himself – and just one other. So Mellis's third boss must be somebody else.

Aileen's logic was on the ball as usual. And so was Stella.

Short Plank's famous mystery partner was still a mystery.

I nodded and tried to save something from the wreck.

'He could still be in partnership with Simmons, or the frigging Dutchman, for that matter.'

When Petesy returned, we all piled into a small Peugeot. First, we dropped off Aileen at Jonathan Philips; she had decided that concocting a convincing explanation for the previous day's sudden departure was her best alternative.

Then we had to stop by Stella's flat in Alcester on the pretext of picking up her spare set of car keys. Petesy and I waited outside in the Peugeot, vaguely hearing the radio and thinking it was taking her an excessive length of time to grab hold of a bunch of keys. Stella's reappearance after fifteen minutes explained a lot; she had also grabbed the opportunity to change out of her business-style suit.

As she approached, I muttered to Petesy, 'Surely that could have waited. She can be back here in her car within a half-hour.'

'You've forgotten what chicks are like, Kenny,' he said, gazing at the approaching Stella with admiration in his eyes. Somehow, I hadn't really thought of her as a chick. However, she was now showing rather a lot of leg and her white top looked at least one size too tight. When she bent down to get into the back seat of the car, it seemed to me that she showed a bit more than the usual segments of breast – a display which was not lost on Petesy.

'Sorry to keep you waiting,' she said, adding, 'I just had to get out of that scabby outfit.'

'No problem,' said Petesy, making full use of his rear-view mirror as he pulled out into the traffic.

The conversation was limited to trivial stuff until we came in among the leafy dual carriageways of Redditch. It was then that I heard a news bulletin begin on the BBC Midlands radio station. I had been on the alert all morning for some mention of a blown-up car, but nothing so far. I turned up the volume – and here it was at last.

A gamekeeper had found it. The wrecked car was burnt out, and contained bodies. No mention of how many. Identification of the occupants would require considerable time and effort, if it could be done at all. A mangled number plate had been blown clear, which identified the car as a Mercedes belonging to the Midlands businessman Gerald Plank who disappeared, allegedly kidnapped, twelve days ago. The police were following up a number of leads, and were confident of making a number of arrests in the near future.

The implication hung in the air, unspoken. But you could tell that the interviewed reporter wanted to get across the idea that Plank had perished in the course of a gangland dispute, without actually saying so.

I asked, 'What are you going to tell your copper bosses, Stella? I mean, you can supply a lot of information that the police have no other way of finding out.'

'Aye, right enough. So why do I not feel like helping Inspector Bastard Cornfoot? Come to think of it, everything useful that I know is hearsay. At the material time, I was imprisoned up to my oxters in a secret location. Anyway, I expect you'll pass on all the evidence to your mate Neil.'

She laughed – a bitter laugh, and said, 'Which goes to show what a stupid idea it was to send me undercover to gain the confidence of a gang of villains. I was about as much use as a cracked wally dug. That Vince Moorhouse must have known what I was all along, or at least suspected.'

'You're not going off back to the wilds of Scotland any time soon, are you?'

That was Petesy, with a touch of consternation showing in his voice. I remembered that Daphne was due back at college in a week or two.

'Well, my assignment here was supposed to be for up to six months, so I've got some time to go, if Inspector Cornfoot doesn't send me packing right away. At least I'll get some proper CID work, now that my undercover role is over and done with.'

I couldn't help having the impression that Stella was talking for Petesy's benefit when she added, 'I quite like it here, by the way ... now that I've got to know some friendly faces. Maybe I could even transfer.'

Friendly faces indeed; maybe she was thinking of Aileen and me. Yeah, right.

By this time we were arriving in the car-park of our destination, and could see that my car and Stella's were both present among the vehicles belonging to the staff of the Ecological Recycling Company. I wondered briefly if they would be surprised when their company and their cushy jobs folded. None of my business really, but I was reminded of my own experience at the lawn mower factory, where the management spent a whole year pretending that business was good and the future was rosy, while the company was swirling down the drain. It was a good thing I made myself redundant before the crunch arrived.

Stella seemed in no hurry to be reunited with her car, so I left the pair of them in chit-chat mode. On my way out, I stopped my car beside the Peugeot to remind Petesy that I would be expecting him back in the saddle at Madigan Motors by lunchtime.

I was already at my desk, starting to have a good think when Petesy came into the office and shut the door with a look on his face that suggested he was enjoying a secret conspiracy.

'Got some interesting information,' he said. 'I was hoping Stella would be the first to leave the car at Redditch, so I could tell you. It's something you might not want her to know ... not just yet anyway.'

I didn't believe the bit about wanting Stella to leave Petesy and me together, but mentioning that fact would just have brought on another bout of waffling. I simply raised my brows to encourage him to get on with it. Which he did.

'It was this morning when I walked up here to get the car ... oh, by the way, I'm going to start using my BMW again ... I mean Moorhouse isn't going to be around any more, and that fat bloke Absalom must have plenty of other stuff on his mind, so I thought—'

I had to interrupt.

'Shut up and tell me what you're trying to tell me, Petesy,'

'Oh, right. Well, as I was saying, I phoned Daphne and guess what.'

He waited.

'What?' I said.

'They've heard from her dad ... her mother, that is, got it through the post first thing this morning. They're back at their own house now. I suppose I can move back into my flat, as well, come to think of it.'

'Petesy,' in my warning voice.

'Well, Daphne is quite miffed about it. She says it's so typical of him, her dad that is ... he has obviously completely forgotten that she goes back to university before long, so it's not much use to her at all. It would have been heavenly, she says, if only he had done this a few weeks ago, but it's for tomorrow.'

'What the bloody hell is for tomorrow?' I had to know.

'The airline tickets and the hotel reservations of course.'

I was very patient.

'Tell me about the airline tickets and the hotel reservations,' I said. I was remembering the bulky envelope I had watched Plank drop into the mail, thereby dropping another piece of his plan into place. He must have just been to the travel agent when I saw him going into the office.

'They're for tomorrow – late tomorrow afternoon. Daphne and her mother. A flight to Nice and a secluded hotel at some place called Cap d'Antibes. No return tickets, so I don't know how long they're supposed to stay.'

'I take it that Daphne will not be joining her mother on the flight to Nice,' I said.

'Oh, Daphne's going all right, but probably just for the week or so that she has left before going back to college. Debra is definitely going because she's still dead anxious about her precious Gerry ... so she will welcome him with open arms no matter where she has to go to meet him. Oh, by the way, it's meant to be a secret ... they're supposed to tell nobody, just disappear without a word. But, of course, Daphne says she couldn't leave without saying goodbye. She says she will always remember the wonderful summer we had together.'

'Thanks for that information, Petesy. That's a nice bit of news to get our teeth into,' I said.

'No problem, Kenny. Do you think we should tell Debra, but not Daphne of course, about her husband being a vicious murderer? That might stop her ...'

He trailed off, noticing that I was shaking my head from side to side.

'Do you fancy explaining that to her, and getting her to believe you?' I asked, and didn't wait for an answer before going on to nudge Petesy away from the subject.

'What do you think of Daphne, the love of your life now? Seems to me she's trying to tell you that you've had a nice summer romance but now it's all over and she's off to sun herself in the French Riviera.'

'Oh,' said Petesy. 'I suppose it could be taken that way, now you mention it.'

'Never mind,' I told him, 'many a man would be very happy to be the temporary plaything of a hot chick like Daphne. So what if she dumps you, you've had a great time together and now it's almost over. You just have to admit it.'

Kenny Madigan with his famous free advice to the love-lorn.

Petesy nodded gravely.

'Funny you should say that. Recently I've been thinking that Daphne is maybe a shade too young for me. I think what I really need is a more mature woman – one who can make her own decisions. Someone like Aileen, perhaps.'

Yes, I thought, or maybe more like a Scottish copper. Aloud, I said, 'Yes, that's fine Petesy, but don't be too hasty. It might be a good idea for you to give Daphne a call when she gets to France. She's been a good source of information. Don't bite the hand that lays the golden egg. Here's a thought – how about this: you go over there tonight, for a last sha— er, a lingering goodbye ... I mean, visit her in her bedroom, just like you've been doing, and see if you can find out any more.'

Petesy was shaking his head, more in sorrow than refusal. There were tears in his voice when he replied, 'I suggested that, but she said she's got too much to do, what with choosing which clothes and bikinis and everything she wants to pack.'

─── CHAPTER TWENTY-FIVE ───

Mr Gerald (Short) Plank is considering the unfolding of his plan so far. A lesson to those who, like Vince Moorhouse, think they can chew up and swallow the hand that has fed them. The news of last night's car explosion has not yet hit the media. When it breaks, he does not expect it to be specific as to the number of charred bodies found at the scene of the explosion.

The police will carry out a minute search of the surrounding woods before getting round to adding up scraps of body parts. Then, with a bit of luck and a bit of imagination thrown in, they will arrive at the correct total. A total which, if factual (as far as Plank knows) will come to four with no fractions left over, though from a strictly Plank point of view, a verdict of five would be greatly preferred.

For Gerald, the most important consideration is that until there is overwhelming evidence to the contrary, he, Gerald Plank, should be assumed among the deceased. Which is, after all, the reason why the explosive charge was so many times greater than was strictly necessary for the job.

For Plank, any kind of organ arithmetic by the police, is merely extra confusion, and therefore useful. But then, he still believes that the explosion started out with four complete sets of human components available for dispersion. He would be disturbed to know there were two survivors. Not only does it dilute the chaos factor, it also leaves alive two people who can in their different ways, bring Plank some degree of unwanted vexation.

He has made sensible arrangements. Like having Debra and Daphne fly to a secret hideaway abroad, in case any members of his former organization should feel sufficiently aggrieved to avenge themselves on his family. The one-day delay before their flight is cause for slight concern, but it is the soonest he could manage in the circumstances.

Already this morning, he has spoken to Debra, so she will know that the impending reports of his death are so much nonsense. He has told her nothing of the previous night's events, his whereabouts, or intentions. He merely repeated the existing arrangement – fly to France, wait, and he will join them in due course. This is standard practice for Plank; if his own family don't know his plans, nobody in the world can force the information out of them.

It is for their own protection after all.

Gerald is also reviewing his own longer-term options. His rise to pre-eminence in his chosen profession has not been exclusively the result of cold logical planning. True, that has been a strong element in his success, but what has really raised him head and shoulders above the few other intelligent criminals has been his readiness to capitalize on unexpected twists of fate. He is a man who is willing to change direction through 180 degrees the moment some new opportunity presents itself – without the weakness of lingering regrets over what might have been.

At this moment, Plank is on the verge of such a change of direction. Prior to the recent wave of unpleasantness, he was preparing to slide unnoticed into a lucrative new enterprise, and that would have been fine, if somewhat boring.

Recent events, however, have convinced him that he is now at a major cross-roads in his life. Look at the opportunity:

1. His wife and daughter, the only people he cares about, are on their way to a safe haven.
2. He has stashed away a fortune sufficient to provide a luxurious lifetime for his family – anywhere in the world.
3. There is nothing to keep him in the UK. His continued absence from his Midlands haunts will confirm the belief that he died in a blazing car.
4. There will be no evidence of the fortune he has amassed. The disc containing the only detailed records of his financial operations, is now in the hands of Debra, who has instructions to take it with her when she flees to France.

Gerald Plank has just finished breakfast in his anonymous hotel room. Now he stands at the window looking down with unseeing eyes at the bustling city of Birmingham stretching into the distance. The decision is taking shape in his mind. Various practical details are being mentally ticked off. Neither remorse nor guilt have any place in his thoughts.

There are his soon-to-be-former associates to shake off, as a matter of urgency. Rod Simmons will not be a great problem. He is your standard villain boss – good at organizing the blowing up of a car and its occupants, but no more imagination than a brick shithouse.

Van Tongerloo is more of an unknown quantity: a lot brighter than Simmons, certainly, and a more immediate problem for a different reason – that reason being that he is present in the same hotel, in a room just along the sixteenth-floor corridor from that occupied by Plank.

Bugger van Tongerloo, he thought. I've moved on and I don't care how enraged he gets at losing his investment and being dumped by his partner. He's just a cheap conman anyway.

Gerald is not one to hang about once the die is cast. Minutes later, he is out in the street, his hotel bill (or at least that of Mr Bryan Thomas, his current alias) paid in cash. Another fast forward, and he has plunged way down-market, dressed in approximate-fitting chinos, T-shirt, un-cool bomber jacket, and cheap trainers, all courtesy of a city-centre discount store. His smart suit and trimmings, inside the discount store's plastic carrier bag, are now rubbing shoulders with last night's plate scrapings in a large green bin at the back of a Chinese restaurant.

Short Plank has joined the junk food, junk outfit society. He could be a taxi driver or a supermarket trolley marshaller. None of his former business or criminal associates would spare a second look for the puny middle-aged guy queuing up to buy a train ticket at Birmingham's New Street Station.

Absalom too, has quite a lot on his mind this morning, and less brain capacity with which to work on it. It is past his usual time of departure to work, but he and his latest cup of tea are still occupying (and nearly filling) the kitchen of his mother's council semi in Studley. Being used to having someone else tell him what happens next, Absalom finds himself in uncharted territory. Last night's miraculous escape from certain death is taken for granted: his concern is with the immediate future.

However, a few facts do stand out enough to be recognized as pointing the way ahead. First, he has worked out that he is now unemployed. Secondly, the cause of his predicament is the death of Vince Moorhouse, his employer and benefactor and a real gent to boot. Thirdly, the person responsible for poor Mr Moorhouse's premature demise, is the traitorous Mr Plank.

His dogged trudge through the above flight of logical stepping-stones has left Absalom's tea to get cold, so he accepts his mother's offer of a refill, and drinks it while putting his gangster instincts into automatic pilot to fill in the rest of the picture. No more hard thinking is needed.

In the world of organized crime, every adverse circumstance provokes the allocation of blame – and blame must be followed by retribution, leading to a continuous spiral of identification, accusation, and vengeance.

Absalom has mentally pointed the finger – thereby allocating responsibility. The next step must be retribution (although he thinks of it as justified revenge). He gets up from the table, kisses his mother goodbye, just like any other day, and is soon on his way, still at the wheel of the Renault he took from Petesy last night.

Briefly, he thinks of the two women he left locked up in the cottage. Delights remain in store there, he remembers. But professional obligation has priority. Business before pleasure. One more day of fretting can only cause the girls to be more prepared – and more grateful – for his eventual appearance.

Absalom is not normally given to flights of fancy, but on this occasion his imagination somehow comes up with the notion that it's just like putting pies in the oven to keep them warm. Stella and Aileen should be piping hot with another twenty-four hours of anxious captivity under their belts.

After all the frantic action I had been through in the last few days, I was grateful when Petesy went off to attend his flock of used cars. It was quite restful to spend some quality time sitting alone at my desk. The trouble was, I couldn't switch off my brain cells; they kept turning over and over all the things that had happened in the last couple of weeks.

As usual, they started coming up with stuff that hadn't occurred to me when I was being faced by urgent questions of protecting and saving myself – or when surrounded by the forcefully expressed opinions of everyone else.

For instance, when Stella and I were reunited with our cars at Redditch, I had looked around in the hope of spotting the red Renault that Fat Bastard Absalom snatched from Petesy the previous night. I mean, we all started out from that car-park in Plank's Mercedes, so Absalom had presumably left his own car there, perhaps even before he nicked Stella's car earlier in the day. I didn't have a clue what vehicle he normally drove, but it must be in that car-park because the Renault wasn't there.

I had to be concerned about the Renault even if nobody else was, on account of I was the one who had shelled out good money in the hope of earning a small profit when it was sold. I made a note to tell Petesy to report it stolen; he would have the necessary documents to hand.

Meanwhile my brain cells were still chewing on Fat Bastard Absalom. I had to admit I would be shedding no tears if he had perished in the Mercedes. As it was, the explosion so spooked him that I could believe he might still be driving, putting as many miles as he could between himself and the murder scene.

I almost awarded myself a grim smile as it occurred to me that what we had here was a classic case of mixed emotions: the good news is, Fat Bastard Absalom is getting further away all the time; the bad news is, he's doing it in my investment.

Actually, as I admitted to myself, I had no reason to think that Absalom was out of my hair for good. He was the loose cannon that doesn't change its spots – it can turn up anywhere and cause Christ knows what mayhem. Especially now that Moorhouse was no longer around to keep him in some sort of check.

But compared to Plank, Fat Bastard Absalom was a clumsy amateur. I mean, Absalom might well be the scariest person I've ever met, but Short Plank was a million per cent more deadly. He was the one I should be worried about. Sooner or later he must find out that I survived his Great Exploding Motor performance. Would he care?

Was he just trying to get rid of Moorhouse? Was it also an attempt to fake his own suicide, or both of these things at once?

I was getting confusing signals about Plank. On the one hand, he was all set up to run a profitable money mill from his office in Leamington; on the other, he seemed to be getting ready to move his family to a more congenial climate. Considering all the cash he had stashed away in Swiss banks or wherever, why on earth would he want to continue with his life of crime, squeezing more and more money out of innocent citizens in a dead boring scam? I suppose that's like asking why the Rolling Stones didn't retire twenty-five years ago, when they only had about £400 million to their name.

It occurred to me for the first time that if Plank were to take up long-term residence in his office, he would soon come up with a reason to complete what he failed to achieve with the car bomb. Namely, the removal of Kenny Madigan from the living world. That video recording Doug Mellis played on the computer screen would present Plank with the whole story of me getting into the office and nicking the disk containing the evidence of his personal crookery. And then, when Plank plays back the recording of me coming back to return the disk – that will confirm that I have understood what it's all about, and quite possibly copied it.

And that in turn means that from his point of view, I will no longer be merely a figure standing on the sidelines. That is when I will be promoted to the rank of prime target in the eyes of the most dangerous man in the country.

Bloody hell, here I was trying to relax and get back to normal, and my own treacherous brain cells have to go and convince me that I'm in as much danger as ever.

Perhaps he was sending Debra and Daphne out of the country simply as a precaution to protect them from any attempted revenge by West Plankers disgruntled by the murder of their boss – or anyone else who might be nursing a grudge. The family could easily move back when the danger had blown over.

Then I remembered that Steve was about to bring in the Serious Fraud coppers, who would definitely aim to take Mr Plank into custody, assuming they knew where to pick him up. So I would be quite safe once he was behind bars. Of course, until then, I would still be in danger.

Now I was getting a clear view of where I was leading myself with this chain of reasoning. I could see it looming over me like a big ugly traffic warden. In order for my valuable skin to remain unscathed, someone would have to assist the coppers to find Mr Plank as quickly as possible. And guess who qualifies for the job of finding him?

Oh shit. How could I do that now? Plank could be with, oh, Simmons, the East Planker boss; or what about the Dutchman, van Tongerloo? Was there some way I could find out Plank's present location, or would I have to go to the French Riviera and watch over Debra until he turned up? It didn't sound promising.

After going over everything once again in my head, I came to a decision: I really would have to track down Short Plank. There was only one possible starting-point that I could think of.

I got to my feet and went outside to where Petesy was pretending to be a real businessman around the Madigan Motors cars.

'Come on,' I said, 'you're the one who got us into this kettle of fish. Let's see if you can grab a spade and help dig us out of it. We'll go in my car. Get everything tidied away out here – I'll be with you in a couple of minutes.'

Then we were on our way. As I drove towards Lower Pebbington, I wasn't brimming with confidence in my ability to coax useful information from Debra. Still, I had to try. And anyway, I thought Petesy might have better luck. If I could keep the mother occupied while he said his tender goodbyes to the daughter, he might well get Daphne to let slip the odd unconsidered trifle.

Arriving at Lower Pebbington, I passed the village school and the village hall, and turned into Friday Street as directed by Petesy.

'It's right at the end of this street,' he said. 'The last house in the village, but it's up a long private driveway – must be nearly half a mile. There's the entrance, the right turn just ahead.'

As he pointed, a car came out of the indicated driveway and turned right. It was a red Renault which had a certain air of familiarity about it. We didn't manage to catch a glimpse of the driver; but we didn't need to.

A bsalom knows the way to Lower Pebbington. He remembers it well from the night when he played a supporting role in the kidnapping of Mr Plank. On that occasion, he was forced to be on his best behaviour – a constraint which no longer applies in a world without Vince Moorhouse.

He has Mr Plank's mobile number stored in his phone. Also the landline number of the house he is now heading for. However, there is no chance that Absalom will call either of these numbers. Every few minutes he repeats aloud to himself the phrase, element of surprise, after which he nods his satisfaction and shows himself a row of yellow teeth in the driving mirror.

He cannot be sure of finding Mr Plank at home. This does not cause him to falter. If Mr Plank is somewhere else, then Absalom will have to face up to another decision. Until such a hypothetical time, no brain exertion is required.

Straight up the drive he goes without even slowing down. No need for stealth on this trip. At the end of the drive, he is disappointed to note that Mr Plank's black Mercedes is not to be seen in the parking area in front of the house. A brief moment of confusion later, he remembers that the black Mercedes was the car whose fiery demise he witnessed.

So that's all right.

He presses the bell-push outside the front entrance.

The heavy outer door is already open, revealing a more decorative inner door bearing patterns of stained glass – which Absalom finds is locked when he tries the handle gently. That doesn't matter, though. He decides to open it anyway. Absalom does not put his shoulder to the door – he performs a very sudden whole-body lean, which causes the door to burst inwards with a loud crashing noise.

The most interesting features of the scene that meets Absalom's eyes from inside the house, are two pale female faces framed in a doorway some distance ahead. The faces are both equipped with wide-eyed expressions. The four wide eyes are merely startled. No sign of fear in them.

That comes later.

Absalom advances towards Debra and Daphne, sweeping them back into the room, which is revealed as a large, comfortable kitchen. He stops and remains standing just inside the doorway. The first shock has passed. The women are both on their feet, eyes and minds filling with uncertainty. Debra is first to speak.

'Who are you? What do you think you—'

Absalom's reedy-voiced question cuts her off. It must be a question, though it does not sound like one.

'Mr Plank.'

Some relief; his ponderous presence is not devoid of reason. Also some anxiety; breaking the door down is not a reasonable act.

Debra says, 'Oh, I'm afraid he's not here. I don't know when he'll be back. Sorry.'

'You sure he ain't here? What about upstairs?'

'I told you … we don't know where he is.'

That 'we' includes Daphne in the reply. It should prevent her being the target for a repeat of the question.

Absalom's gaze swings towards Daphne. Like her mother, she is lightly clad in the kind of flimsy comfortable clothes that women wear around the house, except that the younger woman's attire leaves more acreage of flesh visible – the bare midriff, for example.

Daphne thinks the visitor is seeking confirmation of what Debra has said. She tells him, 'That's right … Daddy hasn't been here for ages and—'

'Scream,' says Absalom.

Before the puzzled expression has time to form on Daphne's face, a podgy little hand reaches out, grips her crop-top by the top edge, and rips it away.

She screams.

Absalom stands still, listening for a response from any other part of the house.

Daphne subsides into a chair at the big kitchen table. She holds her arms crossed over her chest to cover the lacy bra which comprises more gaps than material. Red weals are already appearing on her skin where hems and seams of the destroyed crop-top have put up a millisecond's resistance.

Debra slides into a chair beside that of her daughter. She puts her left arm around Daphne's shoulders in a comforting gesture. Under cover of this move, she uses her right arm to slide a cordless telephone handset across the table towards her. If she continues the motion, she can scrape the phone to the edge, whence it will drop into her lap. Debra is pretty sure she can tap the 9 key three times without having to look.

At the moment of impact she feels nothing. Her right arm suddenly reports zero sensation. It is flung aside. The phone is snatched up and hurled to smash against the tiled wall behind the sink.

In the silence that follows, Debra feels pain pouring into her arm. She is surprised to find she has only partial control of the limb. It must be broken.

Absalom speaks.

'Mr Plank.'

Daphne has sunk lower in her chair, but replies with desperate bravery through her fear.

'We don't know where he is … he hasn't been here at all.'

'He must be some place,' Absalom insists. 'Everybody is some place.'

Debra tries to shrug, but gives up the attempt on finding it too painful.

'He never tells us where he is … look, you're asking the wrong person. You need to get in touch with a man called Vince Moorhouse. He's a business colleague of my husband. I'll give you his number.'

Daphne is nudging her mother urgently with an elbow. She has recognized the intruder as the man who invaded her bedroom the night her father was kidnapped. Unfortunately it is not possible for an elbow to convey the message, 'This man works for Vince Moorhouse'.

Absalom is merely reminded that Vince, his benefactor, has been killed by Mr Bastard Plank, and he is now in the presence of Mr Bastard Plank's loved ones.

'You would get word to him if there was a … emergency,' he says.

A cunning plan is coming to sluggish life in the deep sludge of his mind. Now it grows a tentacle.

'Like … what if she,' – he points a finger at Daphne – 'gets took poorly, and … and needs to be rushed to the hospital?'

He pulls Daphne roughly out of her chair by one arm. She stands cowering by the table. Despite the situation, neither she nor Debra are in tears. Their route to terror bypassed the tear stage.

Tears are too trivial for what is happening to them.

'Well, yes. I suppose … in an emergency I … *noooooo*.'

Debra's shriek of horror is caused by the sight of her daughter being hurled across the kitchen to drop in a quivering heap against the Aga.

'Look at that,' Absalom says. 'That might be a emergency.'

He is feeling confident, capable. Fully in charge. He helps Debra get a mobile phone from her handbag, which dangles from a hook just inside the kitchen door. She clicks left-handed through numbers to reach the one she needs. She hands the phone to Absalom.

He thumbs the call button. Listens to the ringing tone.

Seconds pass. A voice says, 'Yes?'

Mr Bastard Plank. It must be. Absalom wastes no effort on introductions.

'Your bitch wife needs to tell you things, bastard.'

Debra takes the phone with her left hand, the one that still works. She gulps and speaks eagerly.

'Oh, Gerry, is that really you … this Neanderthal here, we've got to do what he wants … he's hurt Daphne … I think my arm is broken …'

Absalom snatches the phone.

'You hear that, Mr Bastard Plank? Now listen to me. We got stuff to discuss, you an' me … if you want to see your pretty little girl and her mother again.'

Pause.

'Yeah. That might be where you would like, but you ain't tellin' me where to go … I'm the one gonna tell you where we meet – an' you let me know the soonest time you can be there. An' just to be sure you don't try no funny business, I'm gonna have one o' your nice ladies with me in my car.'

He goes on to tell Mr Bastard Plank in some detail, exactly where to meet him. The haggle over the timing is resolved. One step done – the end of Mr Bastard Plank is in sight. Absalom ends the call with a clever taunt he has thought up in the last few minutes.

'That bitch wife of yours ain't gonna be interested in your tiny dick no more – not after she enjoys the benefit of a real big-sized man.'

He then makes a mistake typical of the feeble-brained, by explaining the allusion.

'That's me, by the way, Mr Bastard Short Plank.'

After the call Absalom feels even more confident. He relaxes a little and leers around the Plank kitchen. Debra is seated at the table, nursing her wounded right arm, eyes watching him warily. Daphne, still in the corner by the Aga, consists of a pair of panic-stricken brown eyes looking out from a sprawl of bare legs trimmed with brief white shorts and lacy bra. His gaze settles on Daphne.

He beckons her with a crooked podgy finger. She shrinks back against the oven. He beckons again, insistently. She rises shakily to her knees and finally stands shivering in the kitchen warmth, arms ironing out the natural exuberance of her breasts. He points at her chest; 'Off,' he says, making his voice sound almost gruff. She whimpers. Humour him and maybe he'll back off. She unhooks the bra and shrugs it off. It drops unnoticed to the floor. She stands facing him, arms hanging by her sides, nipples hardening in trepidation.

Defeated.

Absalom is disappointed. He has been hoping to overcome some puny resistance and remove the bra himself. He covers the distance between them in two steps.

'Arms up,' he orders, scraping the pine ceiling with his knuckles as he demonstrates. Daphne complies. As she does so, Absalom bends down to grab hold of her shorts, a hand at each side of the waist. His hands wrench in opposite directions, thus disposing of all fastenings. The raggy remnants slide towards the floor. The remaining frilly under-garment is easily ripped away.

Absalom's heavy breathing is not the result of his physical efforts.

He fumbles with his belt and waistband. He slides his zipper down the burgeoning bulge in the front of his trousers …

… he spins around, disoriented, as the world explodes on his head.

Actually, it is the base of his skull that Debra has contacted with last night's empty rioja bottle. Although limited to her left hand, she manages to strike a mighty, and well-timed, blow.

Absalom's spin continues. He staggers, trying to make sense of the revolving kitchen. Instinct takes over. His right hand gropes for the flap-ping pocket of his open jacket. It emerges holding his trusty revolver. He speaks a long sentence comprising mostly gibberish, while placing the muzzle of his gun with exaggerated care between Debra's breasts. His only distinguishable utterance is:

'… dog meat …'

He hurls her backwards, and any other coherent words that might be lurking in that sentence are obliterated by the roar of the gunshot as he jerks the trigger.

Once he has absorbed the blow to his head – one which would seriously inconvenience a rhinoceros – Absalom is again free to concentrate on the task at hand.

Free to turn his attention back to Daphne.

P etesy recognized the car right away.

'That's it,' he said. 'That's our Renault ... the one he stole from me, that big bugger, and my phone as well. Get after him.'

'Never mind him, Petesy – he's not the most important thing at the moment. Right now we need to make sure Daphne and her mother are all right. Christ knows what that psychopath has been doing up there; he's quite capable of slapping a woman around if he feels like it.'

I turned into the driveway as I spoke.

'Let's hope he just came looking for Plank ... for whatever reason. And don't forget why we're here ... we're still trying to get a line on Plank's whereabouts. We can let the cops pick up Fat Bastard Absalom pretty much anytime. He's about as subtle as a bull in a thunderstorm.'

Up at the house, all was quiet. No sign of any commotion. Well, not until we went into the porch and found the inner door hanging in tatters. That set our alarm bells ringing.

'Which way?' I asked Petesy, who must know his way around. But Petesy was already shouting Daphne's name and running straight towards what turned out to be the kitchen. Don't ask me what drew him towards the kitchen. The sight that met our eyes suggested that a certain amount of struggling had taken place, though there was no sign of any people. Then my attention pricked up its ears on hearing a small sound.

A chill shiver ran down my back, and the hair on the back of my neck stood on end. I went round the big pine table that occupied the centre of the room.

There, on the floor was something. I needed a moment to work out that it must be Debra.

'Don't touch anything in here,' I told Petesy. 'Debra's here but she's injured. No sign of Daphne. Go to another room. Call 999 – get an ambulance here as fast as possible. Then call Neil, or Stella. Let the cops work out what to do – all their scene-of-the-crime crap. Get on with it. And after you've done that, check the rest of the house – maybe Daphne managed to hide herself somewhere.'

It seemed to me a bit unlikely that Daphne could be here and not come out of hiding when we arrived, but we would have to check the whole place in case she was lying injured somewhere else. I pushed Petesy towards the door. He went and I knelt down to see what I could do for Debra.

She was sprawled, legs akimbo. Her head and face looked normal, but blood was pooling on the floor around her upper body, which was still clothed. She was naked from the waist down.

I heard that sound again. It was a feeble moan. She was alive – but only just, it seemed to me. Bizarrely, my first thought on finding her alive was to restore some modesty to her. I gathered up various pieces of torn clothing and used it to cover her naked parts.

'Petesy,' I yelled, as loud as I could, and when I got his attention, told him to mention gunshot wounds when he called for the ambulance – matter of life and death stuff. Meanwhile, I made Debra more comfortable with a cushion under her head, and tried to stem the flow from what was revealed as a small, round, dark bullet wound in the middle of her chest. I didn't try to move her in case there was a bigger exit wound in her back.

I leaned down to her ear to whisper comforting words – Christ knows why I was whispering. Help was on the way; she was going to be all right. All that keep-your-chin-up stuff.

It seemed she was trying to tell me something. Desultory speech-like sounds were coming from her, but didn't have enough energy to travel the short distance to my ears. I put some water in a cup and got a few sips into her mouth. I assured her I knew that Fat Bastard Absalom had done this and promised he would pay for it. Wouldn't you just know, Debra's main concern was for her dear Gerry.

It took patience and time, but I ended up with quite a lot of isolated words. Fluttery feeble words, like spent butterflies which barely cleared Debra's lips before falling exhausted to the floor. But enough words so I could jigsaw them together to reconstruct what she wanted me to know.

What I got out of it was that Absalom used threats of violence on the women to force Plank into meeting him. He had taken Daphne. I also managed to get the time and place of the meeting. There might have been more, but Debra sank into unconsciousness about then.

It seemed to me unlikely that much verbal discussion would take place at that meeting between Absalom and Plank. I reckoned that Absalom must have lost whatever precarious balance he might have had. He now simply wanted revenge for the murder of his mates, especially Vince Moorhouse.

Personally, I have no problem about villains killing each other. It seems to me the best possible way of reducing their numbers, if they do it in discreet privacy – so long as innocent bystanders don't get ground up in the gears of their grievance-resolving machinery.

In this case, Debra and Daphne had got caught in the cogs and were suffering horribly as a direct result of their close connection with organized crime. Not to mention a vicious loony in the shape of the dangerously unbalanced Absalom.

I heard Petesy approaching through the hall, and managed to get to the kitchen door in time to prevent him coming in.

'No sign of Daphne anywhere in the house,' he said.

I knew that. It was off the agenda.

'Is the ambulance on the way?' I demanded.

'Yes, and the police as well. I don't have Neil's number and Stella's is gone along with my phone, so I used 999 to get the police and they sounded dead keen to get here as soon as possible and she kept assuring me everything would be all right and I must stay exactly where I am and mustn't touch anything and they'll be with me in a few minutes and ...'

He was still trying to push his way into the kitchen.

'... those bits of cloth over there; they look like some of Daphne's clothes. Let me have a look—'

I cut into his babbling.

'We haven't any time to waste. Better get out of here pronto, before the local fuzz arrive. Come on.'

'But we're supposed to stay ...' Petesy began. I was already guiding him towards the front door. I stopped suddenly, as I had an unwelcome thought.

'Wait a minute ... we haven't got a phone. Is there one here we could take?'

I was remembering about my mobile being blown up in the Mercedes, and Petesy's having been in the Renault when Absalom hijacked it.

'Er, yeah,' he said, 'Daphne's is in her handbag in the sitting room. I used it just now ... see she always leaves it there when she's at home so I knew where it would be. I put it back in her bag after—'

'Get it,' I ordered, 'and hurry. If we're still here when the cops arrive, we'll be pinned down, not able to go anywhere for God knows how long.'

He went and got it. As I hustled Petesy into the car, he said, 'What about Debra? Shouldn't we stay with her till the ambulance gets here?'

I just said, 'There's nothing we could do that would help. The experts will be here soon, with all their equipment. Best leave it to them.'

Sure enough, just as I was choosing one out of about five possible exit routes out of Lower Pebbington, we heard the high-pitched yodel of a speeding ambulance not far away. Quite distinctive, and very different from the sound of police sirens in this part of the country.

I was pleased that they were first, though it was no surprise – I mean, even a pizza can get to your house faster than the cops these days.

At the first opportunity, I stopped in a lay-by and insisted that Petesy should take over the driving, even though he was still a quivering bundle of exposed nerves. It would be good for him to have something responsible to do besides worrying about Daphne. Besides, I needed to concentrate on the phone calls I was about to make. I told him to take it easy as there was still plenty of time before we had to be at our destination.

That delay was interesting; it suggested that Plank had to cover some distance to get there. At least, he must be coming from well outside the Midlands, considering that the venue chosen by Absalom was easily accessible from the motorway system. I wondered how Fat Absalom would pass the time until the appointed hour, and shuddered at the thought of him having Daphne at his mercy.

Anyway, like I said, we were in no great hurry. On the other hand, I thought, we don't want to be too late. It was probably a good idea to get there ahead of the crowd in order to take up a position with a good view of whatever might be about to happen. I mean, it's not as if we would have been able to relax, whatever we did.

Petesy drove us quite gently, though, while I got on with the calls I had to make. First, I called Aileen at the shoe store to get Neil's mobile number, which she would have on her phone (via Sally). I told her something of what was going on (though I let her believe that Absalom had merely beaten up Daphne and Debra).

She got me the numbers and then said, 'Maybe it would help if I give Stella a call just in case Neil is having one of his switched-off days … you know what he's like sometimes, and afterwards he says he was following somebody, or whatever. At least the police will get the message one way or another.'

'Good idea,' I admitted, and filled in the details of time and place. I added, 'Sorry to trouble you at work, but it is kind of urgent. I hope you won't get into any trouble.'

'No, it's OK,' she said. 'I'm stuck with this idiot customer who's spent the last hour in a paroxysm of indecision between two pairs of shoes. This is a relief.'

'Good, Thanks, love. See you later,' I said, and pressed the hang-up button.

I had keyed Neil's private mobile number into the phone during the conversation. I now pressed the call button, while wondering what the hell a paroxysm could be.

Luckily, Neil saved me from having to think about that by answering his phone with unusual promptness. First, I described the horrible scene at Lower Pebbington and assured him that the local police had been contacted and were handling the situation.

'Don't worry, Kenny,' he said, 'I'm already on to that … in fact, I'm on my way there even as we speak …'

'Supercilious bastard,' I muttered, but too quietly to drown out his next patronizing remark.

'… our internal police communications are better than you seem to think. And you're in trouble for not waiting at the scene. But thanks for letting me know anyway; you will be required to make a statement of course – we always appreciate co-operation from members of the public.'

'I see,' I said. 'So I expect your internal communications will have told you where you would be able to find Mr Plank in, oh ... about an hour from now.'

'Is this just some story you've made up ... are you trying to tell me he wasn't killed by the car bomb?'

Pause. I kept quiet, waiting for Neil to think that one through.

'Kenny, if you have any further information, it's your duty to tell me. I'm sure Mr Plank would be able to help us identify the person or persons responsible for attacking his wife and daughter.'

'Yeah, I bet he will,' I replied. 'Well, Plank's got a meeting set up with that person or persons, and it's a meeting he will definitely not want to miss. You won't be wanting to miss finding the two of them together either. It's your golden opportunity to hit both nails on the head with one stone.'

I told Neil the time and place, and hung up. If only he hadn't been so bloody condescending, I would have told him all about Absalom, and about Absalom being an armed and homicidal loony. Then he could have had an Armed Response Unit in position at our destination. And of course he would also have had to get the public cleared out and that would have alerted everyone and the participants would have been kept out like everyone else, so nothing would have happened.

Which would have been fine from a protection-of-the-public point of view, but then nothing would have been resolved either, and the whole thing would just have been put off until another day.

While I was at it, I thought I might as well give Steve a call at his place of work. It would give him a nice break from all that boring insurance stuff he does, whatever it is. Also, it would be a relief for me to talk to a proper human being for a change.

Besides, if I was left to my own thoughts, I might start thinking about the horror of what happened to Debra in the kitchen from hell – and maybe to Daphne too.

'Hi, Steve,' I said, 'I just thought I'd give you a call to say why don't you go ahead and pass on Plank's files to the Fraud Squad ... I know where he is – or at least where he's going to be very soon.'

'Oh, hi, Kenny,' he replied. 'Uh, I meant to tell you, I've already given the evidence to the SFO – yesterday in fact. There wasn't really much point in waiting for you to locate Plank.'

'Oh, right,' I said, trying to carry out a mental reassessment, 'so they'll be wanting to lock him up as soon as possible.'

'Well, it doesn't actually work like that ... not with the Serious Fraud Office. They like to build a case thoroughly, and their targets are not usually violent criminals, so they're not used to a high degree of urgency.'

'You mean they're not going to do anything for ages. It might be too late – he could have been anywhere in the world – still could be if he slips through the fingers of the law today.'

As I said that, I was thinking that Plank's intentions would probably need to change now that his family was – well, the way it was now.

'It's not that bad, Kenny,' said Steve. 'They said they'll probably get on to it sometime next week. They'll start with the files I gave them, and whatever records are to be found in Plank's Leamington office – I told them where it is – and no doubt they'll find the original hard disk if you're right about where he sent it.'

After that conversation, I did have something else to think about, other than Plank's kitchen. Something that carried a more personal impact as far as I was concerned. So I sat there and thought about it.

Meanwhile, Petesy mutely trundled us towards the meeting we intended to gatecrash. He turned towards the M40 which would take us on to the M42 which, in its turn, would lead us to our destination.

'We're going to be early,' said Petesy after a while.

'That's OK,' I told him, 'it'll give us time to look around ... check out the lie of the land ... find the spot where they're supposed to meet, and look for a vantage point we can watch from, preferably without being seen. It would be even better if we could listen – I'd like to know what kind of demands Absalom comes up with.'

Petesy merely nodded, still wrapped in a cloud of misery. I thought I would try to cheer him up with a bit of humour.

'You won't get me to stop for a burger this time; I would hate to throw up over that nice Mr Plank.'

It didn't work. Petesy's face remained as gloomy as ever.

—CHAPTER TWENTY-EIGHT——

'I hav'nae a clue about where places are in this part of the country. Do you know where it is … I mean, how to get there?'

'Yes, of course,' Aileen replies. 'It's only about half an hour from Stratford. If you'd like to come over here to fetch me, I'll come along and show you the way. I'm at the shoe shop; you must know where that is, you picked me up here once before.'

Stella ignores the sarcasm.

'That would be great, Aileen. Thanks for telling me what's going on; Inspector Buggerlugs Cornfoot would never bother to let me participate in the arrest of a major villain like Plank.'

For the second time Aileen walks out of the Jonathan Philips shoe shop and gets into a car with Stella Galloway. She doesn't want to miss out on anything either.

As they move off, Stella admits, 'See what I said before, about Inspector Buggerlugs? I take all it back. He called me when I was on my way here, and told me to make my own way to this place, and he gave me directions. But I thought, och, it would be nice to have company, so I came and got you anyway. Is that all right, by the way?'

'Yes. Thanks, Stella. You couldn't keep me away – I feel as if I have a vested interest in this whole Plank affair. I want to be in at the end.'

Aileen flicks her hair back with that familiar toss of her head, and adds, 'That spooky Absalom being there as well is a real bonus – that could well wrap up the whole thing for good and all.'

Petesy's black mood lasted the rest of the journey, so it was completed in silence. The northbound side of the M40 arrived, and duly merged into the M42, where we once again took the northbound side.

'It's the next exit,' I said unnecessarily, as Petesy had already taken us into the inside lane. We came up on to a vast multiple-lane roundabout, where we turned west towards Shirley on the A34. Only a few hundred yards up that road there is a complex interchange involving several linked roundabouts. Our car traced a devious route through the maze towards the major attraction that has made such intricate traffic management necessary.

We turned into the wide access road leading to what looks like a thousand-acre car-park, past a sign which uses huge lettering to convey the simple message:

HILLCOATS GARDEN CENTRE

This was the place Aileen had been trying to get me to take her to ever since we acquired our new house complete with its potential garden. My mate Steve once told me that if you go to Hillcoats at the weekend, you have to queue up to park, and inside it's as crowded as a big jar of pickled onions. Fortunately this was a weekday, so the parking area was only about a quarter full. Still a lot of people though.

At Hillcoats, they're in no hurry to let anyone directly into the large park-like gardens where they display plants for sale, and give out advice and information (which I would have expected to be their main business). Before you get near any of the traditional garden-fillers, you have to enter their huge building and traverse several acres of indoor sales floors. Not only is there a restaurant so that nobody with a credit card will starve even if they can't find the way out; there are tasteful display areas stuffed full of everything that can be remotely related to the great outdoors (not to mention many things that can't).

We picked our way towards the back through a maze of garden and patio furniture, awnings, gazebos and such – interspersed with gurgling water features. In the back wall of that area were several passages into a large high-roofed hall divided into sections displaying garden tools, books, and clothing; small live animals and birds, tropical fish, and thousands of poshly packaged jars of exotic foodstuffs like chutney, honey, candied fruits, and extremely virgin balsamic vinegar.

Round the sides of that area, was a gallery bearing still more products. We didn't go up either of the staircases to look, but from what I could see from below, I got the impression that the gallery contained both indoor and outdoor lighting as well as ornaments – you know, glass and ceramic objects which are useless except for decorative purposes.

At the far side of the galleried hall, towards the left, there was an open doorway which must have been about twenty feet wide. At last, the open air was in sight.

'This must be it,' I said to Petesy, who was still strangely quiet. He gave me a questioning look. I explained, 'Where Absalom told Plank to meet him, according to Debra ... "at the door out to the gardens". I'm nearly sure that was what she told me he said, but I was struggling to hear her.'

We advanced close to the opening. Through it could be seen a covered area off to the left, full of plants in pots. A tasteful sign told me they were house plants. A similar covered area to the right contained garden machinery – mowers ranging from tractor size, down to little hand-held strimmers, and a load of other machines some of which I recognized and others which I had no idea what they were. More or less straight in front, under the real sky, were several aisles of garden statues and bird-baths which seemed to be made of smooth concrete. Slightly to the right of those was a display greenhouse, the first in a long row of greenhouses stretching into the distance where we could just catch a glimpse of real-looking plants growing in the real ground.

'What do you reckon?' I asked Petesy. 'Is this the "door out to the gardens", or would that be further out, past the white cement maidens?'

'I dunno,' he said gloomily, 'for a start I can't believe that a fat slob like Absalom would choose a place like this to confront Plank ... what would he know about a garden centre?'

'I'll take that as a yes, then,' I said, catching on to the fact that Petesy's input was useless for the time being, 'Let's check for other ways in and out first – and then we'll find a suitable place where we can watch without being seen.'

We did find other ways into the various under-cover areas, and out to the actual garden centre part as well; but they involved relatively small doors and passages. That big door had to be the significant one.

The only other event of any interest was when I spotted my

favourite police inspector, Neil Cornfoot conducting his own survey of the extensive premises. He didn't see us though, because I hustled Petesy and myself through a swing door into the restaurant when I caught sight of Neil pretending to examine a seven-foot-tall patio heater. I had an interesting discussion about the menu with a wait-ress who wanted to show us to a table, and by the time we extricated ourselves from the restaurant, Neil had moved on.

Now there were only a few minutes to go until the meeting. We took up a position in the galleried hall. The curved row of shelved units we stood behind held enough jars of heavily labelled gourmet produce to keep us in reading material for as long as we cared to stay. I did have to slightly nudge an indignant old lady out of the way in order to get a place where I could watch the big door through a gap in the cabinets.

Nothing happened for ages, except that I discovered the ingredi-ents of *Lime, Chili, and Tangerine Chutney*. Still nothing happened. To break the tension, I turned to Petesy and said, 'What do you think anthocyanin is? Sounds like something I wouldn't care to add to my cheese sandwich.'

Petesy opened his mouth as if to reply. But what I heard instead was a screech that cut through the general background buzz. A power screech.

'STAND WHERE I CAN SEE YOU, MISTER BASTARD SHORT PLANK.'

Absalom. Crazy enough to ignore the remains of the crowd, and probably stupid enough to try shooting his way out when the cops get here in force.

There he is. A lump of Stonehenge, at the foot of some steps that lead up to the gallery. Silence drops and stays for seconds. Then, like a belated echo:

'BASTARD SHORT PLANK.'

An even screechier screech from a different direction. A moment's confusion before I realize it's some parrot-style bird in the adjacent livestock area. Absalom ignores the distraction; he is still looking out through the door, where a slight, shabbily dressed figure has stepped out from behind an alabaster garden angel to stand where Absalom can see him.

The whole area is suddenly drained of members of the public as well as garden-centre staff. They recognize menace when they hear and see it.

Plank takes two steps towards the door and Absalom.

'Where is my daughter?' he demands. 'You said you had Daphne.'

Absalom says nothing. Suddenly, his right hand comes forward. It is gripping a handgun. A revolver. Which is pointing at Plank.

There is a thump, which merges into the roar of a gunshot whose echoes almost drown out the sound of crashing crockery. All that soundscape happens inside, on our side of the wide doorway. Nothing moves for a moment, while everyone realizes that the noise has not ceased. It has just changed its focus: outside the door, glass is crashing. It goes on crashing for several seconds while becoming more distant.

I must be among the first to understand what has happened. Something heavy fell on Absalom's head at the moment he squeezed the trigger. The heavy something proceeded to the floor, breaking into many small ceramic pieces. The first effect of the heavy thing was to deflect Absalom's aim, causing him to put his bullet through the glass of the display greenhouse just outside the door. The bullet must have continued on its path through greenhouse after greenhouse down the line, causing both instant and delayed action crashing as pane after pane of glass smashed, some of them with a domino effect into secondary pane smashing.

All this I understand in an instant, without thinking through the details. My attention settles on Absalom who is swaying from the blow to his head. He starts to spin around. I wait for him to slump to the ground. He doesn't. He shakes his head and converts the spin into a simple turn. Somehow he has moved to the foot of the gallery stairs. He points the gun up towards the top of the stairway, which he is now facing. I wince as I see his finger snatching angrily at the trigger.

Another gunshot roars out. A ceiling panel above the gallery makes a brief clatter.

I look around the scene, wondering where the next shot will go. Plank is nowhere to be seen – not surprisingly.

'Did you see where Plank went?' I asked Petesy, not really expecting a sensible reply.

He says, 'He dived out of sight to the right, and I saw your copper friend's face among the pot plants on the left.'

'Right,' I tell him, glad that he's functioning again. 'You get out to the car-park and look for that Renault. Daphne might be in it, tied and gagged … use my car, drive around the parking area till you find it. Break in. Go.'

He goes.

(Actually, I think it unlikely that Daphne is in the Renault; too much time has passed since Debra's house for Absalom to have been just driving around. He must have stopped off somewhere else.)

I look back to Absalom. He seems to have recovered his balance. He is now beckoning with a crooked finger – and still pointing his gun up the staircase.

'YOU. DOWN. HERE,' he says. It is a command. Not shouting now, which makes him sound even more menacing.

Someone comes slowly down the stairs, hands aloft.

Aileen.

Bloody hell. She must be the one who dropped that pot on his head

Now I hear another voice shouting from outside the doorway.

'This is the Police. Put your gun down and come out with your hands up.'

Neil with his usual flawless timing; making the situation more complicated and more dangerous. I have to assume he has not seen Aileen yet. Absalom's reaction is to grab Aileen, who has now reached the lowest step, and hold her tightly in front of him with his left arm.

Absalom has to answer.

'All I want is Mr Bastard Plank. You interfere – this lady gets it.'

Silence for a moment. There's no answer to that. Then Absalom returns to his obsession.

'*PLANK*,' he screeches. '*I WANT TO SEE YOU OUT WHERE I CAN SEE YOU. YOUR LITTLE GIRL IS SOMEPLACE SAFE BUT SHE AIN'T GONNA KEEP SAFE UNLESS YOU DO IT MY WAY.*'

There is a wordless answering screech from the parrot. Maybe a different parrot.

Two facts become suddenly crystal-clear to me.

The first is that Absalom came here with no intention beyond killing Plank the moment he got the chance of a clear shot. If he was going to negotiate, he would have brought Daphne. The second is that if Absalom can be prevented from leaving this place under his own steam, Daphne can be found at leisure.

Plank, being an intelligent man, must also understand these two facts. So he will not be exposing himself to be shot at.

We have a stand-off.

Which could turn into a siege when the cops get here in force, complete with an Armed Response Unit. Neil must have sent for them by now.

Which leaves Aileen in the hands of a homicidal maniac with no visible way out. Well, somebody has to do something.

I pick up a large glass jar of *Abricots preservé en eau de vie Poire Wilhelm*, and lob it high, to smash to the tiled floor about two feet behind Absalom – who whips round to find out the cause of the crash, which sounds like a minor explosion. It must take the thug several seconds to assess the extent of the threat. Long enough for me to make my dash to, and through, the big door to the outside. Once through the door, I dive to the right, to get myself out of the line of fire. I find myself among the garden machinery, still gripping my reserve missile, a handy bottle of Honey-Mead and Cranberry Marinade for Pork.

—CHAPTER TWENTY-NINE—

From my new position I look across to the house-plant display, where Neil can be seen crouching beside a small palm tree and talking urgently into his phone. It seems he has decided to ignore my presence.

Behind me I hear the brief whine of a starter motor, and a petrol engine springs to life. One of the demonstration machines, a ride-on mower, starts to move. Plank is in the driving seat, with what looks like two pieces of wooden palette wedged in, one at each side of him. Another piece of the same is held vertical in front of his face and body. His view ahead must be limited to what he can see through the tiny gaps between the slats of wood.

The miniature makeshift tank comes down the main aisle of the machinery showroom, passes me, and turns left through the door. Towards Absalom – and Aileen for Christ's sake.

I watch round the edge of the door gap. Neil is now watching too, from his side of the door.

Absalom fires a shot, which zings off some steel part of the mower, before realizing that he needed a better angle. Then it turns into something like a slow motion bullfight. Plank charges at Absalom, who stands still until the last moment before snatching himself and Aileen out of the way. Plank's machine charges several yards past, before swivelling round to face his target again. I had no idea these things were so manoeuvrable.

What makes it more interesting is that, on each pass, Absalom tries to get a clear aim at Plank from the side as he passes. Plank is making this a difficult feat by lashing out at the gunman with a tyre iron at the same time. Yet another danger for Aileen. I have to find some way to stop it.

Frantically looking around, I spot a bright yellow plastic object on wheels, with handles at the top end. This is something I recognize because we have one of these in the garage. This one must be set up ready for a demonstration, because it is all connected. I turn the knob that I pray will switch the power on. The machine responds with that chug that indicates it's ready for action.

I wheel it closer to the doorway. Lying down on my stomach, I peer into the galleried area, where the noise of crashing merchandise mingles with the growl of Plank's mowing machine. No more shots have been fired. I am holding the business end of my device as if it were a rifle capable of accurately picking out a long-range target.

Which, in a sense it is, given that I am looking for a target which is only a few yards away. I watch and wait. It won't be long. Very soon their gyrations must give me the chance I need.

I pull the trigger. And hold it down. A jet of water at a pressure of 360 pounds per square inch strikes Absalom's gun hand and arm. Nobody can stand up to that force. The revolver clatters to the floor. I use the jet to make it skitter across the tiles and disappear under a display unit. Well out of reach.

Everything has come to a stop inside the arena. The loud hiss of my pressure hose drowns out the sound of the mower engine. Plank is the first to recover. He starts to charge his machine at Absalom. I point my lethal jet at the mower's engine, which stops, literally drowned out this time.

I swing the jet back towards Absalom, and manage a blast in his face, which rocks his head back. He is now unable to use his eyes, but instinctively turns his back to protect his face from further damage. I take the opportunity to hose his backside, hoping the water jet is powerful enough to drill a hole in his trousers and give him the most exhaustive enema in history.

Absalom is trying to turn round on the piece of floor which has been covered in preserved apricots amid broken pottery and glass, and now also has water sluicing freely around. I would defy anyone to remain upright in these conditions.

Absalom cannot. As he begins to subside backwards, I am hoping that his body is big enough to cover most of the broken glass, especially since he is still clutching Aileen to his stomach with his left arm. In the event, his head strikes the tiles with some force. As Aileen comes down on top of Absalom, I see her use her weight to drive both elbows into his massive gut. That must have hurt

almost as much as the high-pressure water – I know from experience how sharp Aileen's elbows are.

Aileen struggles free, and scuttles away to safety, looking like a
drowned rabbit. Meanwhile I play the hose back and forth across
Absalom, just to make sure he will be too sore to move any part of
his body for a while, not to mention shredding his clothing. After
that, I use the pressure jet to blast the pieces of palette off the
mower so that I can give Plank a good soaking. Being soaked to the
skin is a sure-fire way to prevent someone going anywhere in a
hurry.

I had released the catch on the pressure washer's trigger, and was
turning off the power, when the Seventh Cavalry came to
everyone's rescue. There was a shout from among the house plants
to my right.

'Go – **GO – GO.**'

The whole place was suddenly saturated with coppers wearing
funny jackets and pointing their little two-handed guns every-
where. An amplified yell.

'**ARMED POLICE. NOBODY MOVE.**'

—CHAPTER THIRTY—

The armed cop who was standing over me said, 'I was watching for a bit there. I saw what you did.'

Well, I thought, it's nice to know that somebody appreciates my efforts. I tried to look modest, and said, 'Oh, you know, I had to do the best I could with what came to hand.'

'Yeah,' he said, 'that was your bad luck right enough, mate. You're gonna be bankrupt by the time that big bloke's finished dragging you through the courts for compensation.'

'Neil,' I shouted across to my friend, the detective inspector, 'would you please tell this human pit-bull to back off and let me stand up.'

So the whole thing was more or less wrapped up. Absalom and Plank were both arrested and carted off to be held for questioning by the police.

When Petesy broke into the Renault, he found no sign of Daphne: it was Stella who solved that one by knowing where Absalom lived, having dropped him off at his house – or rather his mother's house – once or twice when they both worked for Vince Moorhouse.

Stella it was also, who was able to explain Absalom's choice of venue. Dirk, Moorhouse's other personal assistant, had told her that Absalom's mother had worked at Hillcoats for years. When her lad was only a schoolboy thug, he used to go there to wait for her after school every day, so he knew it inside out.

Daphne was found in a cupboard in Absalom's bedroom. She was bound and gagged, and naked except for being wrapped in a curtain which must have been torn off its pole in the Plank house. Physically, her injuries were limited to some bruises, but she had to live with the memory of seeing her mother first shot, and then raped. And on top of that there was the worry about what was going to happen to her when Absalom got back. It seems he had described his rather specific plans in some detail. He was saving her for later. Like a spider that wraps its prey and puts it away in the larder to enjoy at its leisure.

Aileen changed out of her sodden clothes into jeans and jumper from the racks displaying the garden centre's clothing range. I took her home in my car, leaving Petesy to bring the Renault. On the way, she told me how it happened that she and Stella had come to the party together.

'How are you going to explain running out on the job two days in a row?' I asked. 'Won't you get into trouble – you must have walked out on your customer?'

'Oh yes,' said Aileen, with a sort of guilty giggle, 'she was getting more and more impatient all the time I was on the phone. When I went back, she got really ratty. She said, "You're meant to be serving me, not gossiping on the phone. I need you to help me decide which pair suits me best."

'Cheeky pillock, I thought. After changing her mind every five minutes for the last hour, and treating me like dirt into the bargain. I wasn't going to put up with it any longer.'

'What did you say,' I asked.

Aileen had this lovely smile on her face when she replied, 'I told her, "definitely those ones with the pointy toes, madam. I think they will be slightly less uncomfortable when you stick them up your bum." Then I walked through the door and waited outside until Stella turned up.'

'Wow, that was great ... I've always wished you would do something like that,' I said. 'but you'll be in dead trouble ... I mean, that woman sounds like the type who will complain to Jonathan Philips.'

'I don't care,' said Aileen. 'I think that might have been my way of resigning from the retail trade.'

She leaned over and put her face close to mine to whisper, 'Now that we have a proper house of our own, wouldn't you like a wife who will keep it nice, and be there for you when you get home from work ... and be there to look after the children?'

I very nearly ran straight over a roundabout.

*

The following Sunday, we were gathered in Steve and Sheila's house having what seemed a bit like an end-of-term party. Besides the hosts and Aileen and me, there was Petesy, Stella, and Neil and Sally.

'What's the latest on Debra?' Aileen asked Petesy.

'They reckon she's going to be all right. Daphne is spending all her time at the hospital. She says all she wants now is for the two of them to get away and have nothing more to do with anyone from here. Not even her dad.'

I looked over at Neil.

'What are you going to do with her dad?'

'Dunno. We're still holding him for questioning, but who knows? We know perfectly well he's responsible for plenty of everything from stealing sweeties from kids all the way up to premeditated murder. But we can't produce a shred of evidence. I'm sure Absalom Higgens could testify against Plank, but he won't co-operate, and anyway, it would be too easy for the defence to prove that he's not of sound mind.'

He looked a bit gloomy. Neil didn't have much time for other parts of the police organization, so his tone was grudging when he added, 'Still, it looks as if the Fraud boys are going to come up with enough to put him away for a while.'

Aileen chimed in with something she regarded as more important.

'What about Absalom then? You'll definitely do him for murder. Right, Neil?'

'Well, attempted murder for sure ... and about two dozen other offences including car theft, armed robbery and GBH. But once again we have no direct evidence of actual murder of any human being.'

'Neil,' I said, kind of tentatively, 'what if I were able to show you a ... well, like a film of Fat Absalom shooting somebody – shooting somebody dead, that is?'

He snapped at me. 'Don't be ridiculous, Kenny. Your warped sense of humour has wasted too much police time in the past, so I'm not going to let myself look stupid by falling for another of your ploys.'

All right then, sod you, I thought. I had been about to make a deal that would deliver Absalom for Doug Mellis's murder, while keeping me clear of any trouble for being in Plank's Leamington office. But what the hell; the computer camera couldn't show me picking the door lock from the outside, which was the only point at which I really committed any technical offence. The fraud investigators would find the video recordings and get the credit for nailing Absalom for murder.

So that was it more or less wrapped up. Life went back to normal. I started taking more of an interest in the garage again, which pleased Senga – on the surface at least, though I'm sure she thought I couldn't run the place half as well as she did while I was occupied elsewhere.

Stella and Petesy became an inseparable item until the end of her assignment to the Midlands, at which point she reluctantly returned to her native Force in Scotland.

Aileen and I are coasting towards marriage, which seems to involve her in a thousand kinds of plans and activities, none of which I can come near to understanding. Well, except the ones that have to do with getting the house fully furnished and decorated to Aileen's demanding taste. The only good result of all this activity is that she has shelved her dinner-party plans until after the wedding.

The garden, though, is still in a rough state. Rough enough to bring the neighbourhood into disrepute, according to the hints our neighbours have taken to dropping. Trouble is, neither Aileen nor I feel much like spending time in garden centres. Maybe that will pass.